By Emem Bassey

A Ridiculous Royal Tale series:
Inside Out
Pristine

Age Is No Bother series:
Fine Wine
Fine Maple
Fine Scotch
Fine Ending

Emem Bassey

First Published in Great Britain in 2023 by
LOVE AFRICA PRESS
103 Reaver House, 12 East Street, Epsom KT17 1HX
www.loveafricapress.com

Text copyright © Emem Bassey, 2023

ISBN: 978-1-914226-51-9
Available in eBook and paperback format

Dedication

To my mother's people in Mkpani, Yakurr Local Government Area, of Northern Cross River State. May this story be a constant reminder to keep peace.
Wofai.

Acknowledgements

My first recognition will always be God for his numerous blessings, especially for the talent and wisdom to churn out beautiful stories.

I'm grateful to Love Africa Press for taking up this story. It is quite dear to my heart as some of the happenings in there were true.

Utmost gratitude goes to Zee, my super editor on this story. She's a writer's editor, making a writer's voice even sharper and the story better told. I'm grateful.

I acknowledge my heritage from my mother's side. I'm proud to be a grandchild from Lekanakpakpa. The people and culture have granted me numerous beautiful stories to experience and write.

Love to my family, especially my husband and our new baby. I love you.

A RIDICULOUS ROYAL TALE 2

PRISTINE

EMEM BASSEY

Blurb

Princess Nkoyo is twenty months into a happy and loving marriage to her soulmate, Prince Onen of Atam Kingdom. Then she begins having nightmares of wars in the wild era of slave eradication, connected to the vintage ring traditionally handed down to all first sons of Atam Kingdom for their wives. The ring has chosen Nkoyo to reveal what was and should be. The past will have its say with visions of a forbidden love story between Nnanke and Okoi—a priestess meant only for the gods and an escaped slave simply seeking a way home to his motherland. But does it hold the key to saving the future of Atam Kingdom?

Prologue

Spirits have always been aware of and, most times, in control of circumstances in the human realm. I say *most times* because I've come to realize a salient truth in man's genetic makeup: the human race just loves complications.

And so, even when the spirits prod and direct and create circumstances to make man take certain decisions that would affect a particular era in eternity, you can be assured someone is bound to rebel from those spiritual plans.

Sometimes, it's a good thing, especially if that someone renegades from a bad spiritual plan. But when it's a good spiritual plan, for the good of all, and a belligerent man insists on rejecting all the prods, well, in that case, destinies change.

While I was able to —

Oh, sorry, I forgot to let you know, this is your favourite tale-bearer, Gossip, with the chosen name Kedei, which literally means love — because I love telling tales. I'm a spirit, one of many roaming the universe. I'm spectral and can decide to be anywhere I please, AKA where an intriguing tale brews.

You must recall my former work, the interesting *Inside Out: A Ridiculous Royal Tale* — the stories about the monarchs of the Atam and Efik kingdoms and how their children unexpectedly found love.

Remember now? As I was saying…while I was able to meet up with my all-time crush, the spirit Trouble, and had a little TLC time with him, I wasn't able to stop the niggling itch in my mind concerning the vintage ring Prince Onen of the Atam kingdom had given to Princess Nkoyo of the Efik kingdom on their engagement, a love match.

Maybe because I had heard Nkoyo's thoughts as she experienced a weird phenomenon of feeling invisible threads weaving hers and Onen's destinies together the instant he slid the ring on her finger.

Oh, one of the perks of being spectral is the beauty of reading thoughts and seeing the unseen. I'd been able to discern, though not clearly but I swear, another spectre swooping around the love birds the moment that ring snugged on Nkoyo's finger.

It'd made no difference at the time until Nkoyo's thoughts of threads weaving destinies together. That made me really look at her and the ring a second time… definitely a story here, one not so ridiculous.

So I began investigating, which meant disturbing higher spirits for the scoop on Nkoyo's ring. And though I've been made to sound like a very annoying nuisance to higher spirits, I didn't mind, for the things I heard led me to realize that *Inside Out: A Ridiculous Royal Tale* only felt ridiculous because I wasn't aware of its foundation—of the prerequisite tale.

Let it be known it's not just humans that plan for the future—the spirits do, too, which is how the ridiculous royal tale could have occurred in the first place.

Therefore, because Nkoyo had felt what I had barely seen, she also shared the niggling itch to find out about the history of the ring. Onen had explained she would wear the ring for as long as it took her first son to turn twenty, when she'd then relinquish the ring to him to be given to his wife-to-be.

An intriguing explanation — you must agree the tale behind it is worth telling.

This tale dates back to a time where man had still been in his wild state. Atam hadn't been a kingdom but a collection of settlements, where the strongest took over the weakest, and it was survival of the fittest. Where deities reigned and the spirits were approachable and man hadn't yet gleaned intellectual wisdom enough to readily reject the spirits' prods…

…a time where true love was an inconceivable notion and man took everything as black and white, with no grey areas. A stark time, a difficult time, a diabolical time…

This is Pristine – a not so ridiculous tale.

Chapter One

It was an era where years, months, and dates as we know now made no difference to the inhabitants of this land which would later be known as Atam Kingdom.

War was on their minds. It made no difference that the language, though slightly different, was basically the same. How could it when the spirit of Greed reigned supreme over this era?

Greed in his tarty robes flew around cackling in glee as he suggested untoward ideas to gullible men, prodding and pushing them to collect the wealth of others diabolically or by force, which meant war.

Another such war was just ending. The little village looked forlorn and deserted in the aftermath of decimation. Smoke billowed up from burning huts and dry animal feed. The last warrior standing had decided to sacrifice himself to give the surviving villagers ample time to flee.

A sacrifice that might be useless if the villagers didn't run fast enough. Even though his arm ached terribly, thoughts of saving the few villagers who had survived the massacre prodded his determination to raise his machete and block the killing blow from the

Umor warrior, who had a ferocious sneer on his face and looked gleeful in his determination to kill.

The last warrior knew it was a useless effort, but he staunchly held off until one other Umor warrior skewered him with a spear from the back. The sharp edge broke through his chest; his eyes widened, and blood shot out from his mouth, drenching the fighter in front of him.

His last sight before life dimmed from his eyes were of the grinning warriors as they stood over him, contemplating if they should strike a finishing blow or let him wallow in his pain.

Death took him, but his eyes remained open and unseeing on the hundreds of other equally slaughtered bodies lying in the pool of their blood which mingled and made a crimson river.

A sickening stench surged through the air as bodies were burnt, but it didn't bother the Umor warriors. Even the fleeing villagers weren't a cause for concern, for they would get to them eventually on the next market day.

In the exhilaration of victory, they raided the store houses and proceeded to get drunk on fresh, sweet palm-wine and roasted bodies of the slain warriors. Yes, you read right: these people were cannibals in this era. They selected the most powerful warriors, especially the last to be killed one, to roast and be eaten. In this full celebration, they believed the essence of the dead warrior's stamina would be transferred to them as they had conquered him and now relished his cooked flesh soaked in palm oil and pepper sauce.

They had conquered another village, and they would many others until they got to their main nemesis, a village called Yakpani, almost as big as Umor and a worthy contender in the war of amassing land.

It made no difference that the people in these lands had once lived together with them as family before they moved to create their own settlements.

Umor wanted to rule them all.

***

My spectral legs were dangling when Nkoyo woke with a petrified gasp from her horrible, reoccurring nightmare. As usual, nausea from the gory sights attacked her. Who wouldn't be sick after so much blood, urrg! I'm a spirit, yet I gagged a little every night she described such horrors. I pitied Nkoyo as she repeatedly wondered what she'd done to deserve this unusual punishment. Could it be her past as a painfully entitled individual? However, I agree with her it wasn't worth this daily plague.

The princess couldn't understand why she kept seeing wars and soldiers eating their slain contenders. Quite scary, indeed, especially as she'd never thought about such things or even read macabre books, nor watched such movies.

There was nothing I, Gossip, could do as the couple of months' old situation bothered Nkoyo and her husband, the Crown Prince and heir of Atam kingdom. At the beginning, Nkoyo had thought it a rare case of typhoid and she'd treated herself accordingly, but it hadn't stopped.

I wish I could tell them it wouldn't stop as this was a spiritual matter. But then, they would ask for a solution, which I didn't have. Besides, not like they could even see me.

Nkoyo rolled from the huge bed she shared with her ever-loving husband, Onen. Usually, she was so terrified, she woke him to stay with her while the jitters of fear subsided. However, today, the sight of his innocent face in deep sleep tugged at the strings of her heart.

Aww, I do love love. Additionally, I understood why she felt that way. After a full day of work at the mill, which had been expanded over the twenty months she'd been married to him, plus his kingdom responsibilities, Nkoyo surely wouldn't have the heart to wake him. The man needed his full night's rest and some.

Hurrying from the room, I floated behind her, just in time to witness her lower her head into the ceramic toilet bowl before vomit exploded from her mouth. She expelled what she'd had for dinner until she had nothing left in her stomach, yet, the heaves wouldn't stop.

"Jesus Christ! Nk! Sweetheart!"

My spectral heart melted as Onen rushed in looking distraught. Usually, he was awake with her. Despite being so tired he hadn't heard her wake, guilt suffused his heart, struggling for space with worry at the unknown problem bothering his wife.

Onen slammed to his knees beside her, his hand immediately rubbing her back in a circular motion. The stench of vomit or the sight didn't bother him, but it troubled Nkoyo that he saw her this way. So, when she pushed him off slightly, he didn't argue, and left to get her chilled water to calm her upset stomach.

I hung back and watched her flush her mess, brush her teeth, wash her face, and sit on the edge of their massive bed by the time her husband returned. Close to her, he could perceive the scent of mint from their toothpaste. He smiled through his worry, admiring how she was strong and unnecessarily independent sometimes. Onen understood she was still fighting to erase the image she'd created around herself, before she'd met him, a time she'd been regarded as a lazy, self-indulgent princess.

Hmm, I recalled how arrogant Nkoyo had been, so much that her parents, the monarchs of Efik kingdom, best friends with Onen's parents, had conspired to send her over to Atam to be tamed. His sister, Wofai, had also had complex issues and had, in turn, been sent over to Nkoyo's parents to be healed in kind. Oh, I'd loved telling that complication!

Everything had turned out good after all the drama that followed—like Wofai falling in love with Nkoyo's fiancé. A long story, but I know Onen was glad his parents had made the ridiculous decision that had brought him the love of his life.

In the silence, his eyes didn't leave her face until she finished the glass of chilled water. After, he gathered her into his arms and held her wholesome figure to him. Nkoyo's head nestled on his massive, muscular chest, the thumps of his heart slowed from its worry and comforting her as it reverberated through her body, her own heart aligning and beating with his.

"You should have called me," he whispered into her hair, and kissed her temple tenderly.

The love in that room, in any room these two were, was stifling. Yet, I wouldn't be anywhere else in this moment.

"I didn't want to disturb you," she whispered back.

Onen pulled her face from his chest so they could really look at each other. He wanted her to see the sincerity in his eyes. "You could never disturb me, darling. I love you with every beat of my heart, and I want to share in this struggle with you. I want to help...I will help you," he concluded determinedly.

Aww, dear God, the romance in this room proved too much.

It didn't help that they'd decided to keep this strange phenomenon to themselves. I wonder why. However, thankfully, Onen thought it time to speak to his father about it. He thought the nightmares were obviously something from the past since his wife had described the soldiers as having nothing more on except loin cloths and weapons of machetes and spears.

Obviously, he couldn't wrap his head around the cannibal part. Onen knew of the history of his people — of parts that had eaten human flesh as meat. Despite getting rumours of such a thing happening in recent times, his father, the king, had done some investigations with no success. Those must be things that had occurred centuries ago.

Yet, none of us could explain why his wife was having nightmares about eras past.

Back to the romance.

Nkoyo's eyes softened at the love shining from her husband's gaze, and she didn't miss the determined glint either. She had reached her wits' end, and she wouldn't argue over whatever method he deemed fit to help her.

"Besides, if I had waited to wake you, I would have expelled everything on the bed," she joked, her palm cupping his cheek. She loved the feel of his one-day-old beard scratching her palm softly.

I would love that, too, if Trouble—my crush—bothered to keep a beard. Cue eyeroll.

Onen chuckled and drew her close, settling his lips on hers and convincing himself she was okay. Her fingers grazed his naked chest and went round his neck, effectively aligning her lace-covered bosom on the expanse of his chest as they embraced passionately.

His arm rounded her silk-covered waist and drew her closer, a groan of pleasure slipping. But then, he recalled she'd woken from a nightmare, and he had to hear what she'd dreamt this time.

Thank God, my eyes rolling again. I needed to hear, too, even though I knew the general idea of it; I needed specifics. Daily, I catalogued her nightmares, making sure to check for any changes.

Slowing the kiss to pecks around her face, he settled her in his arms as they lay side by side, facing each other, but without much space between them. His semi erection brushed her stomach, but he ignored it, concern for her taking precedence over his base desires.

Onen was sometimes shocked at the purely innocent things that could spark passion between them. He felt lucky and blessed to have found his soul mate, the one he would love forever and had to protect from whatever disturbed her. When she hurt, he hurt right along, and he wouldn't survive if something were to happen to her.

With a little breezy nudge, I helped him squash the morbid thought as he smoothed tendrils of hair from Nkoyo's face.

"Same dream?"

"Yes." She shivered in what could only be described as fear spasms upon recalling the gruesome images.

I sighed wearily, wondering what the plans of the spirits were if they were only giving Nkoyo the same recurring nightmare. That was just boring. Would I have to visit the spirit of Dream to get a heads up on what came next on this story? I grimaced — I'd been banned from Dream's floaty abode. Urrg! I was stuck getting this tale the hard way.

Stuck with these lovebirds for the foreseeable future.

"I'm here with you, Nk, nothing can hurt you. We will figure this out together," he assured while gathering her closer in a bid to protect her from even the spasms of fear.

I nodded at Onen's assurance because, truly, we'd be figuring this tale out together.

Nkoyo nodded, wrapping her arms around him and holding tight for dear life. Even though the situation was unknown, and therefore solutions might be impossible, she still believed her super husband. If anything could solve her issues, he would go to the ends of the earth to find it.

"I love you, my man of steel." She placed a soft kiss on his chin, grazing it a bit with her teeth. He groaned as pleasure thrilled through him and tightened his hold on her. In the silence of the room, they fell asleep in each other's arms.

Hmm, their marriage of almost two years had been bliss until a few months back. There was something of utmost importance unfurling here. It might not be pleasant, but processes for a better future hardly ever were. I knew this from swirling around in eternity.

In case you were wondering — and also to inject a lighter note into the tale, for I feel it's too early for gloom; there's time for that later — Ekong and Wofai, Nkoyo's former fiancé and Onen's sister, had of course welcomed their 'premature' baby boy, who at almost five pounds was anything but premature.

This memory made me giggle into my palm as the happy parents maintained their child had been conceived in wedlock. Who were we to counter that?

Everybody agreed and ignored the very obvious time of birth five months after the wedding. Nobody told them it would be a medical miracle for a baby as healthy as theirs to have spent only five months in the womb.

Anyway, Ubongabasi Ekong was going on two years, and his parents were already expecting, hopefully, not another premature baby.

Chapter Two

So, a little background tale is in order. As we wait for what is definitely unfolding, let's visit some surrounding tales in brief.

When Prince Onen turned twenty, his parents hadn't just gifted him with the traditional vintage ring which he'd given to his wife when he'd proposed; they'd also given him his own house, a mini palace.

It had frustrated them when he'd refused to furnish the house and had preferred to maintain his suite at the Atam palace. The frustration had only lasted a while as the monarchs loved having their children with them anyway.

However, when Onen finally acknowledged he was in love with Nkoyo and had been ready to fight for her hand, despite assuming she'd still been engaged to her fiancé who was now his sister's husband, he had made all the necessary calls to have his mini palace furnished.

I shook my head wondering why people still doubted the power of women.

In a show of insight, Onen only furnished the house with the basics and allowed articles that would give the mini palace its unique character to be chosen by the bride he'd been planning to fight for, despite the gloom of a possible political clash between kingdoms.

Thank God it hadn't come to that.

He'd been pleased to know Nkoyo loved him as much as he loved her. And she had already broken off her engagement with her fiancé; a decision made easier since said fiancé, a prince of Ibibio kingdom, had already fallen head over heels in love with Onen's sister.

Onen loved his wife. He loved his home. He loved his life. But at the moment, after another night of unexplainable nightmares seeming more ferocious than the last, he had put off work and made an appointment with his parents, and he was going with his wife.

Finally!

Obviously, these nightmares were interfering with his marital bliss. Thank God for sex in marriages. These days, his carnal desires for his wife came with guilt. Onen felt like he was adding to her stress. Though she had no idea he felt this way, he suspected she might not be as passionate for him as he was for her all the time when a string of nightmares hung ominously over her psyche.

Eh, not really—nonetheless, we can all agree his concern for his wife proved commendable.

"Are you sure you're okay with this?" he asked her again as they settled in one of his cars, a Range Rover SUV. "Because if you aren't, we can explore other channels."

"But there aren't any other channels, love," she replied with a reassuring smile.

Onen huffed in frustration. They had decided to keep a private home and life. They'd handle issues themselves, but they were breaking that decision now, in opening up to his parents.

"You know they are going to prod into our private life, right?"

Nkoyo nodded. "I know, and it's a small price to pay to clear off the nightmares."

"I'm just so worried," he grumbled, his eyes expressing the emotion, especially because his beloved, curvy wife seemed to be losing weight every day.

"We'll be fine," she assured, her hand reaching out to grab his comfortingly. He only nodded before turning the ignition and driving through the gate held open by a security man.

Finally, dear God, if I wasn't invested in getting every news, every nuance from this couple, I'd have floated over to the palace instead of sitting grumpily in the back seat.

Fifteen minutes later, he drove into Atam kingdom's palace. A minute after, his mother exclaimed at Nkoyo's weight loss. The fact she'd noticed right away made Onen terrified of what was eating his wife from the inside.

All through the telling of the bizarre dreams and circumstances, Queen Jesam held her daughter-in-law to her side as though to protect her from all harm.

Don't we all wish for great mothers-in-law like Queen Jesam? Don't lie.

Yet, in all that time, Onen's leg bobbed nervously because he wanted to hold his wife the same way. He wanted to convince himself that even though she looked ill, she was still okay. He wanted to be her sole protector.

Ha, one would wonder where Nkoyo had gone to wash her face with everyone loving her this passionately. The woman was simply blessed, I guess.

They had decided to use his parents' suite—their massive bedroom which would shame that of a five-star hotel in size—for privacy. They sat around in white leather seats while Jesam held Nkoyo sitting on a three-seater couch.

"Why didn't you tell us this the moment it started?" Jesam admonished, her eyes flashing her worry.

Onen swallowed with difficulty, then unable to help himself, gave in to his itch and surged to his feet, moving rapidly to his wife's side. Nkoyo knew him and what he was thinking, so she calmly extracted herself from her mother-in-law's arms and went into her husband's own.

And instantly, everything in him calmed and settled. Suddenly, he could breathe easier, and his rapid heartbeat slowed. Nkoyo was the centre of his life, his balance. He tightened his arm around her and silently willed her to be okay.

I know this is a serious situation, but their love was killing me softly.

"You should have told us, son," King Liman said in a calmer voice, his eyes assuring his own wife that everything was fine.

"We are sorry. At first, it felt like hallucinations from typhoid fever, but after the treatment..." Nkoyo left the sentence unfinished.

The king and queen exchanged a knowing glance. Though afraid of what it would mean to Nkoyo, Onen didn't hesitate. "What is it? I've seen that look on your face, and it means you know something."

My spectral head swivelled to Jesam as she cleared her throat.

"Well, I went through these same symptoms when I was pregnant with you, Onen, though they weren't this serious."

Say what now? Nkoyo was with child?

Nkoyo sat up, her eyes widening in hope. "So what did you do to make the nightmares stop?"

Onen nodded, silently concurring to her question.

Unfortunately, it was obvious the young couple weren't listening to the nitty-gritty of the matter, which was the pregnancy.

The monarchs noticed this and exchanged a telling look again, this time with a frown. Their son seemed to catch up quicker.

"Pregnant? But Nk isn't pregnant," he pointed out.

"She must be, son. You see, we'd have told you to expect these symptoms when you announced a pregnancy, but..."

"But I'm not pregnant!" Nkoyo exclaimed.

Poor woman didn't feel pregnant, just listless and tired all the time because she wasn't getting enough sleep at night. Should we tell her? Let me explain that Nkoyo is ignoring all the obvious signs of being pregnant because by all means, she shouldn't be. How could she be pregnant when she and her husband had decided not to have kids yet? Especially with her mother, the queen of Efik kingdom, who had recently given birth to her brother; he was still a baby, and she couldn't be pregnant yet.

"How do you know, darling?" Jesam asked kindly, her hand unconsciously reaching out to comfort the dear girl.

"Well...we...we...I..."

Onen cleared his throat, cutting into his wife's stammers. "We decided not to try for a kid just yet, so Nk was on the pill," he explained gruffly and held his wife to his body.

Now we all, including Nkoyo, understood why Onen had worried about their privacy being pried into. It had been about the judgment they might get for their personal choices. And Nkoyo was feeling appropriately judged simply by viewing the shocked expression on Queen Jesam's face.

I'm feeling pretty judged myself and wincingly thanking God I'm a spirit. Damn, if looks could kill.

"You what?!" Jesam exclaimed with no censure to her emotions.

Well, the woman was both hurt and disappointed, not just at daughter-in-law but at her son, too. Yet, her eyes remained on Nkoyo, which made it seem like she was angry at her.

"Jay, sweetheart..." Liman called in warning while leaving his seat to go to his distraught wife.

I could see the wise king understood his wife had been looking forward to cradling Onen's child, so to find out they'd consciously thwarted it from happening was a tough blow to take. Additionally, I could sense her slight envy that her friend, the queen of Efik kingdom, just had a baby boy. So, Queen Jesam had really been looking forward to having a baby at the palace. She'd been worried and concerned Nkoyo might be having issues getting pregnant and had even wanted to help, but Liman had stalled her from doing so. He'd told her to give them more years before concluding it was a problem.

Apparently, it hadn't been a problem but a conscious decision.

Liman was sure Jesam might react in a way that would be difficult to forgive later, so he approached her. However, Jesam jumped from the seat as though by sitting close to her daughter-in-law, she risked the contamination of a vile virus.

Don't go off judging the queen—her actions only looked that way, because Jesam was too kind to have meant her actions that way.

Oh, but Nkoyo and Onen saw it differently.

"Mother…" Onen called in a warning tone, glad his father reached his mother and held her, shushing and whispering to her to calm her reaction.

But it was too late. Nkoyo's lips quivered as she tried not to cry, yet tears filled her eyes and spilled down her cheeks, dripping down her chest. She was appalled at her weak attitude, not understanding why she was suddenly crying. Jesam's reaction hurt her, of course, but she'd always been good at maintaining decorum and controlling her emotions.

Can someone tell this woman she was pregnant already!

It was therefore understandable to feel Onen become so furious at his mother that he was shocked at how tempted he was to scream at her for hurting his wife. I agreed with his thoughts that it was solely their decision if they were ready to have kids or not and nobody's business what they wanted with their life. Yet, there is no way a marriage can exist on its own without opinionated family members; at least, not in Nigeria.

Onen caught his wife as she abashedly turned into his chest to hide her face from the monarchs. Her shoulders heaved, and his worry for her increased. He knew his wife. She wasn't into emotional displays, so he couldn't understand why her sobs were growing loud and frantic. Was it the stress of the sleepless nights?

Why is no one listening to me? She's pregnant!

Nkoyo looked up at him then, her eyes drenched with tears and full of confusion. "I'm sorry," she heaved and stammered.

Apparently, she couldn't understand why she was crying so uncontrollably either.

The prince was thinking if someone had punched him in the sternum, it wouldn't have hurt as much as it hurt him to stare at her tear-drenched face. It twisted his heart to see her so forlorn, and the pain travelled down his stomach into his bones.

"Oh, God, Nk…" he rasped, helpless, trying to wipe her tears because he didn't know what to say. She shook her head, stood, and fled through the first door she came upon, which so happened to be the bathroom.

Onen followed her, but she'd already shut the door and locked it. He stood there, his head on the door, effectively sharing in her pain. "Nk, my love, please," he begged, not remotely concerned his parents watched on from behind him.

"Give me a minute," she called out, her voice muffled by the heavy oak door. "I'm fine, I…I just want to repair my make up."

He swallowed hard. "Okay, baby, take your time. I'm right here," he announced, wanting to assure her he was on her side — they were in this together.

"I know…thank you," she called back.

His heart — my heart, too — totally melted at her tone and gratitude. In the same vein, I could feel he was also angry at his mother for making Nkoyo feel as though she'd done something wrong. Grinding his jaw, he turned to face his parents.

Jesam moved forward, her expression full of remorse. "I'm so sorry. My God, I can't believe I reacted that way. Jesus, Onen, please, don't be angry, I'm really sorry."

Well damn, a humble queen, ladies and gentlemen.

I turned to Onen. His mother's apology had totally depleted his anger and the itch to vent his fury. He had no idea what to say to her, particularly because she looked extremely contrite.

The door opened behind him, and his parents were forgotten as he swivelled, rushing to Nkoyo. "Hey," he whispered, his hands cradling her cheeks while he looked into her eyes to find out if she was okay. Nkoyo peered back and seemed to have regained her composure.

When they turned with his arm on her shoulders, his mother moved forward again. Ignoring her son's fierce frown, she grasped Nkoyo's hands in hers.

"Please, don't take it to heart. I really was looking forward to holding your and Onen's baby, and your decision was just a shock to me. You see, I'd been worried that, maybe, you were having difficulty taking in, seeing as —"

"Jay," Liman called, instantly shutting her up from what she'd been about to say.

Don't panic, I'm here. The queen had been about to refer to Nkoyo's mother's difficulty in taking in, too, when she'd newly married. I'm sure we can all agree with Liman that titbit is not necessary here.

The queen read his gaze and sighed instead. "I'm still excited about holding your baby," she enthused and hugged Nkoyo who still looked flummoxed from the apology.

"Mother—"

"But I'm not—"

Jesam cut off their simultaneous refutes. "Oh, but you are," she declared, excited. "She really is," she said in an assuring tone to her son.

Liman nodded at Onen when he turned to his father for confirmation. Nkoyo looked flabbergasted and speechless, definitely wondering what happened to her consecutive pill popping for pregnancy prevention.

Even though it hadn't been their plan, suddenly, Onen could think of nothing else more beautiful than seeing his wife plump and swelling with his seed. Cue eyeroll—men, with their one-track mind. It was almost disgusting how the thought was so exhilaratingly erotic, he was instantly hard and longed for an extended alone time with his wife. Onen was deliriously happy at this new, unexpected development.

I'm happy for them, too, but can someone get on with explaining the nightmares? Thank you!

"Your mother had nightmares similar to that of Nkoyo, but they hadn't been this vivid, and they'd only lasted the first month of the pregnancy," Liman explained.

Onen's gaze met Nkoyo, his eyes widening in realization. Did this mean she was almost four months pregnant? They were definitely having a silent conversation with just their eyes that I'm here to expose. We'll visit a doctor soon, they decided with a nod and returned their attention to the monarchs.

"How do we get it to stop?" Onen wanted to know—his main concern. Now with Nkoyo pregnant, he didn't want anything stressing her.

Jesam cleared her throat.

"We had to visit the oldest woman in the kingdom." Oh, finally, something interesting. "I cannot say how old she is, but she barely had any teeth left. She'd explained the nightmares stemmed from the power of the ring wanting to share history and reinforce what the ring had finally been made to represent."

"What...what had the ring been before; what does it finally represent?" Nkoyo asked almost breathlessly, like she had to know or suffocate if she didn't.

She can't have been more eager than me to find out, but she sounded that way.

I frowned as Onen gave her a quizzical look and was shocked to see her almost bending out of her chair in a bid to get an answer. Umm, she made a picture of pure eagerness in that moment. Come on, that should be my act, not hers, I pouted.

"I—" Jesam noticed her eagerness, too, as did Liman. The queen thought how strange her behaviour was, like her life depended on knowing. It left Jesam confused and uncertain, and she turned to her husband helplessly.

Liman decided to respond. "The old woman never told her. She'd said it wasn't hers to know."

Nkoyo's gasp of disappointment rang so loud, it couldn't have been mistaken for anything else. Onen was instantly concerned, frowning at her and silently asking if she was okay. She nodded in assurance.

I felt a sudden presence in the room. Hey, there was another entity here apart from me. I should have been able to see it, but I saw nothing. If I had a physical heart, it would be pounding as my gaze swivelled from corner to corner, searching for the being with the heavy presence.

All I got as reply was Nkoyo's thoughts as her eyes fixed on the ring. Her heartbeat echoed strong in my ear as I swooped closer.

Nkoyo realized her ring suddenly seemed snug on her marriage finger. For some reason, she had the swift knowledge that she wouldn't be able to pull it off if she tried. How she knew this, she couldn't fathom.

I nudged her to prove it to herself, so she fiddled with the usually free ring and tried to twist it upward...to no avail.

Her heartbeat picked up speed as I gasped. In that moment, she also felt something unexplainably larger than life surging to existence. If I wasn't watching her like a hawk, I would've missed the only sign indicating what was happening in that moment. The simple cut of the diamond stone on the ring twinkled as though winking at her.

The ring was the entity?!

"I want to meet the oldest woman in the kingdom," Nkoyo blurted out as though it hadn't been her will to do so.

Did the ring make her? Oh, my, this was definitely more than a ridiculous tale. Things were getting deeper than expected.

"Wait a minute, Nk, we don't even know if this is safe. Is the woman even still alive?" Onen, of course, didn't like the direction of the conversation.

"She is," Liman replied.

"I want to see her. How soon can I see her? Maybe tomorrow —"

"Nk —" Onen refuted. He wasn't one to barge into unknown situations.

Honestly, though, I can tell you for free the prince had never been comfortable with anything stinking of the supernatural. If he'd known the ring hadn't been just an old piece of jewellery and would be causing this much complications, he wouldn't have given it to Nkoyo in the first place. With that thought in mind, he turned to shoot down the whole 'visiting the oldest woman in the kingdom' idea.

I surely wouldn't have allowed that. Come on, I needed to know what was going on. However, Nkoyo turned to him, too. And Onen swore in his thoughts that for a second, his wife's eyes swirled and flashed an aqua colour. Really? How did I miss it — what did it mean?

To be sure, Onen closed his eyes as I leaned closer to Nkoyo's face. When he opened them again, Nkoyo's eyes were their usual hazel hue, yet, to me, it held a certain knowing glint. Then without warning, he felt an overwhelming surge of love for Nkoyo in his heart. So powerful, he knew he couldn't deny her anything she asked.

I stood back, shaking my head in consternation. Uh, no way I'd mess with this entity. This was something stronger than I'd ever encountered in my spectral existence.

"Please, darling, please," she begged, even managing to pout.

I frowned as her voice took on a certain musical quality. Right before all our eyes, Onen couldn't resist smiling at her. Even to me, Nkoyo looked so alluring; talk more of what she looked to her husband. In fact, Onen was feeling lucky to be married to her.

"Of course, my love, anything for you," he whispered with an infatuated look.

"Are you okay?" Nkoyo asked with a slightly worried frown, eyes narrowed on her husband's face.

Onen snapped instantly as though rousing from a dream. His eyes widened at his wife. It was still Nkoyo, but a moment ago, she had been…more…he couldn't explain it.

I couldn't explain it either, and it was driving me crazy.

"I'm fine." He nodded and shook his head slightly to clear the webby feeling in his mind.

"So we can really go?" she asked for confirmation.

"Mm-hmm." He nodded, still trying to get the weird vibe off him. "But we should visit the doctor first of all and make sure you're fine," he rallied back again, seeming in control.

"We should go now. I'm so excited. I know it isn't what we planned, but I want this baby. Are you happy, my love?" she whispered, suddenly realizing he hadn't reacted to the news as yet. Was he happy or… She couldn't complete the thought.

Onen saw the uncertainty in her eyes and leaned close to her ear to assuage it. "If I give in to my emotions right now, Nk, my parents will be scandalously shocked. I've been hard for you since I heard."

His voice was pure seduction, pure sin. Her turn to look dazedly at him with total surrender and love.

"We should go now, and I don't mean to the doctor's," she whispered back urgently, her eyes flashing desire as she stood up with a ready smile.

The fire ignited in his stomach and began burning. He wanted his wife so much at that moment, it was all he could do not to grab her and return to his suite in his parents' palace. But then, everybody would know what they'd been doing because it would definitely be apparent on their faces afterwards.

Oh, he was refusing to add that they could be quite loud in their passion. I've had to step out of their room a couple of times.

Well, to the monarchs of Atam kingdom, they made the doctor's appointment excuses and fled from the palace. The monarchs exchanged a knowing smile and went right ahead to discuss the arrival of their first child's child. The grandparents were ecstatic about a third baby in the family, but they were also worried about Onen's reaction when he got to see the oldest woman in the kingdom.

Let's give the lovebirds some time alone while I find the scoop on the oldest woman in the kingdom. Wouldn't you want to know? She sounds fascinating.

Chapter Three

She was a small, shrivelled, old woman with one foot in life and the other in death. Mmatami was on her death bed and had been for the better part of several months. Each time, her caregivers announced she wouldn't last the night as she kept whispering names of long-dead relatives. Yet, against all odds, her narrow chest kept rattling up and down, crankily inhaling and expelling breath.

Her caregivers and family—grandchildren and great-grandchildren abandoned by their parents at the old woman's compound in search of greener pastures—had enjoyed a certain prestige when Mmatami had been functional. She'd been the eyes of the gods and spirits, and people from different kingdoms trooped down to enquire for solutions and directives in their challenges.

But then, she had taken to her death bed—and never died.

An admirable trait, though: they watched out for each other and worked together to farm the massive lands which would be theirs when Mmatami finally deigned to die.

Apparently, it wasn't today, I thought as I snooped around.

While the family gathered at the massive square courtyard, peeling the giant heap of cassava from a successful harvest, they got the shock of their lives that early morning. Mmatami walked out from her room, albeit leaning feebly on her walking stick, which was taller than her.

From all I'd gathered and seen, that feeble woman shouldn't be walking at all! She hadn't done so in ages. She should be dying. Or maybe she was dead already, the children thought.

At this frightening thought, the girls and boys fled in all directions, scattering their slippers, some swiping the babies from the ground on their way and howling 'ghost' at the top of their voices.

Okay, I have to confess this was the funniest thing I've experienced this year. Surprisingly, though, instead of neighbours gathering as expected from the screams, nobody, not even one person, came out. It was as though the compound had become insulated — no sound went out.

Oh, well, it was to be expected, after all. The woman did work for the spirits, and they were fully at work here.

Ignoring the antics of her family, Mmatami took coordinated steps towards her favourite rocking chair in her opened space receiving area. A mini hall, she'd used it to receive guests when she'd been a functional channel for the spirits.

In disuse, the space had dust and cobwebs everywhere.

Mmatami could not speak English. As such, all her communications were done in Lokaa, the native language. But she went a step further, since she was practically a spirit these days — she willed her family back from their rat race. They returned to find her rocking in her chair.

Without wasting time, she gave directives. "Clean this room from top to bottom," she said in a voice rusty with disuse. "Make sure my inner sanctum is cleaned even better than this room. Use that fine smelling water you usually pour on your white cloth, so that the room will smell fresh."

"Do you mean bleach, mama?" the oldest grandchild ventured to ask. And the look Mmatami gave her clearly pointed to her disinterest in the name of said washing chemical.

I'm giggling my head off here.

The family went into a whirlwind of activities; they wiped and cleaned every surface. The inner sanctum was Mmatami's shrine, and they took great care in cleaning out that room. The eldest grandchild went a step higher to spritz a bit of her perfume in the room to give it a flowery smell.

The sanctum was more of Mmatami's office. Where every other floor in the house was cemented, it had a mud floor, and it had always been that way.

Mmatami directed three hens be slaughtered and a sumptuous native meal be prepared. Then she asked one of the teenage girls to run her a hot bath, where she sat right in the middle of the courtyard to take. The boys were noticeably absent at this epoch-making event.

I can't blame them. Nobody wants to see the shriveled flabs of flesh that used to be breasts and buttocks hanging from their grandma's bony frame. That was a sure libido killer, and we know these boys needed their libidos at their age.

Her great iron box was opened, and her ceremonial white lace, floor-length gown was withdrawn from the camphor cocoon. She was dressed, her teeth cleaned, at least, the few remaining ones, and her white, baby soft hair, which resembled poofs of cotton, was combed.

Then Mmatami retired to her sanctum and rocked on her chair.

The family stood around, uncertain, not understanding what all the preparations were for. One of the boys finally asked.

"I'm expecting a guest," she replied in her whispery soft voice.

We can all guess who the guest will be.

***

Onen pulled his hands from the pockets of his trousers when his wife strolled out from the Atam palace. His eyes smouldered at the sight of her. His body heated up, his immediate urge to take her home for more down time. His desires seemed doubly fuelled since they'd returned from the hospital the previous day. It had been confirmed—she was completing her third month, and yet, her stomach seemed the same.

The previous night's nightmare hadn't been too bad; it hadn't made her nauseous. As though the ring realized they were making plans to do the needful, whatever that was. Onen refused to think about it.

Where he refused to think about what was to be done, I, on the other hand, couldn't stop wondering and anticipating what would be done at the old woman's place.

They had arrived a few minutes ago apropos Queen Jesam taking them to see the oldest woman in the kingdom. Nkoyo went inside to find if the queen was ready. Even as I flitted about excitedly, I noticed her eyes immediately locked with that of her husband's as she walked out.

"Stop looking at me as though I'm a juicy piece of meat and you're a lion." She smiled coyly as she moved towards him in a white, chiffon, knee-length kaftan and matching trousers, with flat shoes.

Oh, that coy attitude got his heart hammering. This couple never stops with the lovey-dovey. He approached her, grinning and making a playful growling sound as his arms rounded her waist. Her scent inundated his nostrils, and he held it in, enjoying the warmth of her body.

"You shouldn't look so deliciously pregnant then," he suggested in her ear and nipped it tenderly, enjoying the full body shiver of pleasure racking her torso.

"But you caused it. Your—" Nkoyo lightly cleared her throat, and I rolled my eyes understanding what she wasn't saying. "...defied my contraceptive pills and nailed my poor egg." She pouted, and Onen laughed heartily at her joke, instantly attracting the gazes of the palace workers.

He leaned on his car and drew her close, aligning her body on his. "You should never have called me super man." He smirked, his eyes glinting pure male satisfaction and pride in his virility.

"If you lost your mouth-watering muscular physique, and a bit of your height, and surely your great stamina in bed, I might be tempted to stop—"

He kissed her then, silencing what she'd been about to say.

"Don't you dare," he whispered when he raised his head, his eyes gazing into hers with tenderness.

Nkoyo shook her head. That kiss had melted her limbs. *I* had not been kissed, but just being in the vicinity meant I felt melty even in my spectral form. Nkoyo leaned heavily on her husband's body and momentarily wished they weren't on an important mission today.

"I would never—" she whispered the same moment Queen Jesam walked out dressed in a free, long white gown.

"Nkoyo," the queen gasped in pleasure. "How did you know to wear white?" she asked as she approached the disentangling couple.

My interest perked up at the question, immediately noticing the coincidence. Surely, it was a coincidence, right?

"Err, I didn't know, I just..." Nkoyo shrugged self-consciously. "This was the only thing that seemed extremely comfortable to me."

"She has it in all the colours," Onen teased with a grin. "Good morning, Mom."

"Good morning." Jesam turned speculative eyes on Nkoyo again.

All right, it definitely wasn't a coincidence if the queen's pulse was racing with that speculative look in her eyes.

Nkoyo shrugged again. "I don't know, the white just called out to me."

"What's the significance of the white?" Onen asked off-handedly, as though he wasn't feeling terribly uncomfortable with the conversation. He had made up his mind not to freak out about whatever might unfold in this strange expedition, and that meant taking every ridiculous thing said casually.

Jesam was aware of her son's loathing for the metaphysical. "It's just lovely to wear matching colours," she replied, and Onen rolled his eyes with exasperation, causing the women to laugh.

"So, I take it this woman is still alive, then?" he asked, because his mother had promised to reach out to those closest to the old woman to check if she was still functional.

Jesam cleared her throat, and Onen narrowed his eyes. Whenever his parents cleared their throat in an uncomfortable manner, it was a harbinger for the delivery of unpleasant news.

"Well…she isn't dead, but she isn't exactly alive either."

"Mom…"

"Then why are we going?" Nkoyo beat her husband to the question and looked extremely worried, almost scared.

"Hope, children. Hope is why we are going, and it's not like we have a lot of options," she pointed out and went towards her car, where the driver opened the door for her.

Sighing in exasperation, I muttered my thanks to the queen's positive outlook on the situation.

Onen sighed, too, and opened the door for his wife before turning to the driver's seat and following his mother's car.

***

Mmatami had been rocking for the better part of forty-five minutes. The family had given her nervous glances and wondered what was next. Even though she looked as though peacefully dozing, the chair continued rocking.

Oh, things with this woman would be entirely too interesting for my poor heart. I couldn't wait for the shock of the royals when they find her awake as opposed to being a vegetable.

Of course, her grandchildren could explain how she'd been able to walk, when she'd been half dead as of that morning. Twenty minutes into the rocking, the family had been lulled back into a semblance of relaxation, but they never left the vicinity. Everyone found a vantage point and vigilantly kept Mmatami in sight.

Then, without warning, she stopped rocking by thumping her smooth, solid walking stick on the hard mudfloor.

The sudden silence was eerie. Even my spectral skin itched with static. The family sat up and looked nervous. The eldest girl rubbed hands over her arms as goosebumps spread over her flesh. She'd been about to ask Mmatami what she might need but was interrupted by the woman's rhythmic whispers in tandem with the thump of her walking stick.

Kakalakakakakalakaka – kuwee
Kakalakakalakakakalakakala – kuwee
YanenwobolOjilopon – Ofuken
Wenwobol; WenwoOjilopon – Ofuken
YanenWenwobol – Ofuken
Nnanke! Yanen- woyee, wofai, woObasenfawa – Ofuken.

Wow!

I'm laughing because I can imagine your confusion. Ahem, throat cleared…Mmatami is, until she dies, one of the maiden leaders in a female-only tradition called Kebolabola—it could be called a female cult, responsible for some traditional rites in the process of installing a new king. Oh, and the women go topless during these rites, whether young or old. Don't freak out, this is Africa, after all.

The reason for this background exposure is because of the first two lines of her rhythmic chant. Those are descriptions of drum sounds that begin the song of the king's procession. So, Mmatami used it as the spirits whispered the arrival of royalty in her home. The family heard and understood her chants, and they fled to the front yard just in time to see Onen, Nkoyo, and Queen Jesam step out of their cars.

Rushing forward, the eldest granddaughter genuflected in greeting to the queen and prince. The other kids did the same, eliciting smiles from the royals. Onen recognized two of the elder boys who had recently begun work at the mill. Their eyes bulged in awe that the prince of the kingdom was at their home.

They were immediately led to Mmatami's hall, and her whispery chants flowed and carried on the wind to where they stood.

Jesam smiled in acknowledgement as she understood the woman's chants, even though she frowned in confusion at the supposedly half-dead woman's strength and the mention of the name 'Nnanke.'

Goosebumps broke out on Nkoyo's body from her scalp to her soles and up again. Then the ring seemed to tighten and release on her finger. When she looked down, the diamond illuminated and the sapphire flashed bright. Her heart thumped as she knew, without fathoming how, the ring was acknowledging whatever the yet unseen woman was chanting.

"What is she saying?" she whispered to Onen after shifting unobtrusively towards him and grasping his hand.

Onen felt the cold sweat on his wife's palms and immediately looked down with concern. She seemed okay, except for the slight look of apprehension on her face.

"She's welcoming us, I guess."

"I need the words, Onen. I've heard 'Obol' in that midst, and that means king, right?"

He nodded. "Yes. Well, if you really must know, the first two lines are just some instruments sounds, like drums. Then she says, 'YanenwobolOjilopon – Ofuken.' This means the king's woman and queen of the village is coming."

"'Ofuken' means 'is coming'?" Nkoyo asked for clarity's sake.

"Yes; 'Wenwobol, WenwoOjilopon' means 'son of the king,' 'son of the queen.' Then 'YanenWenwobol' —"

"Oh, that's me, right?" she whispered with an excited smile that endeared her to him more. He grinned and nodded.

"That means 'son of the king's woman or the prince's woman," he explained and liked the sound of it so much, he wanted to kiss her there, especially with the adoring look she was giving him.

Focus, I snapped even though they couldn't hear me. This was serious stuff, not the time for romance.

"I like being your woman," she whispered in his ear.

"I like being your man," he replied and winked, tightening her hand in his. "Then there is 'Nnanke.' It's a name, and it means 'I received from God.' And this Nnanke is a good woman. 'YanenWoyee,' a woman of peace—'YanenWofai,' and a woman that God has blessed—'YanenWoObaseNfawa'."

"Who is Nnanke?" she asked with a frown.

"I have no idea," he replied the moment the old woman ended her chant.

The thump of her walking stick heralded her approach from the small room. Her poof of white hair broke through the drapes first before her shriveled body dressed in white.

I grinned because I'd been waiting for this moment. I turned to the prince, and he stiffened. Onen immediately knew his mother's explanation had been a lie about the significance of the white wears. His heart hammered in trepidation, but then, he calmed himself when he recalled he was there to help Nkoyo.

Mmatami shuffled slowly, so slowly, Onen wished he could have gone to help her. But the little woman needed no help because she ignored assistance from her grandson. Her gait was unequal, like someone suffering from one lame foot. She made her slow way directly to Nkoyo. Without sparing her any glance, she went for the ring on her left hand.

"Nnanke! Awonke."

She welcomed Nnanke, who was apparently the ring! Oh, I get it now.

In fact, to the shock of everybody in that hall, guests and family alike, Mmatami carried on a one-sided conversation with the ring, even though to Nkoyo and myself, of course, it wasn't so one-sided because she could feel the ring hum on her finger as though replying the woman.

The whole conversation to everyone, except Nkoyo who didn't fully understand the language, entailed Mmatami catching up with a woman named Nnanke. It was a strange situation, and Onen kept wondering when they'd get to the part of helping his wife.

Patience, my prince. We were here now and fully invested in unravelling this mystery. Now, I needed to know who Nnanke is and why she's in the damn ring.

Chapter Four

Mmatami's one-sided conversation ended after ten minutes, then she ordered her granddaughter to bring in the *'Yedamblongh'* – the welcome tray basically meaning *'enjoyment.'* It contained a small wooden bowl with palm oil and pepper sauce, and other smaller bowls of long-shaped chopped kola-nut, garden egg, shredded smoked fish, edible cow skin, and *okaana*, which some people know as the afang leaf.

Nkoyo struggled not to grimace. Even after marrying Onen for this long, she'd still not gotten used to the tradition of eating kola nut and garden egg wrapped in raw afang leaf, dipped in palm oil/pepper sauce. Raw afang! A travesty to eat raw afang. She wondered how the people of Efik or Ibibio kingdom would react when presented with raw afang to chew. She almost smiled recalling Ekong's face during the marriage rites to Wofai: of course the tray had been presented – it was tradition.

And like her, he'd been shocked. The only use for afang in Efik and Ibibio was for soup, sliced, pounded, or ground before being cooked into soup.

But she did it all the time—tradition required it. She girded her imaginary loin cloths and did it. But she had a system: she preferred to wrap the smoked fish, seasoned cow skin in her okaana leaf, get a good amount of pepper and oil, and chew the mixture. Nothing could make her touch the kola nut. She'd always had a sweet tooth, and kola nut was the bitterest thing on God's green earth as far as she was concerned.

She could never understand how the queen and Onen managed to relish it. Silently, she thanked God as the tray was cleared after just one wrap, and a sumptuous spread of boiled yam and another kind of chicken sauce was arranged before them.

Onen was shocked to see Nkoyo wasn't allowed to eat. Apparently, the food was for himself and his mom. Mmatami dragged Nkoyo into the small room she'd come out from, and the couple's eyes held until the garish drapes closed.

Guess where I'll be, folks?

"She'll be fine," Queen Jesam said, touching her son's arm and breaking his gaze from the closed drapes.

"I thought you said she was half dead. She looks very alive to me," he pointed out.

"I was confused, too, but the granddaughter spoke of a miracle this morning. After several months of being half-dead, she just suddenly got out of her bed this morning, ordered everywhere be cleaned, dressed up, and told them she was expecting a guest."

Onen's mouth hung open from shock. He was recalling the old woman was already calling out their persons before she'd even seen their faces. He didn't like strange situations at all; he preferred things that could be clearly explained and seen.

Huffing in frustration, he frowned as he joined his mother in eating. He couldn't taste the food. He might've been eating sawdust from the bland taste in his mouth. Rather, he worried for Nkoyo in there with the strange woman.

***

The room was small, with a mud floor, Nkoyo noticed the instant she got inside. A tiny window opened into a vegetable garden, the only furniture two wooden seats facing each other and a table by one of those seats, with tiny wooden bowls carrying indeterminate colours of liquid substance.

Nkoyo had the peripheral feeling they weren't alone in that room. Well, I was here, yet, I could also feel another presence. Could it be Nnanke, the ring, or something else? The thought sent another rapid spread of goosebumps all over Nkoyo's body. This time, the goosebumps felt alive, like it had tiny insect feet skittering on her skin.

She shivered and had the pressing urge to swipe her whole body with a piece of cloth to get the feeling off. But she didn't need a piece of cloth because Mmatami did something that totally took her mind from her uncomfortable feeling.

My eyes widened as the old woman softly thumped her walking stick in front of the seat with the small table beside it, and the stick just stood there, on its own. Nkoyo's eyes bulged in their sockets. She immediately went to check if the stick was imbedded in the mud floor, but the abnormally long staff stood there alone with no support.

Her heart began hammering at what she was seeing, about to hyperventilate when Mmatami placed a tender hand on her stomach and smiled amiably.

"*Eyaeee…Wen-Wenwobol, awonke! Wol-idiyanoo?*"

Nkoyo wasn't totally ignorant of the Atam language. She knew simple greetings and so, mentally, she interpreted what the old woman was saying to her baby. "*Yes o…the child of the prince, you're welcome! How is the body?*"

"*Wol-itawatawa,*" she answered. At least, she knew that one, meaning 'the body is well.'

Mmatami raised her white head with a smile. "*ApueLokạạ?*"

She was asking if Nkoyo understood Lokạạ, the native tongue. Nkoyo shook her head, and the woman cackled in old people glee, her eyes glinting mischievously as she directed Nkoyo to sit down while she took the opposite seat and repositioned her walking stick beside her…still standing alone, unsupported by any seen thing.

Nkoyo took the seat, immediately captivated with the woman's chants, which she didn't understand at all. Then with her gnarly hands, Mmatami reached out for Nkoyo's left hand—specifically, for the ring. She looked down as the old woman spoke and rubbed the ring with reverence.

The ring's design entailed three gold bands, seemingly banded together by very thin gold vines with delicate flowers on them, and then the centre held the considerable sized, kite-shaped diamond.

It was no ordinary ring. Nkoyo knew that now and watched, fascinated, as Mmatami seemed to coax the ring from her finger and then dumped it in one of the wooden bowls that carried a thick, yellowish clay substance.

Without wasting her movements, Mmatami reached into another bowl, and her fingers came out stained by white clay mixed into a gooey consistency. And without permission, she shoved her stained fingers into Nkoyo's mouth.

Oh my God, I gagged at her unprecedented action.

The woman had the effrontery to expose her toothless gums in a wide grin when Nkoyo gagged in disgust at the slightly salty taste of the clay substance.

"You speak Lokạạ now," Mmatami said with a smile while fixedly watching Nkoyo control her gag reflex.

Wait, what? I turned to stare at Nkoyo, wondering if such a miracle were possible. However, I shouldn't have wondered, seeing the wonderful things this old woman had done so far.

It took Nkoyo a while to realize Mmatami was still speaking the native tongue, but she understood her fully. She gasped in surprise and widened her eyes, nodding that she indeed understood what she was saying.

"Good. Now you will see…"

"See what?" Nkoyo asked, testing her newfound language and surprised it didn't feel awkward on her tongue.

"You are the one to see what the ring was and what it now represents," she explained.

Mmatami dumped her finger into the yellowish substance that had the ring. She stirred it and then pulled the finger out and made a dot on the centre of Nkoyo's forehead, close to her hair line, then another over her left eyebrow, and another over her right eyebrow.

The yellowish dots formed a pyramid shape on Nkoyo's forehead, and Mmatami asked Nkoyo to do the same to her face. Nkoyo followed the process as it had been done to her. The old woman nodded her pleasure at Nkoyo doing it right. The ring was brought out, the diamond flashing blue fire, the gold glinting orange sparkles even as it dripped yellowish gooey substance on Mmatami's white dress.

Words were spoken—gibberish as far as Nkoyo was concerned because her eyes were riveted on the amazing sight of her ring. She followed it as the old woman extended it to her forehead and then she couldn't see it any longer…she could only feel it.

Oh, but I saw. You didn't think I would miss this epoch-making event, did you? Oh, yes, I saw…as Mmatami's hand holding the ring extended to Nkoyo's forehead, the three dots illuminated on her skin, glowing the same orange sparkle on the gold bands of the ring.

Nkoyo felt like the neurons in her brain were suddenly humming, vibrating as the ring drew near. Her breath picked up, her body hummed right along, and she closed her eyes to try and contain the very palpable power flowing through her veins.

Her hands clasped the handles of her wooden chair, so tight, she imagined she heard a crack in the wood. But she dispersed the ridiculous thought even in her struggle; she didn't have such strength, not after months of sleepless nights.

After valiantly trying to tighten her lips and keep it contained, she gasped aloud at the sheer wave of energy surging through her. Then Mmatami placed the ring on the centre of her forehead, and it stuck; the circle of the ring in the middle of the yellow dots' triangle and the flashing diamond face down, wedged in between her eyebrows.

"Don't fight the power," Mmatami said as Nkoyo's hand splintered the wood of the seat handle while expelling grunts of effort.

"Breathe and take it in…allow it to control you, and then you will control it. You will be one and the same," she said calmly.

Nkoyo heard Mmatami's voice in echoes, like she was drowning in a turbulent ocean wave, hence why she couldn't breathe. If she took a breath, water would rush into her mouth. But then, the old woman continued whispering, encouraging her to breathe. At the end, the life-preserving urge to take in air finally made her breathe.

Oh, and it was a large inhalation, one that felt like Nkoyo and everything that was her dropped away in a dark hole swirling so rapidly, she physically swayed at the dizzying effect it caused.

"Let it in, Nkoyo, stop trying to control it. *Komaạ!*"

At Mmatami's authoritative shout of 'stop' in the native tongue, Nkoyo let go. And as she did, her head flung backwards, her face pointing to the ceiling, her mind taking in the furious speed of centuries swooping back through time.

Centuries of war and peace, love and lust; centuries of betrayal and lost tradition and knowledge, centuries of slavery by the whites and then the blacks…a river of blood, dead bodies, discord, a spirit shrouded in dark, tattered cloths, prodding men to evil, a black man in the sea of white people, and then an unwanted baby, abandoned and saved by a poor family.

The swooping stopped, and Nkoyo took another large inhalation of oxygen, her face still pointing to the ceiling. Suddenly, her eyes opened, and it beheld the same flashing sapphire colour of the diamond in between her eyebrows.

Yellowish gooey substance dribbled slowly down her face from the ring firmly stuck on her forehead, but she didn't feel it. Nkoyo's eyes were open, yet she saw nothing in that small room. She inhaled what Mmatami burned in one of her small wooden bowls, and her consciousness went further, deeper into the era of her nightmares.

It was a waking dream—a vision of the past.

Finally, we are going to my kind of world.

Chapter Five

The Past

The elders of the different *kepun* — patri-clans that made up Yakpani — gathered round the *Binah's* shrine. It was a small hut at the edge of the biggest forest in Yakpani settlement, surrounded by a collection of objects, pottery vessels, curiously shaped stones, and carved wooden figures.

The binah — priest — sat on the ground in front of the entrance of his hut and listened to all the refutes coming from the elders concerning the decision the *ase* — fertility spirits and ancestors associated with Yakpani — had taken.

Their arguments came because they thought as men, and it was a large difference from how the spirits reasoned.

"Binah, this cannot be. Our women are specifically for child-bearing."

"And the gods are aware that we are still sacrificing all we have to the fertility spirit to bless our women who have been suffering barrenness for too long."

"Too long since we left Lekanakpakpa, the ancestral land, and settled at Umor."

"And we thought it might have been something caused by the Umor's abomination of eating human flesh. But after the conflict and we moved to make Yakpani..."

"Our women still suffer barrenness..."

"Well, except Ibiang's wife who seems be to shitting them like goat droppings."

"It was after she found and picked that girl child in the forest which everyone thought was a baby witch. But after so many years, Ibiang and his *lejimo*, his matriclan, have prospered both in farming and children."

"Maybe they are blessed by the *ndet* which they place in their compounds."

"But we place such carved figurines, too, in our compounds, yet our women miscarry their pregnancies, don't carry at all, or when they deliver, the interval between is too long. It is like we pour our seeds into unfertile wombs."

"So, it must be his matriclan; it must be the fact that he traces his descent from a woman."

"He is not the only one with a matriclan descent in the village, there are others, and they find themselves in the same barren distress."

"Enough about Ibiang. There is the war approaching, quickly and surely towards us. You know Umor has not forgiven the trick we played on them, and then we left to make Yakpani before they could revenge."

"This war is not about revenge. Umor just wants more land and power. They do not like that we have prospered on our own and our women are more beautiful."

"Every woman is to be protected; we cannot lose any of them, not even to the gods. *Lesouletaotoba* – 'a large population is more powerful than a machete.' We must pledge to work hard at night to fill our wives' bellies with our seeds and hope that as we fight in the approaching battle, sons will grow in their wombs to take our places if we fall."

"May we not fall!"

All the elders nodded in agreement to the prayer.

"Even the warriors are to find a maiden they like, and we, the elders, will pay what is required to make her his wife. We hope their young seeds would prove more powerful than ours. Yakpani needs to overcome this barrenness in our women."

"We do not see why we need another binah, and a female one, at that. You are the binah we know and trust, and we see your strength. The gods speak clearly through you, and you always lead us right."

Binah Yakpani stared at the group of fourteen men who had just expressed their misgivings at the decision of the spirits. "Okuo, you have just said the gods speak clearly through me, and yet, you people disbelieve today's words."

A murmur of explanation rose from the group of men dressed only in woven wrappers around their waists. They tried to tell the priest that their words didn't mean they disbelieved him.

"It's okay, *komaa*," the priest advised them to stop their murmuring in a calm voice. He waited, and they did. "The gods have spoken, and there is nothing I can do about it but follow. After two nights, we will gather here again, rub our hands and legs with *ekoo*, the mystical yellow clay, before entering the village in search of this woman."

The elders gasped as one in shock, their eyes widening. "You mean, the woman might come from any of our *kepun*?"

They feared the chosen woman might be one of their wives or daughters.

Binah smiled knowingly. "There are two sides where we trace our descent. The matri-clan, *legimo*, and the patri-clan, *kepun*. No matter the war, Umor, Yakpani, Ekori, Nko, Idomi, and the other smaller settlements are from one ancestral land — Lekanakpakpa or Akpa, as you have decided to call it.

"It is just that we have made the patri-clans so dominant, it seems the matri-clans have no importance or use, and their descents practically disappears," Binah said while using his forefinger to dig a hole in the soft sand.

Several brows furrowed in confusion.

"Are you saying this woman might come from a *lejimo*?"

"She might..."

And the elders sighed as one in relief.

"...or might not," Binah said, his eyes focused on what his finger was doing. "The gods will decide after two nights."

When the elders left, their hearts were heavy with the weight of their recent discovery. There were only three *ajimo* (plural for *lejimo*) in Yakpani, and in those three, only Ibiang's own had a girl of marital age. The rest also suffered the effect of barren women. And as Binah had rightly said, the *ajimo* was of little importance and therefore might be exempted.

Since the gods and spirits would choose from anyone, it might end up being from a *kepun*. Yakpani had fourteen *yepun* (plural for *kepun*), and they had an abundance of marital-aged women.

Each elder silently slunk into the night to their compounds with the decision to pray to their *ndet*, that their women be spared from the responsibilities of the spirits.

Binah had explained the chosen woman would never know a man till her death. If she did, the punishment would be instant death, or else the land would suffer for her transgressions. So, said woman would never give birth, and each elder wanted as many children and grandchildren for his *kepun* as possible.

Apart from the general aim of expanding the population of Yakpani, the elders were also conscious of the prestige of a large family, which invariably meant larger lands. And larger lands resulted in power and status and being respectfully heard at council gatherings.

But in two nights, each elder feared their aspirations might be destroyed.

***

An unmitigated cry of terror wrenched from his throat and invariably roused him from his nightmare of being branded with a glowing red iron straight from a blazing fire.

A nightmare that had been his everyday life but from more than two years ago when the white man decided that slavery was indeed inhumane. Some of the white men anyway, not all, grew consciences and created the anti-slavery movement which curbed the exportation of African slaves.

It had been like a dream, an unbelievable miracle, when liberated Africans, former slaves, were given their freedom and Christianised in Europe. Okoi only wished his mother had been alive to see the era of the black man not treated entirely like cow dung on an elegant breakfast table.

With the abolition of slave trade in 1833, many of the former slaves, himself included, headed to Africa on the missionary ship. He'd heard of ex-slaves who'd been liberated from a slave ship having a settlement at Sierra Leone. He'd heard that those who could trace their roots in Nigeria could emigrate back to their homeland.

Okoi sighed and shivered from both the cold and the memory of the white man's vicious face in his dream as he had approached, his aim being to place the hot iron on his manhood. Shivering again, he muttered under his breath, "Thank God for freedom," and then grimaced as the actual branding scar on the back of his left shoulder throbbed painfully, reminding him of the horrors he'd just been liberated from.

Because of the stories his mother had told him about the land she had come from, he'd been among the people who had decided to follow the missionary ship from Sierra Leone to Nigeria in the hopes of tracing their roots. The ship had berthed at the shores of Onitsha, the east of Nigeria, where Samuel Ajayi Crowther was valiantly trying, together with Doctor Blake and other white missionaries, to Christianize the locals.

Having stayed at the settlement in Sierra Leone for more than a year and grown used to the cries of men, women, and children suffering from nightmares, Okoi enjoyed the calm and quiet of the mission house at Onitsha. He envied the people who'd been lucky not to experience the horrors of slavery and so were accorded peaceful sleep.

He also admired Samuel Crowther, an equally liberated slave who had been an understudy with the missionaries for so long and now was selflessly determined to spread Christianity all over Nigeria.

He could still remember his words clearly to the black men that worked with him; "*May this be the beginning of rapid over spread of Christianity in the countries of the bank of the Niger and in the heart of Africa, through native agents!*"

Sighing wearily as he had that great sunny day at the wharf before the missionaries began their spread of Christianity, he thought as he had that day, too, that the spread of Christianity in native Nigeria could only be a miracle from the white Jesus who was called the son of God.

Okoi heaved himself from the pallet which he'd been sleeping on and made his way outside the mission house. A sliver of moon decorated the sky but did nothing to relieve the heavy darkness covering the land in the early hours of the morning.

As opposed to the houses he'd been used to in Europe, the ones at Onitsha, which was considered a city, were mere enclosed verandas in oblong squares of mud walls without rooms. Apart from the white missionaries and of course Samuel who rented bigger homes, the rest of the workers, like Okoi, slept in those mud-enclosed verandas.

He had over the months given up hope of finding his way to his mother's land. He had preferred to settle here and hope for the best while doing God's work.

Groaning in pleasure of finally relieving his bladder against a tree in the bushes, he didn't hear the crackle of dry leaves as someone stealthily approached.

The heavy wood slammed the back of his head and sent him flailing forward. Okoi lost consciousness before his body hit the ground.

Slavery might have been abolished legally, but there was still a long way to its total eradication.

Chapter Six

The sheer *lesou* — populousness — of Umor gave the giant village the confidence they were powerful enough to take over all the other settlements and be as big or bigger than the ancestral land they had all migrated from.

And what put this idea in their collective minds was their Binah. The man stood in his shrine, grinning as he knew the elders approached to report the success of another raid. His eyes, which had been total dark pools moments ago, returned to their natural hue when the elders threw out a collective greeting but waited paces away from the shrine.

No one approached here unless summoned, and that rarely happened, except when the binah had need of the warmth only a woman could provide. He refused to take a wife but had several concubines in his sleeping hut.

Though it was against the norms to have such amount of concubines, especially if some of them were other people's wives, but nothing could be done as a binah was the highest authority in the governing council of every village. The binah of Umor was above the law, and all feared his power and viciousness.

Their binah hadn't always been this way, but Umor people were okay with it; they were left feeling more entitled than the other villages.

"I see the ambience of victory as a feathery cloud shadowing your approach, elders," the priest said with an affable chuckle as he withdrew from his shrine.

"*Eyaaee*…yes, this is true, Binah," the elder at the front of the group replied in obvious excitement while the others agreed with vehement nods.

The priest nodded and chewed on the fat stick in his mouth, his expression that of contemplation.

"And bounty?" he asked, without looking at the group of elders—he shaded his crafty eyes from their view.

"Oh, Binah, plenteous," the elder replied again, the others murmuring in agreement.

Another elder took up the narrative. "There's much cattle, palm wine, healthy tubers of yam that will fill up Binah's barns and some warrior bodies."

"Women?" Binah requested.

He could sense the instant nervousness among the elders. They shifted their weights from one foot to the other, their movements rustling the dry leaves littering the compound.

The first elder cleared his throat. "The warriors relay the unfortunate event of the few they had captured dying from their wounds, and the rest had conspired and succeeded to kill themselves during the night."

"But they speak of the body of a most vicious warrior, who had stood his ground, sacrificing himself for some of the villagers to flee," another elder rapidly added.

"This is good. I shall follow you to the square to share this bounty."

"You would share, Binah? Oh, how kind of you."

"This is victory for the whole village, we shall celebrate. Tell your women to prepare trays of *yedamblongh* and be brought to the square."

"We shall do as you say, Binah."

"And tell the warriors that they shall rest for a while. Let the terror of their exploits saturate the souls of the other villages as they wait their turn." Binah declared this, his voice rising as his spoke, and his eyes turning into dark pools in his excitement.

But the elders couldn't see because night had fallen, and they were eager to return and share the good news of a celebration.

"*Eyaaee*, Binah, we shall do as you have said."

"The warriors will be happy."

"And we thank you very much — *sameh*, Binah," the last elder said as they hurried into the night to announce the celebration.

With his eyes still dark pools of deviousness, the Binah of Umor remained where he stood and roared a laugh into the sky.

"I shall rule the land," he said. "I shall rule all these lands!"

***

On the first night at Yakpani, urgency permeated the village, and the need to find the chosen woman escalated exponentially.

"*Komaa!*" the warrior commanded the yet unseen but numerous treads beating the bushes, approaching the boundaries of the Yakpani village. "Do not come any further!"

The warrior moved in a wide berth which would enable him see far off. His eyes met those of several women and children, some wounded.

Not trusting anything these days, he whistled for his fellow warrior guard in the trees and was glad to hear him jump nimbly from tree to tree to see far into the forest.

"Forgive us, warrior, but we flee from certain death and seek sanctuary in Yakpani," the middle-aged woman begged while pressing a young boy to her side.

Before he could make his reply, an urgent whistle blasted from up above. That only spelt trouble. The warrior guard instantly pulled his sword from his animal skin scabbard, the women and children's eyes widening in terror.

He moved to defend Yakpani from any kind of hostile intent, even the ones dressed as women and children. After all, they had heard of the powerful binah at Umor who could do anything, maybe even make warriors look like women.

But before he took a strike at the screaming women and crying children, an old, diminutive man wobbled from the back of the group to the fore.

"Hold your war arm, son!"

"I am not your son!"

"You would slaughter defenceless women and children?"

"They aren't defenceless with the long line of warriors behind them," the warrior guard of the trees immediately replied, joining the face-off. "You thought to sneak up on us. This is Yakpani. We are always ready, and this moment, we have you surrounded."

"It is cowardice for warriors to hide in the wrappers of women," the warrior on the ground said snidely to the old man, and spat out to show his disgust. "And you deserve the death you shall get," he said and raised his machete to smite the old man who made no move to save himself.

"*Ke ka nung!*" *Do not do so* was the command that stayed the war arm of the warrior guard. When he turned, he was shocked to find the binah behind him with a wrathful expression. "You aim to kill an *ase* priest? Have your senses escaped your skull?"

The warrior looked instantly shocked. "I apologize, Binah, but I saw no signs he was one," he stammered in explanation.

"Did you allow him to speak? And if you had stopped being hot-headed for once, Uben, you could have seen the marks on his staff," Binah Yakpani pointed out.

And truly, Uben could make out the ancient figures ingrained on the smooth body of the staff. The rest of the warrior guards blended into the bushes to avoid the binah's chastisement, leaving Uben alone to bear the brunt. Even the guard in the trees had disappeared without a flutter of leaves to mark his move.

Binah Yakpani hit his equally smooth and engraved staff on the back of Uben's head; the fierce warrior was immediately rendered a child in front of the visitors. The old man laughed at the show even though the women and children behind him remained uncertain.

"I have warned that you find a wife to expend some of your energies. You might just stab yourself one of these days in your urgent need to fight," Birah Yakpani continued his harangue.

"I found a woman, but she would not speak nor look at my face," Uben grumbled while sheathing his sword.

"It is hardly her fault that you are plagued with the ugliness of your *ajimo*," the binah joked, and the old man barked out a laugh.

"You cut me deep, Binah," Uben said, hiding a smile, grateful the priest didn't seem so angry at his costly mistake, for to kill the representative of *ase* is sacrilege.

"And you're lucky that's all I'm doing," Binah said, eyeing him in exasperation.

"You may be more favourable tomorrow when I carry wine for the hand of my woman?" Uben said in excitement.

"I doubt that, Uben, but I'm sure it will be an especially good night for you. Now apologize."

"Forgive my rashness of before, Binah, it is the anxiety that follows the approaching war," he said humbly.

The old man touched his shoulder with his staff and accepted his apology, before turning a wide smile to his counterpart. "Binah Yakpani, I am grateful for this acceptance of me and my people."

"Binah Ekori, forgive the exuberance of our warriors again. They speak truth about the coming war."

"*Eyaaee*, they do, and I am glad I have made the right decision to flee and join forces with Yakpani rather than stay and be conquered like Nko and his village." Binah Ekori's eyes settled sadly on some of the wounded women and children.

"Such sacrilege. Binah Nko is dead?" he asked in shock.

"Burnt and probably eaten by those savages."

"*ObaseWoden!*" God Almighty, he exclaimed while waving his hand at Uben, the sign giving the warrior permission to lead the displaced villagers into Yakpani. "This is terrible. What has come over Binah Umor? Why is he doing this?"

"I have no idea, but I have sent scouts to the binah at Idomi, Agoyi, Assiga, and Nyima."

"And what will this solve?" Binah Yakpani frowned, shifting to the side as the wounded villagers filed by, heading to the village.

"I hope they are smart enough to hearken to my message and join forces with us to win this battle. Umor must not win, or we shall all be slaves in our lands, and it will be worse than when the white man came to Akpa."

Binah Yakpani nodded and led his friend towards his hut. "I agree with you. But this night, the palpitations of my heart will rub me of sleep, so I must consult *ase* and *ndet* for the way forward."

"I will do the same with you, if you will be kind enough to grant me space for my shrine."

Binah Yakpani slapped his friend on the shoulder. "Of course, this can be done. And by morning, mud and palm fronts will be gathered to build huts for your people."

"*Ase* grant you power and sight," Binah Ekori greeted with gratitude.

"And you, too. You must be hungry from your trek. I have a bit of roasted yam, dried bush meat, and palm wine that has been in the soil under the giant tree of shade."

"*Eyaaee! Sameh!*" he enthused gratefully, and followed his friend into his hut.

And that night, the spirits were not allowed to rest, and so they directed the priest to seek out the chosen maiden by morning, a night earlier than spoken.

***

Unknowingly, two groups of men processed towards Ibiang's compound the next day. Both groups sought the same thing but for very opposite reasons.

Uben the warrior, his age grade, and elders from his *ajimo*, carried wine for the hand of Ibiang's adopted daughter, the one that had been picked from the forest by his wife.

The child even Ibiang had been afraid to touch, and because of the conversations with his age grade, had considered killing at night. But every time he'd planned and determined to do it, sleep proved especially, unavoidably delicious that night.

He'd always suspected the villagers might be telling the truth when they called her a baby witch. And since she was unnaturally fair-skinned, her hair soft and curly even as she grew to a woman, she was called a spirit from the river. Her quiet nature, unusual ways, and disquietly sonorous voice didn't help to refute these claims.

But Ibiang's suspicions slowly dissipated as prosperity filled him home. Even his cattle were fruitful, his tubers of yam were giants, and his traps caught fat bush meat. He wasn't surprised when Uben insisted she would be his wife, and he was glad to add yams to his barns and cattle to his herd for her hand in marriage.

Shortly after Uben and his people arrived and were welcomed at Ibiang's compound, even the tray of *yedamblongh* had been presented and was half-eaten, the second procession of men treaded the same beaten path towards Ibiang's compound.

This procession, unsmiling, was of two priests, Binah Yakpani and Ekori, both bearing small white chalk-painted calabashes and followed by the fourteen elders representing all the ajimo of Yakpani.

Smoke emanated from these calabashes, and the limbs of all men in that procession were painted with *ekoo,* the mystical yellow clay. Bare upper-bodied and carrying fat, unpeeled chewing sticks in their mouths, they branched into Ibiang's compound and caused a flurry.

Women flew into the huts, grabbing their children as they went while the men stood in respect and trepidation; they all knew why the priest was there.

Binah Yakpani knew who would be chosen this day, but as the spirits had directed, he was to give the head of the house a choice. When he got to the centre of the compound, he blew the smoke from his calabash and proclaimed peace on the household and everybody.

"*Ase* requests a woman from your household to bear the responsibilities of the spirits. This is a privilege, and blessings will follow this sacrifice," he declared and waited.

The elders behind the priests exchanged glances, thinking the same thing. They would not begrudge Ibiang his added blessings, even though he'd had more than most. They were just glad it wasn't any of their women that had been chosen.

Ibiang cleared his throat and refused to glance at the forlorn look on Uben's face. Everyone in the marriage procession knew who would be offered this day. "I am grateful for this privilege, and I accept the blessings of *ase*."

After the official acceptance speech, Ibiang was quiet and looked deep in thought. This was allowed, for it was considered a difficult task to sacrifice one's family member to the spirits, a family member that would live the rest of her life in the forest and may never be seen.

Ibiang was definitely not going to sacrifice any of his two wives. He liked his first wife's cooking too much, and his second wife was young and nubile and able to accept his rigorous plays at night as many times as he requested. He was glad his children were mostly sons, and the few daughters were just beginning to bud tiny breasts. Of course, the spirits wouldn't want them, so that left his adopted daughter.

All he regretted was the wine and tubers of yam he would miss from her potential husband. But he didn't lose out completely because the spirits would bless him.

Making his decision, he looked up, cleared his throat, and again ignored Uben's furtive head shake. He wondered if the young warrior expected him to give up his wives for someone he hadn't even had...for someone that hadn't once spoken to him.

Yet before he could make his announcement, the woman of interest emerged from the hut. Her knitted wrapper glowed brightly like the fresh cotton buds in the fields. Its knee-length showed off rounded calves, and the snugness of the wrapper did nothing to hide the large curve of her breasts and buttocks. Her unnaturally long hair had been twisted into tiny strands and woven together in one fat braid dangling down her back.

Her fair-skinned beauty made the men gasp, Uben the loudest. Her lashes grew long and shaded her strange eyes which swirled with the colour of the sky on a sunny day; eyes that were knowing and full of secrets.

A hush fell as she made her way towards the priest in the centre of the compound. Her bare feet made no sound as she walked—even goats ceased bleating and no bird chirped. Her gaze did not waver, and she showed neither fear nor hesitation.

She had almost reached the priest when she was stopped by the half-sob wrenched from Uben's throat. It had been an unconscious reaction when he realized he would never get that which he sorely coveted.

"Nnanke, please!" he exclaimed, taking a step forward, but was immediately held back by his kinsmen.

She turned then, and for the first time, her eyes met Uben's, and his knees buckled beneath him. The sheer force of the emotion he felt for her at that moment was so much he could kill for her. Then her plump, berry-coloured lips opened, and her voice hypnotized everyone.

"I belong to no one, Uben. You shall find a wife soon, and she shall bear many sons. Yakpani shall bloom with children from today," she said softly but was heard by all.

It was as though her voice echoed in their minds, since she hadn't been shouting her words.

Nnanke turned and continued towards the priests. When she arrived, the smoking calabashes exploded with blue flames. The spirits had accepted Ibiang's sacrifice.

As Uben sobbed shamelessly, totally forgetting he was a warrior, Nnanke walked calmly and quite regally in the middle of the two lines of men escorting her to her new home—a home she had always dreamt about, and a life she had been born to live.

Chapter Seven

Binah Yakpani paced his backyard, under the giant shade tree where he usually buried his calabash of palm wine for chilling. He was agitated because the spirits were conspicuously silent.

"I see you have beaten a new path in the grass," Binah Ekori commented as he neared his friend from the hut.

"It has been koke — six market days — since we led her to the sacred cave, and not a word has been shared with us."

"Well, let me share a word with you. Binah Assiga has refused to flee his village and has called me a coward for suggesting it. My scout was tired and so I couldn't send back a defensive reply," Binah Ekori commented with a wide grin.

His humour infectious, it drew a slight smile from Binah Yakpani for a moment before the old man returned to scowling.

"What is she eating?" He worried and began pacing, and his friend sighed wearily while leaning his naked upper body on his engraved staff.

"Fruits and berries ase provided every morning," Nnanke replied, suddenly there when, a moment ago, she hadn't been.

Both priests startled and shifted several steps backward from her. She seemed to glow with an ethereal light, power crackling about her. The two were speechless and stared as she approached from a path in the forest. Wherever her feet touched, tiny flowers bloomed from the soil. A phenomenon, it only meant one thing: the ase of fertility had favoured her with abundant powers.

"Do not be shocked, Binah," she said as a form of greeting, her blue eyes twinkling with humour. "Ase has said much in those days, and there is much to be done."

Her voice came out in a melodious tone, the priests experiencing the feeling of peace as she spoke.

"I must perform a ritual with all the females of the village. This ritual will be at the time old day and new day changes, that peaceful time where all is calm and the spirits come out to play."

Nnanke turned, her eyes falling on the objects in the priest's shrine, one in particular.

"It is a gift to you. More beautification to the woman of the spirits, first of its kind," Binah Ekori explained and rushed to bring out the big, copper rolls of bangles, the annular irons clanging against each other.

"I shall wear them for the ritual." She smiled at Binah Ekori, and the old man had to place a hand on his chest to calm his palpitating heart.

"And here is mine." Binah Yakpani presented a pair of heavy brass anklets that he proceeded to tie around Nnanke's fat ankles.

The jewellery gave her leg such beauty, and she couldn't wait to wear the copper bangles later that night.

"My fathers, may ase grant you wisdom, power, and sight," she said and then reached for each of their palms and blew on them, whispering wofai—a blessing of peace in their lives. The priests felt it like a cool breeze on their leathery skin.

"Send out a town crier. Let all women wait outside their compounds and all men remain inside. As I pass, they shall follow me."

"To where?" Binah Yakpani asked with a frown, having never done such a ritual before.

"To the sacred river by the sacred cave," she calmly replied.

"The river of the spirits! No one dare enters there, not even you," Binah Ekori exclaimed.

"I do as I'm told, Binah. Remember, all men, even you my fathers, will remain inside at this time."

***

Only nocturnal sounds permeated the calmness of the chill night, during the time of the spirits, and they frolicked as night animals and wispy insects glowing in the light of the moon.

Chang, chang, chang, chang, chang, chang...the leg bangles clanked from each step Nnanke took as she made her way into the sleeping village.

The annular irons piled loosely around the length of her legs up to beneath her knees, her white wrapper barely grazing the top. She looked like a goddess in the glow of the moon. Her hair spiralled down her back in its usual braid. Her hand handled a staff similar to the ones held by priests, and she clanged her way with every step she took, announcing her arrival.

Women of Yakpani shivered not in cold but in sudden awe when they heard the approaching clang and then looked up to find the apparition walking the village paths that crossed their compounds. The clinks from her walk sounded like accompaniments to the chant of peace Nnanke whispered as she walked by the women, and they followed her. After every three rings from her steps, she whispered wofai, and to the women, it sounded like she was singing to the accompaniment of her leg bangles.

A crowd of women followed behind her with their female children, even babies, when Nnanke branched into the forest path. On this night, even the warriors standing guard at the boundaries of the village were not to be seen.

When she entered the sacred forest, her eyes glowed a blue light.

"Do not be afraid, you are with me," she called out when she heard the terrified whisperings of the women. They would be afraid because they had entered the territory of the gods, and the sounds in this forest were different and blood-chilling.

Nnanke called out to the spirits in greeting; she chanted praises and hoped for blessings as she led the women to the river.

They knew they neared it when mist began to coil through the forest floor. It became a thick white cloud as they neared the edge of the water, and the women wondered how Nnanke was seeing.

Then, she stopped, exactly at the edge, and the mist seemed to dissipate from the centre of the river, making a cloak at the edge. If anybody were to be walking through the forest, the person wouldn't be able to see the river or what was happening in it.

With the mantle of mist surrounding the river, the moon seemed to shine its light brightly on the water, causing it to glimmer and glisten. The sight was so ethereal, the women sighed.

Nnanke waded into the water until she got to the middle, and there, she chanted and asked and pleaded for the fertility of the women. The crowd watched in abject fascination as she swirled gracefully in the water, her hair moving as though it had life.

Then, she called out to the women and female children to strip their wrappers and wade into the water. They hesitated for a fraction of a moment and then did as she'd commanded. They had expected the water to be extremely cold because the night was frigid, but when they stepped in, holding their breath in anticipation of the shock, they were surprised the water was comfortable.

When all the women got in, the ones with babies dipping the infants up to their necks, Nnanke disappeared under the water and swam around them, putting them in a circle. She did it six times before she swam out and sat on a ledge by the river, watching them bathe and have fun.

Then, she heard an echo saying fuken—come. She cocked her head to the side to listen more to the whispery sound, so far away yet clear about the command.

Fuken...

Nnanke's eyes, which had dimmed after the ritual in the river, instantly glowed again as she turned sharply to stare into the forest...

Chapter Eight

"Fuken!" Mmatami exclaimed quite loudly.

Nkoyo gasped long and loud, her body returning from the forest and the sight of those glowing blue eyes.

Her own eyes instantly lost its glow when Mmatami removed the ring from her forehead and replaced it on her marriage finger. Nkoyo sat limply, her mind still struggling to return to reality while the tale of the past swirled fresh at the fore of her mind.

Onen rushed in when the old woman called out to him. His heart hammered when he saw his wife sitting limply in the chair, and he also saw the damage her hand had caused on the wooden handle.

How could that be? Nkoyo was a lot of things, but she wasn't strong enough to crack wood with her bare hands. But the evidence was right there. Her palms still grasped the destroyed wood, and blood caked part of her fingers from scratches she'd gotten from the splinters.

Onen wanted to rail at the old woman for putting her through this. Didn't she realize she was pregnant? He also wanted to take care of his wife, feed her, bathe her, and cuddle her while she rested.

As though reading his mind, Mmatami limped into the room. "*Kou yanenkedei.*"

Give your woman love, she said, and then she grinned knowingly at Onen.

Okay, I'm loving this old woman more and more.

Despite his anger, Onen was suddenly abashed since he knew what the woman really meant. No way was he doing that with his seriously weak wife, yet he nodded, rose from his crouch, and lifted Nkoyo, who seemed to have fallen asleep, into his arms.

It used to take some serious effort to do that when they'd newly married, but she had lost some weight, and it proved a bit easier for him to carry her to the car.

Thank God I could float. After all we'd seen in the past, I'd be weak, too, if I were human.

***

I watched Onen's anger unfurl after he'd assisted his wife in having a hot bath, effectively washing off the disconcerting yellow clay from her face. He held it at bay as he fed her, and later laying her on their giant bed to rest. Only then did he express his rage, pacing his sitting room while his mother tried to explain why the whole inexplicable situation was necessary.

"Darling, calm down."

"I can't, Ma. Did you see how weak...how totally depleted she was?" he cried out. "What did that old woman do to her?"

Jesam sighed and waved her son into a seat. "When I was pregnant with you and began having the nightmares, the chiefs directed we go see the old woman. She's a channel for the spirits.

"Mmatami explained that each queen is the symbol of peace, love, and unity in the kingdom. And for her to understand the importance of this, she had to know what war had once done to the kingdom.

"Most of these towns are filled with hot-headed people who are ready to fly into wars at the slightest provocation, you know this. And as a queen, leading beside the king, one has to know what sort of advice and decisions to give to the king to maintain the peace.

"We are one people, with the same tongue, but some unscrupulous individuals still find it fun to disrupt the peace by unearthing trivial matters that had long been buried and settled," Jesam postulated angrily as though recalling a slight.

"What are you saying, Mother? Is there unrest in the land?" Onen sat up, alert. After moving from the palace into his own place, he hadn't been privy to much information, especially the ones his parents tried to hide from time to time.

At this point, Jesam regretted her outburst. She and her husband had decided to keep the brewing unrest from the prince a little while longer. Liman had been sure he'd be able to settle all their grievances before it became public. How difficult could it be to settle a land boundary dispute? But it was rearing to be extremely difficult, as though both parties didn't see peace and settlement as an option — only a communal clash would solve the issue.

She often wondered why men were so stupid at times. Of what use was a communal clash? Innocent people will die, decent people will be displaced from their homes, nothing would be solved, and then the next generation would want a go at another clash just to display superior strength and war strategies.

If she were king, she would summon army generals and ask that those who want war be forcefully recruited into the army and taken straight to Siberia or Syria, any of those war-torn countries where Nigerian soldiers helped out. Then, she'd want to be an insect on a leaf watching them and seeing how much they loved the real war.

Truly, I was with the queen on this one. What was war good for, anyway?

"Mom?" Onen prodded again when she hadn't answered his previous query.

"There's a giant possibility of it, Onen." She sighed wearily, leaning back in her son's very comfortable chair and wishing she could close her eyes and when she opened it, the kingdom would have reset itself to peaceful times.

"And no one told me?" He looked aghast at his parent.

"Well, I just did," Jesam snapped, not in the mood to be judged by her kid right now.

Onen reined in his anger, sighed, and endeavoured to be patient. "So, how does this link to what Nkoyo is going through? You said yourself that yours wasn't this intense and it had ended after the first month."

"That's true." Jesam cleared her throat and sat up a bit straighter in her chair. "Mmatami says Nkoyo has been favoured to see the full strength of the ring."

"Favoured?" Nightmares weren't a Favor, no matter how twisted one looked at it.

"Chosen, then. The old woman says she is going through training—"

"For what?" he gasped out in frustration, rubbing his face with an opened palm.

"For...difficulty ahead," Jesam answered slowly. Her heart had skipped fearfully when the old woman had said that, and she suffered for her son, too, at hearing such terrible news.

"What?! Like...like this isn't difficult enough? And what is this difficulty?" Onen asked, his heart hammering as though he'd just completed a marathon.

"She didn't say..."

"Of course, how would it be sufficiently difficult if said future difficulty was known?" he asked, scoffing in anger. What had he been expecting, that they...whoever 'they' were, would make this easy?

Whatever the case, all he cared about was his wife, his child growing in her, and the safety of the kingdom as a whole. He didn't want to bring up his child in perilous times, and he didn't want his parents, the currently reigning monarchs, to fail in protecting the people of the kingdom from harm.

His mother sighed, quite heavy and tiredly, and Onen saw the stress she was facing. Suddenly, she looked her age, and his heart hammered in fear at the realization that his parents wouldn't always be there — they would die at some point.

He was terrified of that natural phenomenon and wished it would never happen. And he felt guilt for adding to her stress and worry. Shoving his anger down, he showed some concern to his mother — he offered food, which she rejected, but he helped her to her car and the waiting driver.

"Take her there tomorrow, Onen. If not for anything else, let her finish off the so-called training at once, so she can have a peaceful night's rest," Jesam advised but with a pleading tone. She knew her son and his hate for the traditions.

"Of course, Mother. I will do that." He didn't like it, but he would do it. One less thing for his mother to worry about, and he was glad he could do it for her.

"Thank you," she said reverently and hugged him before climbing into her car.

"I need to know about everything, Mother...Tell Father that," he admonished, and the queen smiled and nodded before her car zoomed towards the gates and out into the night.

Sighing wearily, he hurried inside, instructing the maid to lock up the house while he rushed up the stairs, two at a time, to get to his wife. He bent over her, kissed her brow, and she sighed in her sleep which looked marginally peaceful. Then he stripped, took a bath, and quietly joined her in the bed. Onen curved himself over the length of her back and cuddled her warmth, with his hand around her torso curbing a luscious breast, and the other settled protectively over her stomach and his child. He was soon asleep.

You would think I'd leave now that they were asleep. However, there was a possibility of more dreams. Wouldn't you want to know about it?

Chapter Nine

War waged in the small settlement of Idomi, the smallest of them all. Warriors were cutting down the enemy with sharp machetes and throwing equally sharp spears that either missed or wedged in its mark, a body of the enemy.

The villagers fled into the forest while Yakpani warriors rushed to join the mêlée, fighting against Umor warriors. It should've made a difference—the Yakpani warriors, added to the paltry handful of Idomi ones. But soon, it looked as though Yakpani warriors were weakening, and Umor took delight in cutting them down.

Nnanke hid behind a tree and watched the curious fight. She had run from her sacred cave and had carefully followed the jogging warriors as they made their way to Idomi.

She had told Binah Yakpani she had to follow them to war even though she couldn't say why, explaining it as just a feeling. The priest had refused. It had never been heard of a woman, especially one belonging to the spirits, going to war.

Holding her anger in check, she'd returned to her cave only to grab her engraved staff to follow the warriors without their knowledge. Now, her staff hummed, vibrating in her hand and prodding her to enter the square.

Nnanke took a deep breath and let it out, also letting off her will and allowing the spirits to use her. Her eyes instantly glowed the flashing blue of the sky as she walked slowly from the trees right into the middle of the fight.

Before the men could react to her sudden appearance, she opened her mouth and sang. They couldn't decipher if the language was theirs, but her voice soared, lilting and bending, sounding as light as a breeze, the rhythm heart-wrenching and bone-numbing...

It took a few moments before the Umor warriors fell to their knees after experiencing weakness in their limbs. Yakpani and Idomi warriors stared in amazement as they fell despite the struggle not to fall written all over their faces. It was as though someone took away their will and strength.

They didn't know if the spirit song would soon affect them, too, but it didn't, so they picked up their weapons and proceeded to kill every one of the warriors.

Well, everyone except one. Nnanke discovered him lying wounded by the forest while she returned to it. Her eyes were still glowing, and the wounded warrior shivered in terror at what he was staring at and knew he would die.

But Nnanke smiled. A bunch of warriors were approaching and would've killed off the wounded soldier. However, she raised her hand while still smiling at him and redirected the warriors who decided halfway to use another bush track.

Nnanke widened her smile into a grin at the warrior's shock. "Wofai," she whispered — peace — as though a farewell greeting and walked regally into the forest, leaving the man to stare after her in shock.

***

Onen gasped awake, disoriented.

This was new. Usually, it was his wife who jerked awake in the middle of the night. It got me curious.

He discovered his face wedged between the bountiful softness of her breasts. He inhaled her beautiful scent and burrowed his face deeper into the pillowy comfort.

Even in his present state, the prince frowned. Something important hung at the periphery of his mind, but he couldn't recall it. Nkoyo's left hand lay on his forehead as though she'd been caressing his head and had slept off leaving her hand hanging there limply.

He flicked out his tongue unconsciously and tasted his wife's smooth skin. I groaned at his one-track mind. He'd just woken up from sleep, for God's sake. His tongue ached to pull up her breast and suck on her nipple, but he seemed too sleepy to bother. I was more interested in the peripheral thought which he wasn't giving much attention.

A nudge from me sent that soporific feeling fleeing, and he recalled the dream he'd just woken from. Onen jerked into a sitting position on the bed, the sudden movement jarring Nkoyo awake.

Yep, that's it how it should be, I thought, grinning and floating closer because my skin prickled with the nearness of a good tale.

"Honey, are you okay?" she queried with a small frown and in a husky, sleep-filled voice. She sat up and turned on the light. A swift look at the wall clock told her it was the same time she usually woke from her nightmares, a few minutes past one a.m.

"I think I just had your nightmare," he told her in shock, swivelling on the bed to face her.

Interesting, but how did that happen?

Nkoyo frowned. "I don't understand—"

"Did you dream?" he broke in and watched as she frowned. Then she widened her eyes in realization, shaking her head in the negative.

"Then it is confirmed, I just had your dream." Onen didn't know whether to laugh or be worried. Was it because of his anger at Nkoyo's apparent weakness yesterday? Was this a test?

Nkoyo crawled close to him, her brow furrowed as she inspected something on his face.

"What's this?" She traced an indentation on the side of his forehead, very near to the centre of his head. It looked curiously like the design of her ring. "Did I hit you in my sleep?"

She'd never done that before, but anything was possible these days.

Onen chuckled despite the worrying situation. "No, you didn't..."

"Then why do you have the indent of my ring on your forehead?"

He reached up and traced the mark. "Your hand was there when I woke up."

As though someone slapped the realization into her, she recalled the visions she'd seen when the old woman had placed the ring on her forehead.

"Oh my God," she whispered. "Tell me the dream," she prodded, her hand settling softly on his arm.

Yes, please, do tell. I floated even closer.

He told of the dream about a young man who was a sex slave to a white woman on a ship and how he finally escaped.

"Okoi..." she whispered in realization.

"Huh?" Onen asked, unconsciously bending forward to hear her.

"Okoi is his name. He was a freed slave as a result of the anti-slave movement that curbed slave trade at Europe," she explained excitedly.

"How do you know this, and how come he was still a slave in a ship owned by a white woman?" he asked curiously.

"He followed the missionaries from Freetown in Sierra Leone to Nigeria in the hope of finding his people. But he was kidnapped at Onitsha by the white woman's workers..."

"And he became a sex slave," Onen concluded, recalling the very erotic detail of the dream.

"Not really. The woman was going to bury him alive as a sacrifice with her dead husband. But in the meantime, she decided to make him her plaything. How did he escape?"

"The mast broke on the ship, and the woman sent him ashore with a search party to find wood. But he was cunning and saw his way out. He trapped small rodents and used their blood to simulate that he was mauled and carried off by a wild animal, leaving his torn, blood-stained shirt behind. The rest of the men carried that as proof to the white woman. When she realized he had played them all, she laughed. And then I was thrown into a different dream entirely, of war and death and an unbelievably beautiful woman with glowing blue eyes…"

Nkoyo couldn't help the small squeal of excitement she emitted.

"You saw my dream! More like a vision; the ring showed you my vision. That's the story the ring is telling, and the unbelievably beautiful woman is Nnanke," she said, enjoying the shock on her husband's face.

"The same one the old woman was conversing with while touching the ring?"

"One and the same," she confirmed and laughed when he groaned in disbelief, pulling her down on the bed with him.

"Christ, what happened to good old-fashioned mathematics and reality," he grumbled while nuzzling her neck.

She giggled at his ridiculous comment while burrowing deeper into his body and enjoying his warmth and caresses.

"So, if you go back to that old woman's—"

"Not if but when," she corrected firmly.

"Yes, when you go back there, would the vision continue from where I stopped or from where you stopped, which is where I started from?"

For once, I totally agreed with the prince's question. We were all invested in this tale now. I could feel Nkoyo wanted to chuckle, but she saw the seriousness on her husband's face. She thought it cute, which proved weird and unheard of in someone so tall and muscular like Okoi.

She gasped in realization, the same moment my gaze focused on the prince, seeing what she was seeing.

However, Nkoyo desisted from revealing that he might be a descendant of Okoi. He would only worry that his ancestor had been a sex slave to a white woman—something extremely shameful to men so full of pride in this kingdom.

So she kissed him softly and looked into his eyes. "I think the ring recognizes that we are a unit, you and I..."

"And the baby," he whispered seductively while his large hand caressed her belly.

Her heart melted at the deluge of heat that suffused her. She loved this man so much, she couldn't even explain it. "Yes, and the baby. A tight knit unit, one and the same, which is why I believe the vision will continue from where you stopped."

Her words brought a smile to his face, and to mine. However, his hand slipped round her neck and caressed her nape while I shifted from the heat they were creating on that huge bed.

"God, I love you, Nk," he whispered.

Her reply was to scoot even closer to him. She rubbed her body seductively on him, undulating her hips against his until he gasped and tightened his arms around her while pressing his impressive erection on her belly, so close to where the heat would be warm and molten.

Instantly, the prince recalled the old woman's toothless grin and her advice to give his wife 'loving.' Onen knew what she'd meant from the leer she'd given him, but he'd mentally sworn not to do anything, not when his wife had looked like she'd been in one of the ancient wars of her dreams...or vision.

Now, he found himself torn between keeping his mental promise or taking his eager wife, whose leg had crawled up his hips, conveniently sliding up her sleek nightgown and exposing the warmth of her core. The tantalizing scent of her pheromones drifted into his nostrils, making him salivate. Sweet mother of God, he wanted to taste her.

Hey, guys, I'm right here! Have some decorum.

Nevertheless, Nkoyo saw her husband's nostrils widen as he took a giant breath, his right hand creeping slowly and surely down her hip to her exposed thigh and towards the ache of her centre.

I groaned because what woman wouldn't want his fingers buried deep in her? Nkoyo wanted more, but he seemed to be fighting an internal battle as he kept pausing, although his hips undulated helplessly against her.

I scoffed. If the prince thought his wife hadn't noticed how he'd curbed his desires for her these past nightmarish months, he had another think coming. She hadn't called him out on it because she knew he was first and foremost honourable and caring and that was what drove his attitude. Plus, she'd mostly been tired and terrified of what was happening to her.

Not anymore. I felt as guilt chewed at her for having made him take such a tough choice; a choice he was considering at the moment even though his body blatantly said otherwise. Sighing, I saw her determined face as she made a decision.

Nkoyo purposely rubbed her breast on his arm as she dragged herself upward, aligning not just her face with his but also her aching lady part with his hardness. She moaned at the thrill of pleasure that shot through her when she felt his hot, hard length rub against her.

Ha, this woman was a pro at seduction. I should be taking notes for when I meet Trouble.

"Nk…" he groaned, moving forward once, twice, and gritting his teeth to control the barely controllable passion driving him for his wife.

"My man of steel," she whispered alluringly, nipping his earlobe and enjoying the full body shiver wracking his big, muscular body. That she had such power over this man was still a thing of awe for her; that she could bring him to a point of losing control, which hadn't been for a while, gave her such utter joy.

"You aren't strong—" he attempted to refute.

I rolled my eyes. Man, please.

"Sshh," she admonished, her mouth in his ear, then she pulled back and made sure he looked at her. "I noticed you held back, and I'm sorry you had to make that decision—"

"Nk, stop. Why are you apologizing? You shouldn't—"

"Because I should've stopped you when I first noticed your restraint." Her eyes expressed utmost sincerity.

"I had you after the doctor's visit," he mumbled breathlessly because she moved a bit, allowing the liquid heat in between her legs to rub over the swollen head of his erection. She knew she was torturing him, and she would do it until he gave in.

"Even then, you held back," she panted, her own torture getting to her because he seemed to have taken over the movement. He had reached in between their undulating bodies and rearranged the swollen head of his penis to hit directly on her clit every time they moved. "Remember our first time?"

"I'll never forget our first time," Onen panted, suddenly wanting to tear off her nightgown to get to the soft succulence of her body—a pressing urge he just had to have.

Reaching down, he roughly pulled her nightwear upward, causing a whimper of eagerness from his wife who immediately straightened her arms to enable a swift removal.

His eyes focused instantly on her erect nipples as he flung the nightgown over his shoulder and licked his lips imagining how they would feel and taste in his mouth. Nkoyo swallowed imagining what he was picturing. Impatiently, her hand rounded his head and pushed him towards her aching breast. With a groan, he went forward, his mouth puckering as he sucked a nipple into his mouth, both of them moaning at the sensation that shot through their heated bodies.

"I missed you," she panted as he frantically released her nipple with a pop and went after the other. She revelled in the feel of his big body, enjoying the ripple of his muscles as he balanced in between her widened legs.

"I missed you," he finally replied with vehemence, his eyes hooded and clouded with a wild hunger for her body.

"I'm all yours, baby," she whispered, her hands caressing the overnight beard on his jaw.

Onen sucked in a breath and pulled himself upward, aligning his engorged phallus to her wet opening while leaning down to capture her mouth in a kiss so hot, her arms tightened around his neck. She moaned loudly, her legs mirroring the actions of her arms around his hips.

The movement invariably widened her dripping core, and nothing could've stopped his next action. Onen reached down, grabbed his impossibly hard phallus. He had to pull from the inflaming kiss because looking down as he joined with his wife would be way better.

Nkoyo whimpered her protest at losing the seductive tangling of his tongue with hers. But then, her eyes rolled into her head with ecstasy as his thumb slipped into her sleekness and found her pleasure nub. Her cries echoed in the room as he rubbed her clitoris rhythmically, his right hand still holding his engorged cock, using the swollen mushroom head to tease the cream-drenched entrance of her cunt.

Nkoyo's hips bucked from the bed at the euphoric rush coursing through her body in waves, making her quiver violently as her orgasm happened on her without warning. Body tightening, she gushed warm cream, completely drenching her husband's hand as he continued his brand of pleasurable torture.

"Oh, that was beautiful," he gasped, his eyes glazed over in lust as he watched her pant from the powerful orgasm he'd given her. Male pride surged through his mind at how limp her limbs became as the high of the climax dissipated.

"Babe, darling, there are so many things I want to do to your body—" he stopped and swallowed, his mind flashing so many ways he could give her pleasure, which invariably meant getting pleasure, the mind-blowing kind.

Nkoyo twisted and smiled seductively, her hands leaving the bed sheet she'd been clutching when she'd climaxed to languidly grab her large breasts. She gasped and moaned as her thumbs rubbed her overly sensitive nipples. She gave her husband a hooded look, enjoying how dumbstruck he seemed, his eyes clearly widened in lust as he followed the movements of her hands massaging her breasts.

"My body is all yours, my man of steel. And we have all night. Do with me what you please," she declared and widened her legs, one hand leaving a breast to creep slowly towards her pussy.

Onen growled, a sound purely suited for an animal. His caressing hands tightened on her fleshy thighs as he pushed them upward, bending them so far, they touched her breasts, invariably exposing her dripping cunt to his consuming gaze.

This woman and everything about her drove him crazy with a maddening hunger that nothing else had ever elicited from him. She was his life, his hope, his future, the only one that balanced him. Joining with her had always been a visceral experience, and he had missed it. He had missed the 'no bars' of their lovemaking, the inferno they usually created when they joined, and most of all, the lightening of their souls afterwards.

"Nk –"

"I want you now, super man," she sobbed, her hand reaching and caressing his broad, muscular chest while her legs rounded his thighs and pulled him nearer. He didn't hesitate this time.

"You're going to feel me fill you, baby—" he declared just before he bridged her entrance, watching as her eyes widened and her mouth formed a silent 'o,' taking the full length of him. Then she moaned loudly, the pleasure eviscerating all inhibitions, for she didn't care if the maids heard her scream.

"Oh, lord," Onen groaned, holding himself stiff, his eyes closing momentarily since the sight of his wife's enjoyment would surely end their lovemaking before it even began.

She thrashed about, silently demanding he move. But he groaned again.

"Nk, please," he begged, shaking his head at her when their heavy eyes met.

She whimpered, panting, almost sobbing because she understood she wasn't supposed to move when all she wanted was to feel the inexorable glide of his hard length filling her and turning the ache in the pit of her stomach to mindless pleasure.

Finally, he moved, just a little, and she bucked from the bed to get more. She arched her hips to meet him halfway as he began plunging, settling into a rhythm that had her gasping aloud each time he slammed into her.

"Yes!" she rasped, her inner muscles tightening as she felt the onslaught of a powerful orgasm begin with unfurling heat and tingling in her womb.

"Oh, Nk! God, I love you," he panted, feeling she was close, and the knowledge only made his pleasure gather momentum at the base of his spine. It was going to be a gigantic one, he could feel it.

His movements lost rhythm, and he rutted into his wife like an animal. His hips pounded against hers so fast, he was barely even pulling out before slamming back in.

"Come with me, darling, come with me," he gasped as he twisted his hips, slightly changing position to get to her deepest G-spot. Her increased screams and mindless thrashing told him he'd succeeded. He still reached down in between their bodies and flicked her clit with his middle finger, satisfied when she shouted her climax, drenching his plunging penis with molten cream and dragging him over the edge, too.

Onen expelled his essence deep into her womb, groaning and growling and not able to stop his plunging movement until every drop of him had been squeezed by the swollen nerves of his wife's sweet cunt.

"Thank you...thank you," Nkoyo gasped, rolling after her husband as he slid out of her. Their arms circled each other tightly, both of them panting as shivers of pleasure wracked their bodies at intervals.

"I love you, Nk, I love you so very much," he whispered with reverence, kissing her neck and tightening his hold on her.

"I love you, too. I love you beyond words, my super man," she whispered, and they slept that way till day break.

Ahem! Why is it so hot in here?

Chapter Ten

As you well know, usually, I always make myself scarce when my people are *'loving.'* I'm cousin to Jealousy, and I tend to display some of her traits at times. Additionally, I hate missing my all-time crush, Trouble—that guy is fine sha. Nevertheless, last night, I was caught off guard. Forgive me.

If this line of conversation is confusing to you, then you really need to read my previous story. If you haven't, then you're sitting on a long thing.

Anyway, it's six-thirty a.m., and despite the very explosive 'loving' that had occurred in this room, Onen had other things in mind. Other things against his basic instinct of staying in bed, wrapped up in the warm, fleshy softness of his wife until it was time to visit Mmatami again.

However, he was a prince, and he worried for the king, his father, and his people. After listening to the worry in his mother's voice yesterday, thoughts of the problems that might be brewing hung on the periphery of his mind and prodded him away from the comfort of his wife's body.

Sometimes, reading people's mind could be a problem—too much information. I cannot say here the things going through the prince's mind to do to his beautifully naked wife this morning. I can only confess the man has a dirty mind, though. I mean, I'm a spirit, but I feel the urge to blush at the pictures flashing through his brain.

I'm proud of him anyway because, even though his 'lower body' had risen to attention at his erotic thoughts, comfortably wedged in between his wife's considerable backside, the prince groaned and *reluctantly*—notice the emphasis—got up and went about preparing to visit his father at the palace.

This is the kind of attitude that makes for a good king, and Onen will be that…if he stays alive long enough. But let me not spoil the story for you.

***

The Atam palace could pass for an ordinary, wealthy man's house for all the ceremonious fixtures it didn't have. It had been this feature that'd shocked Nkoyo when she'd first been sent over by her parents, the king and queen of Efik kingdom, on the pretext of learning basic leadership skills. The monarchs had hoped their friends, the rulers of Atam kingdom, would be able to instil humility and the reality of what leadership should be in their daughter.

A smile lifted Onen's lips as he strode from his car into the palace, recalling his first sight of his wife. After a harrowing day getting here, the shock of the palace looking like a peasant's home compared to that of her parents' and discovering her luggage was missing, courtesy of his mom, Nkoyo had later told him that his discovering her half-naked on the floor had been as a result of waking up with a start and not realizing she'd been sleeping at the edge of the bed.

He shook his head, his smile widening into a grin as he followed a palace attendant. Warmth suffused his heart at the intense love he felt for his wife. She'd been the most self-centred, entitled 'bitch' when he'd met her, but after going through his mom, she'd changed. Who would've thought they'd be soul mates when they'd started off hating each other…at least, publicly, since both of them had later confessed to their inability to stop thinking about the other.

It had been Nkoyo's opinion the palace was less than royal when she'd first arrived, especially when no one waited on her as she was used to at home. The palace was actually gorgeous but in an understated way, especially when compared with the Efik or the Ibibio one.

Dressed in jogging clothes, with the hope of exercising after speaking with his father, Onen nodded his thanks at the palace attendant and knocked on the door of the king's library, waiting to hear his directive before entering.

"Good morning, Father." His words came out stiffly, pissed his parents had hidden kingdom matters from him.

King Liman sat at his impressive desk, the glow of his table lamp illuminating his face and the papers scattered on his table, so it was easy for Onen to see the slight arc of his eyebrow at his intonation.

"Father?" he asked with a mild smile, mimicking the stiff tone while looking over the spectacles perched on his nose at his son.

"Well, my dad did refuse to tell me the challenges the kingdom was facing. You said I had to learn a lot from you, especially the diplomacy involved in conflict resolution. How do you expect me to succeed you and be as good as you when you hide important issues from me?"

Onen didn't realize how worked up he'd become until he stopped talking. The silence after his outburst was deafening, a huge contrast to his just raised voice.

King Liman sighed and dropped his pen. His heart was heavy for he knew his son was right. As a king, a leader of many, he should've been used to people misunderstanding some of his decisions. Nonetheless, this was his son, his blood, and his blatant anger at him caused a twinge of hurt in his heart.

Onen was more hurt than angry that he'd been kept out of the loop by his parents. He couldn't imagine why they would do such a thing. He knew his father always had reasons for every decision he took, which was why he was beginning to feel the onset of guilt for shouting at him.

The guilt blossomed when he noticed that his once impressively stately father had lost some weight, his shoulders stooped as though he carried the weight of the world on them. Despite the overall soft lighting of the library as opposed to the brilliance of his table lamp, Onen was able to see new groves of wrinkles on his father's face as he approached him. Even his gait seemed less confident. He had always been a bit taller and more muscular than his dad, but it'd been unmistakable that his physical attributes had been inherited from his father. Right then, though, he just seemed like he towered over the man.

It was as though he was seeing his father with new eyes. His intense concern for his wife had totally taken all his attention, leaving all other things he'd usually been able to pick out with observation invisible. He hadn't noticed his parents' stress or any discord in the kingdom, and he felt he was less of a prince for not noticing, like he'd failed at his basic duty.

"Sit down, son," Liman said wearily as he neared his first born and heir.

Onen wasted no time in respectfully dropping into the couch strategically placed in the library. A place that had become one of his favourites in the palace because Nkoyo had agreed to marry him there; she had accepted his ring, the heirloom ring, while sitting on that same couch. It seemed like a far-off memory, but the image was as sharp as ever, especially since the heirloom ring had become their present issue.

Liman watched his son take a deep breath and shake his head as though to clear his thoughts. He sighed because he did that a lot, too. Sometimes, he just had to let a lot of other issues go to enable him keep a clear head for his kingdom; other issues that included alienating his beloved wife.

"I'm sorry, Dad," Onen whooshed out as though the words had been constricting his throat.

"Nothing to be sorry about, son." Liman sat down beside him.

"I shouldn't have snapped. I should've recalled that you always have good reasons for your decisions, and I should've asked with a cool head," he insisted.

Liman chuckled as his son flung the lessons he'd learnt over the years on leadership at him. Though it was important a king keep a cool head in heated situations, he didn't blame Onen for being angry. The boy would be perfect for the throne, and Liman was sure he would do greater things than him when he ascended as king of Atam kingdom.

"Your mom did warn me to expect you, but not this early," he began calmly, then coughed to clear his throat while arranging his house coat over his pyjamas.

"I hope to exercise later before checking out a few things at the mill. I still have to take Nkoyo back to Mmatami today." Onen ended with a grumble.

Liman chuckled again, understanding how much his son hated the spiritual side of their culture. "How did that go?"

"You mean, Mom didn't tell you?" Onen asked with a slight raise of his eyebrow, a tint of playful sarcasm in his voice.

"She did," he replied with a wide grin. "But it mostly contained her opinion. Now, I'm asking yours."

Onen groused, folding his muscular arms over his equally muscular chest. His father's smile widened because his adult son resembled a petulant child at that moment.

"I don't like it. There're just so many unexplainable details. Last night, she was so depleted after her ordeal, Dad. I didn't also understand how my soft wife could have been strong enough to crack the arm of a sturdy wooden chair."

Liman's eyes widened in blatant shock.

Onen nodded. "Yes, Dad. When I went in to carry her because she'd practically fainted, her hands were clasped over the cracked arm of the chair, and she had tiny slices from the splinters."

He huffed in annoyance, the same that had consumed him the previous evening when he'd stared at his fatigued wife.

"Your mother's own hadn't been that severe. In fact, hers had ended at just dreams that had lasted only the first month."

Onen sighed. "I...did you ever have Mom's dreams?" he asked, sounding confused and actually looking vulnerable for such a manly man.

Liman's brow furrowed in confusion. "I don't understand."

"Exactly. But at about one a.m., about the same time Nk usually screams awake from her nightmares, I awoke from one of it."

The king's eyes widened again. "That's a new one. Are you sure it wasn't just psychological?"

"I wish. I told Nk about the dream, and she confirmed it was the continuation of the vision she'd been made to see at Mmatami's place. Apparently, her marriage finger, with the ring on it, had mistakenly landed on my forehead in her sleep..."

"So, you saw the vision. This confirms it," Liman said with a proud mien as he stared at his son.

"Confirms what?"

"This confirms, Onen, that you're special, which is why your wife is also special. And only special persons become great kings," he declared sagely.

"Dad, that means you're special, too, because you're the greatest king I know, and I hope to be able to do half the things you have done."

Liman chuckled and slapped his son's shoulder companionably. "Of course I'm special, I sired you, didn't I?"

"That you did," Onen agreed with a smile of his own, his heart surging with love for his parent.

"I know you hate the issue with the ring, but the old woman coming back to life just because you and your wife were visiting should be a sign that some powerful spirits of destinies are at work here. As kings, there are some things in the traditional etiquettes that are against our personalities, but those things still have to be done. 'Give to Caesar what belongs to Caesar'," he quoted, pleased that his son nodded in understanding.

Liman took a giant breath and let it out with a whoosh, and Onen knew he was finally getting to the kingdom issue. Said giant breath also told him the issue was heavy, with probably no solution in sight.

"There is land dispute," Liman reported, his expression becoming pensive.

"I thought that dispute was reconciled six months ago," Onen pointed out, physically turning on the couch to face his father.

"You're right. The land dispute between Idomi and Abini had been settled six months ago. This one is between Umor and Yakpani," the king confessed soberly.

"What?" Onen exclaimed in righteous anger. "People would dare to cause trouble in the royal community of Yakpani? Isn't that an abomination? The palace should make Yakpani the safest place to be; it should be a haven for displaced people from other communities as it has always been in times past."

Liman nodded in agreement. "Of course, son, that is also right. But I have reached my wits' end. When the clans involved were called for resolution, I got the feeling they both didn't want peace. I got the weird feeling they wanted war or nothing."

"That's preposterous," Onen said without much conviction in his words, because his father had always had good instincts, which he'd confessed had saved his life several times as a young man.

"You know better, son." Liman smiled sadly at his heir. "There's something else at work here. I don't know what, but I'll find out. Yakpani and Atam as a whole must remain peaceful."

"How can I help, Father?" Onen asked eagerly, desperately.

"Nothing much," Liman replied. "And that's why I didn't tell you. I didn't want you to worry when a line of action hasn't been identified and you were, still are, worried for your wife."

"It doesn't matter. I still want to do something, Dad. This is serious."

"It is, but there's nothing to be done yet. Some trusted elders are out there investigating possible causes of this dispute. With a cause, a solution is imminent."

"True."

"So, continue to keep that mill running. There's no need to cause panic among the people. If there's trouble in Yakpani, then Atam kingdom crumbles, and I cannot let that happen."

"We will not let that happen, Father," Onen stated with conviction, his hand grasping his father's shoulder and squeezing in support.

The men shared an understanding look, and their relationship in that moment roped stronger. The royal men were ready to fight for their kingdom.

Chapter Eleven

Onen made the turn on the untarred path that would take him back to the mill. He couldn't run as long as usual because the meeting with his father had taken up some of his exercise time. He'd left his father a little past seven a.m. and had driven to the mill. The main office hadn't been opened, but he'd spied some early workers on the farmland as he parked his car in front of the first factory which still housed his personal office.

He currently ran along the wall that fenced in the old mill. In the previous years, more land had been accrued, making the mill and its surrounding farmlands more than ten thousand square meters. More factories had been built; more heavy-duty food processing machines had been added and were still being shipped over from foreign countries, to increase production.

The kingdom was single-handedly feeding other kingdoms, especially Efik, Ibibio, and Oro which were the closest. King Liman might've started the place to make food processing easier and cheaper for the community, but Onen had a vision for it. A big one that included exportation to China; recent research discovered China was the leading consumer of processed cassava at sixty percent, plus the increasing demand for cassava as a biofuel; his father had gladly handed over the reins.

He'd turned the place into an independent money maker by buying more lands to produce the raw food in bulk, apart from the ones bought from petty farmers in the kingdom. He'd imported more machines and had employed mostly youths to farm the land and women in the parts of the processing plants that required them. He still had more ideas, which involved accumulating more lands. He also hoped to package and brand processed food that came from the kingdom.

He wanted the mill to become the largest employer of youth labour, both literate and illiterate. He wanted less bad gangs and more responsible young adults. He envisioned adopting, at least, two young men into his council of chiefs when he became king. It was time the youth quit being youths; they needed to take up more proactive roles in the leadership of the kingdom rather than wait at the periphery to cause strife and discord when dissatisfied with a particular royal decree that rubbed them the wrong way.

"*Oda wenwobol.*" It is the prince.

"*Eya-eh.*" Yes, I agree.

Onen sighed at the loud whispers of the women approaching him. He'd lost count of the group of women he'd passed this morning during his jog as they went to their farms. Unfortunately, he had to respond to their enthusiastic greetings — part of why he couldn't run for long, and the main reason he preferred to run on the forest path behind his house.

Granted, he had to run really early before the farmers arrived, but even when they did, they would be hard at work, deep in the farms, away from the path he usually ran on.

"Wenwobol, aploka!" the approaching group of women with their farming implements chorused. He even spied some of the young women giving him shy looks.

Their words meant 'good morning, Prince,' but literally interpreted to 'Prince, you have risen?' which he replied in the affirmative, *"Eya-eh, aploka."*

It would've been too easy to assume the greetings would end there when the morning greeting in Atam kingdom was a fixed process of questions and answers. It's what he'd been doing all morning. He was sure his thirty-minute run only included fifteen minutes of actual running; the rest of the time entailed him acknowledging greetings from his subjects.

"Wol idiyan o?" How's the body, one of the women threw at him with a smile. They all were happy to be conversing with the prince, quite a rare occurrence.

"Wol itawatawa." He replied that the body was well; said body was currently pumping with unused energy from an unsatisfying exercise session.

It should have ended there, but a feisty old woman commented at his reply. *"Nkurke."* I have seen, she said, giving him a leer which was funny coming from such an old woman.

"Eya-eh!" the others chorused in agreement and laughed raucously to his eternal dismay.

Onen was shocked to find these women were flirting with him and openly ogling his obvious muscles through his sweat-drenched T-shirt. An awkward situation, and the women clearly saw his embarrassment even though he laughed along with them. He was grateful for the man who came out from his house, obviously going to his farm, and shooed the women along, allowing him to return to the mill.

Greetings from workers erupted from the farms and factories as he ran by—he made no mistake to stop. He simply waved and put on a burst of speed to get his heart pumping. He used the speed to run through the first-ever built factory, up the iron stairs and into his office which faced the open floor where work happened.

He'd gotten used to the heavy, starchy smell of cassava in the early stages of processing, so it didn't bother him any longer. However, he closed his heavy, iron door anyway. At least, it blocked out some of the noise from the machineries, especially the cassava graters. The vibrations, though, were another thing entirely.

Breathing heavily from his last-minute speed run, he first checked his phone for calls from his wife. Before he left to see his dad, he'd dropped what he hoped would pass for a love note, and his last words had been for her to call him immediately once she saw the note.

After kissing the corner of her mouth, he'd slipped the paper into her slacked fingers so he was sure it'd be the first thing she saw when she woke up. When he didn't see any calls from her, he smiled in gratitude. It meant she was still asleep, and she needed all the rest she could get. He couldn't bring himself to feel bad about how wildly passionate she had encouraged him to be with her, but he could help her rest as much as possible.

His mind swerved to the land dispute he'd just heard about this morning from his dad. It was impossible not to worry with a communal clash imminent. Everyone knew Atam men could shame a civil war with the bloodiness of their communal clashes. It was why his father tried as much as possible to resolve all conflicts peacefully.

Onen prayed the situation never got to a communal clash, especially as it involved the two biggest communities of the Atam kingdom. From history, these two powerful people had always tried to best each other in everything. During his father's reign, though, everything had stayed peaceful, until now.

Shaking his head, he settled down to check the production book. His father was right—with no clear solution in sight, he had to maintain appearances, and that meant running the mill smoothly.

A knock came on his door before it opened and his head foreman stepped in. After pleasantries, they discussed how work had gone on the mill the previous day.

"Why is Eja's hydraulic press still covered?" Onen asked.

The hydraulic press, the biggest in the factory, was used to squeeze moisture from bags of grated cassava before it was shifted to the vibrating sieves and then to the automatic garri fryers. Though some people specifically required the manually made garri for the local flavour, so some of the sieved cassavas were pushed to the women to roast in large, wide pots which would turn them to garri.

The foreman sighed wearily. "He still hasn't returned. Yesterday, I asked one of the boys that lives on his street, and he said he has not seen Eja for some time. I'm worried we might not find someone soon enough to run that hydraulic press. He'd been the only one who knew how to manoeuvre it."

Onen knew they needed the biggest hydraulic press to work since it could carry multiple large bags of cassava pulp at a time, making production swift. They wouldn't have worried if they could pull some boys from the farm to work the machine, but they needed those hands at the farm—they couldn't afford to pull the boys.

He could have employed more people, but of recent, applications weren't forthcoming as compared to a few months ago. He really needed Eja, and the young man knew he couldn't just leave work without some sort of permission. He knew the punishment for such infraction, but Onen was willing to overlook it if he would just return to work the hydraulic press. It'd been covered for days now, and the other smaller cassava dewatering machines weren't producing much.

"I'll go to his house," he declared, reaching into the cabinet to pull out the mill's employee register which would have Eja's address.

"But, Boss...don't worry, I'll do that," the foreman immediately offered, his eyes wide—it was unheard of for the prince to personally visit a lowly worker for being absent from work for a few days.

"Why, because I'm the prince?" Onen asked with a mocking smile.

"Well, yes..."

"Maybe Eja needs royal encouragement then. What would be the point of my royalty if we don't deliver on contracts given to us? The whole integrity of the kingdom is at stake here," he concluded and used his smartphone to snap the address on the register.

The foreman got to his feet when Onen did the same.

"I'll visit this morning. Call me if you need any assistance. I still have royal duties today, and it might take the whole day," he said and ushered the man out of his office, locking the door behind him.

"Of course, my prince," the foreman shouted to be heard above the heavy machineries on the factory floor.

Onen nodded his acknowledgement and followed the fit but middle-aged man down the iron stairs. He was proud of his homeland. The men were all warrior materials, old and young, which was probably why they were always eager to show their prowess in clashes. He sighed wryly.

It was difficult to find any fat and lazy men in Atam kingdom. Everyone worked mostly as farmers, hunters, artisans, traders, and of recently, many had joined the police force in droves. Probably why there was a noticeable dwindle in job applications at the mill.

He really hoped Eja was okay and the reason for his absence something he could easily solve.

***

It wasn't something he could easily solve.

Eja seemed to have run away from home with no one the wiser why he'd run or his destination. Onen was at a loss as to what to do for his poor infirmed mother.

The idea of young adults leaving the kingdom for greener pastures wasn't far-fetched. In fact, it was usual, and these youths mostly ended up at Efik kingdom first, mostly in pursuit of grandeur and the partying lifestyle.

With nothing to do but watch Eja's mother sob into her wrapper, Onen returned to his car, grateful his phone rang at that moment. He smiled when he saw his wife's name.

"Darling, I'd hoped you'd sleep longer," he crooned, the pressure he'd been feeling moments ago subsiding at her voice in his ear.

"I love you, too, super man," she murmured with a smile in her sleep-induced husky voice. "I got your note."

Onen laughed, and the pressure disappeared completely.

"How's the mill?" she asked softly.

And the pressure surged up again, but he wasn't letting it affect his tone, not when he didn't want his wife to worry about anything. "It's running."

Nkoyo sighed in his ear. "I'm sorry that I've not been helping with the accounts lately."

"You soon will," he encouraged brightly. "We just have to take care of the ring issue, and everything will be fine. I'd probably prefer you do the work from home—"

"Don't you dare baby me, Onen Liman Ikpi!" she snapped, and he chuckled at her fire. "I'm pregnant, not ill. *Okuo*, that is your plan, to keep me at home as your baby mama, it will not work."

The pressure slunk away at this point as he laughed whole-heartedly. "Did you just use my language in between speech? When did you get so fluent, or is that the only word you know?" he teased lightly.

"I know *obandi*," she murmured seductively, and Onen sucked in a large breath as warm pleasure tingled through his body, basically pooling in between his legs.

"You are my sweetheart, too, the apple of the eyes," he said, interpreting the word.

"Are you heading home soon?" He heard blatant need in her tone. "We have at least an hour before going to Mmatami's place," she crooned, her voice serving as a siren that drew him in, attracted him like iron to magnet.

Onen was turning the ignition of his car before even replying. "I'll be home soon, baby."

"I'll be waiting," she encouraged huskily.

And indeed, she'd been waiting…naked.

No one should ask me how they are still this hot for each other after more than two years in marriage.

Chapter Twelve

Okoi hung on a branch, watching as the party he'd landed with scurried through the forest, racing down towards the waiting boat that would take them back to the ship. He patiently waited until they were far into the sea before he climbed down from the tree.

Making his way in between tree trunks, he grabbed his boot and pulled it on, then searched the shrubbery for a particular leaf he'd learnt at Onitsha was good for clotting blood and healing wounds. To add to his ruse, he'd had to cut his leg to smear more blood around the spot where he'd led the men to believe he'd been mauled by a wild animal. It was either that or return to the ship to be shackled in Eugenia's room so he could pleasure her by licking her privates many times a day and rutting with her at night, to then be fed morsels of white man food like a dog after the act had finished. And then when they'd reach the south of Nigeria, he would've been buried alive with Eugenia's husband, the Baron, sent into servitude with him to the afterlife.

Risking it all to escape had been worth it, no matter what.

When he found the leaf he was looking for, he squished and rubbed it in between his palms until it emitted green juice which he squeezed into the cut on his thigh. For good measure, he squished more of the leaf and stuffed it into the wound, using part of his torn shirt to wrap the leg, holding the medication in.

Okoi returned to the path, watching with relief as the boat carrying the others got tinier the farther they went. Distantly, he wondered what Eugenia would say when she received the news that he'd been killed by a wild animal. He imagined she would say he'd always been destined to die. But her opinion wasn't important anymore—he was free, and he had to decide which way to start his journey.

The left of the river led to new Calabar, and that town crawled with white people synonymous with slavery, so he couldn't go that way. The right was where Eugenia's ship had been headed, to Brass. He didn't know how far Brass was from the forest, but he knew that direction held certain death where he'd be buried alive with the white masters, so it was a no-go area, too. The only direction remaining was back into the forest.

Okoi was aware he was in the south, the part his mother had said she'd been grabbed as a slave. How fortuitous that Eugenia's ship brought him this way, but he had no idea how to get to Akpa, the ancestral land.

With a determined breath, he grabbed the food bag which still had food to last a couple of days. He reached for his machete where he'd hidden it in the bushes and turned, marching with strength and blind faith into the forest of uncertain fate.

***

The wounded Umor warrior, the only survivor from the battle Umor had been winning at Idomi despite the addition of Yakpani warriors but drastically lost because of a song, finally arrived at Umor village square and collapsed.

He'd been slowed by the large, bleeding gash on his thigh. In fact, he'd not thought he would make it home, not with the fear that the female spirit with eyes like the sky would change her mind and return to finish him off. He should have been dead, just like his fellow warriors, lying butchered and scattered all over Idomi village square where the battle had occurred. He would have died if Binah Umor had been the one to discover him beside that forest, but the blue-eyed spirit had saved his life. For what purpose, he wondered.

How could they have lost that battle completely with just a song? These questions whirled inexorably through his mind as he stumbled his way home. Still, it was his delirious mind that answered that the song had come from a spirit—a beautiful spirit, and men couldn't stand where spirits kneel.

It'd gotten dark when he'd finally bridged the boundaries of Umor, and he went straight to the village square as per the firm instructions of the binah for warriors returning from war. When he stumbled and fell gratefully at the square, he momentarily thought he was hallucinating when elders immediately surrounded him in concern. It was late and really dark; nobody should've been awake at that time.

As he sighed heavily, his eyes drooped, and as peace stole through not just his body but his soul, his limbs began stiffening. But he was rudely shaken by one of the elders which made him groan in pain. Blood gushed from his wound, and his eyelids rose lazily, their questions seeming like far away echoes in his mind.

"What happened?"

"Where are the other warriors?"

"Are they behind you?"

"Did you run from them…?"

"…do they need help, is that why you're here alone?"

"Speak, warrior."

"Speak, warrior!"

This particular demand wasn't ordinary. It thundered through his body, shocking him awake despite his fatigue. Fear gripped him, and it showed in the widening of his eyes — eyes presently focused on the dark pools of Binah Umor's eyes.

Binah Umor's stormy eyes…

Which did nothing to hide his fury. Even the wind picked up, wiping branches of trees wildly at his vexation.

"Speak, warrior!"

This time, the demand echoed in his mind. The voice sounded like a legion made the request. But it could not be, as his eyes were only seeing the binah. However, his mind became heavy and full with tendrils of black smoke, and the same demand to speak echoed in so many drippy whispers in his head. It felt as though his soul were being clawed with the demand to speak.

In abject terror, the warrior began panting. His heart palpitated so hard, it felt like it was pounding right out of his chest, and then he started screaming.

The elders took several steps back at the blood-curdling scream. They were tempted to cover their ears just like the warrior was currently doing. The sound in the fiery night of biting wind sent chills of terror down their spines. This was a strange occurrence, and they were glad to have the binah there to take care of it, since they had no idea what madness had taken over the warrior's body.

Binah Umor saw the warrior's eyes roll into his head, and he knew the man would never speak. In fact, he was dying, and he couldn't allow that—not when for the first time, Umor warriors had been soundly defeated by little Idomi soldiers, an impossible feat. He had to know what had happened. And it wouldn't be from the warrior's tongue. He had to see with his dying eyes.

With determined purpose, Binah Umor grabbed the warrior's head with both hands and blew black wispy smoke from his mouth to his face.

"Let me see," he demanded both vocally and in the dying warrior's mind.

The wispy smoke wiggled into the warrior's nose, making the dying man twitch violently. His hands dropped from his ears, and he lost control of his body as it shook with the force of the oily darkness currently prowling his mind for answers.

He knew he was dying, and all he wanted was peace.

As though the gods heard his wish, the image of the blue-eyed spirit flashed in his mind: he saw her whisper 'wofai'—peace. And his soul immediately reached for the almost tangible aura of peace that surrounded the beautiful spirit. He felt it. He floated in it and sighed as the spirit whispered again, 'wofai.'

Binah Umor was staring at eyes the colour of the sky. He'd never seen such eyes before, yet he knew their owner was the cause of his defeat. He wanted to know more of those eyes, but the light from it stole the warrior's soul from his grasp, quite easily. His soul just drifted away peacefully, a totally unacceptable situation. A man that died in peace had nothing to offer. A warrior that died in peace was a travesty, a waste of meat that could have filled him with more power.

The binah was furious.

"Binah." One of the elders dared to creep close. "He is dead," he observed unnecessarily as the binah continued to stare into the vacant eyes of the dead warrior.

A sacrifice was in order, Binah Umor thought snidely. He had a need to investigate and find out who owned the eyes of the sky, and when he did, he would destroy that person. A sacrifice was in order, and the stupid elder creeping close towards his elbow would do.

Binah Umor sank his claws into the eyes of the dead warrior and excavated both slippery balls, ripping them from his head. He dragged and dragged the bloody, squishy tendons that seemed like an endless rope coming from the warrior's head. Impatiently, he clamped his teeth on the ropey nerves that connected the eyes to the head and severed them with a snap. Pieces of tendon and drops of blood hung from his untidy beard and around his mouth. Then his tongue slipped out, licking as far around his mouth as he could, his eyes shining evilly.

The elders gasped and stepped away from the unsavoury gore they were seeing. But it was too late for the elder that had dared to step close earlier.

Binah's hand snapped out sharply and rounded the elder's throat.

The others ran, scattering like dead leaves in the wind, but Binah Umor didn't care. With the eyes in his palm and a sacrifice in his grasp, he strode through the darkness to his shrine, logging the choking elder along like a piece of wood.

Without finesse, and with impatience, he carved up the stupid elder, dragging out his entrails and throwing each major organ into the fire as he murmured incantations that should make him see through the warrior's eyes, yet he saw nothing.

Finally, he flung in the heart and growled out the incantations, willing the dead eyes to show him what he wanted while slightly believing he wouldn't be shown, but then…he saw.

He saw the whole battle. He saw what defeated him. Peace defeated him.

"Wofai!" he spat in disdain, his fury building beyond manageable proportions. He looked up to the murky skies and roared his fury and a promise of revenge.

***

Nnanke gasped awake from yet another horrible dream. Her chest rose and fell rapidly as she looked around the sacred cave, her home since she'd been accepted by the fertility spirit to be her binah.

After cleansing the women of Yakpani at the spirit river, just before she'd defied Binah Yakpani and Ekori and followed the warriors to the battle at Idomi, she'd begun having strange dreams.

She was used to the spirits whispering to her, giving out instructions of things to do. But the dreams had no explanations and no pattern.

Sometimes, she would have nightmares about a bearded man. The engraved staff in his hand made him a binah, but his essence was of deep darkness, as though his soul had been shrouded by a dark force. Nnanke had no idea what these nightmares meant, and the last one was so real, so close, she could almost feel the hot breath of the evil binah on her face as he roared in anger.

Then there was the other dream, about a handsome man.

She sighed and folded her knees into her body as she lay on her pallet, under a wrapper. At the thought of the handsome man, calm stole through her body, the panic and terror of the nightmare instantly melting away.

She had no idea why she was being affected by this strange, unknown man. Was he a spirit? It was the only way she could describe him since thoughts of him, from the first moment she'd dreamt of him, generally calmed her body. Though, there was a time she'd dreamt that he held her in his arms tenderly, then his lips had slowly moved across her skin, sending curious shivers of pleasure through her body; pleasures she'd never known before.

Pleasures that had made her nipples hard and her eyes flutter close. The strange man had then lowered his mouth until he'd found her hard nipples engraving her wrapper and sucked one through the fabric. The bliss from his action had been sharp and white, and it had shocked her awake.

Just like when she'd dreamt of the handsome man, her breath came in pants but not from terror. Furthermore, thoughts of him caused the secret place in between her legs to secrete moisture, confusing her. It only happened when she recalled that dream. The spirits weren't whispering to her about this man or the evil binah, but she had faith they would soon.

Her eyes roamed the dark cave—a smooth, white stone shaped like a snail's shell—a giant snail's shell. She could imagine how the outside looked without seeing it. The snail-shaped cave had been covered in green shrubbery, making it almost invisible in the dense forest of trees and greenery. Nnanke had thought it looked too green, so she'd touched the surface, satisfied when wild flowers, of different bright colours, spread through the green shrubs that covered it.

As though the spirits could read her mind, which they did, the wild flowers grew until it draped heavily over the opening, making it look like a giant mound of wild flowers. It was beautiful and practical because the drape over the opening kept the chill of the night out.

Nnanke sighed, pulling her hand from the cover of her wrapper and touched the smooth cave wall in front of her with her fore finger. A tiny rope of wild flowers grew, swirling beautifully on the smooth surface. It was the first of its kind in the stark interior, and she realized if she did the same all over the wall, the place wouldn't look so bland. She was excited about her discovery, her mind swirling with different colours of wild flowers and where she'd put them.

Despite her decorative epiphany, she was still worried about her dreams. She considered telling Binah Yakpani and Ekori, but the men were currently furious with her for defying their instructions not to go to battle, most of all Binah Yakpani.

She'd tried to explain the overwhelming push she'd had to follow the warriors. Nnanke couldn't understand why they couldn't see that all the warriors would have died and the battle would have proceeded to Yakpani if she'd not been there. With a sigh of frustration, she wondered why the spirits hadn't spoken to them about the rightness of her actions.

Turning on her pallet of soft grass, she lay looking at the smooth, curved ceiling, imagining drooping flowers from it. Deep down, she was angry at the belligerence of the binah — they both refused to acknowledge that she'd saved the day just because the spirits hadn't detected it to them, just because she was a woman. Sometimes, she felt that men where quite stupid, but she would never vocalize her thoughts.

Nnanke's mind returned to the handsome man. Who was he? Why was he in her dreams? Why did he cause these warm, pleasurable feelings in her? Feelings she couldn't explain; feelings that both scared and excited her.

Just recalling his face now sent tingles through her body. She pressed her legs together to relieve the curious ache she'd begun noticing in her core whenever she dreamt of him. Stranger still how she referred to him as handsome. She had never felt the need to refer to any man as handsome — they all kind of seemed the same to her. None had ever made her giggle like her age mates had when warriors passed the square on a market day. But just the thought of his glistening, dark complexion, the definition of his muscles, the fierceness and intelligence in his eyes, and the warmth with which he stared at her in those same eyes, just made her want to surrender to him, body and soul.

And that was the scary part. How could she want to surrender to a man, body and soul, when she knew she belonged to the gods? Nnanke knew she could never be with any man, not if she wanted to live and protect Yakpani, which was her destiny.

Determinedly, she closed her eyes, deciding there was no need to tell Binah Yakpani and Ekori about the strange dreams, especially about the handsome man and his effect on her body. She would desist from thinking about him at all; the dreams probably meant nothing.

But just before sleep took over her mind, she was reminded that from an early age, her dreams had never been random. They'd all meant something.

Chapter Thirteen

Okoi's knees weakened at the sight approaching him. The machete fell from his useless fingers in defeat. This was different from outsmarting an animal. He was tired, hungry, and quite honestly, after everything that had happened to him, he lacked the will to fight any longer.

For a man who had no idea where he was headed, he wondered why he'd even bothered to survive this long. Several times, he'd wondered if his being captive on Eugenia's ship hadn't been better than his exploration into the forest to the unknown.

Right then, he wondered which would be better: slavery by the white, or slavery by his own people. He was about to find out anyway.

***

He had traipsed the forest, making sure he'd maintained a straight path from the river. Okoi's aim had been to walk until he happened upon a village or settlement. That he lacked basic local parlance was brushed off with sheer will in favour of a blank mind and energy to make the trek of indeterminate distance. He couldn't worry about what he couldn't change; he would use sign language as he'd seen done by the missionaries back at Onitsha.

The paltry food in the cloth bag held close by drawstring had by disciplined rationing sustained him for more than four days. It would've made it to the sixth day, but then it rained—a source of much-needed fresh water he'd promptly taken advantage of, filling his water skin. Nevertheless, the rain had destroyed his refection. The bread had melted right before his eyes, the cheese, too, and just so the food wouldn't waste, he'd gobbled the whole mess up, left with just the bag, a skin full of water, and his machete.

The lack of food hadn't deterred him at this point; he was in the forest, after all. Wild fruits everywhere had sustained him, seemingly giving him more energy than when he'd only depended on the bagged food that had gone stale long before its destruction.

Okoi had kept track of the days spent in the forest by scratching out the number as sticks on every tree he'd decided would be his bed for every night. By day fourteen, his mind had become delirious from the fever that wracked his body, and he'd lost count because he'd stopped walking for an indeterminate number of days.

He'd been lucky his body had finally succumbed to the mosquito-induced fever close to a river. All he'd done for days had been to reach out and pluck wild, edible-looking plants and then drink as much as he could from the river. He couldn't even be bothered with climbing a tree at this point—his precaution against wild animals, not when he'd had to crawl to the river bank to drink water because his legs had gone boneless with the fever.

Having totally lost count of days, he had no way of knowing how long he'd spent in the forest. But when his body had regained a modicum of strength, and his limbs didn't feel as though they were about to melt under him, he'd taken a very long swim in the river, rinsed out his weakened, white cotton cloths, filled his water skin again, and continued his journey, making sure to maintain a straight path.

A path he wasn't even sure was straight any longer, not when he'd had to divert from really dense bushes where his machete would've been useless to clear the way. Or when he'd heard the growl of wild animals and had made the decision to skulk through another trail in the forest.

All he knew was that he followed where the sun rose every morning.

Daybreak made everything better...or was supposed to.

Okoi had barely gone a hundred feet, his leg dragging from fatigue, pain, and lack of sleep when he happened upon chaos. Having to endure excruciating pain, he'd not been paying much attention to his environment.

One moment, he was mentally prodding himself to, at least, make it to the next big tree he could lean on and rest. The next, tall, dark men surrounded him, their bodies and faces haphazardly smeared with native chalk. They all carried spears, some of them with dead, bleeding men hefted over their shoulders.

That's when the will to survive left him. His hand loosened its hold on the machete, and his legs weakened beneath him. He'd been miraculously surviving all challenges, even escaping being swallowed by a python and ending up with a dislocated arm, but Okoi knew his luck had run out.

The mean faces around him meant certain death, the language they spoke gibberish to his ears. His broken English would be the same to them, too. Okoi knelt, resting his buttocks on his legs, and awaited to die.

Binah Umor broke through the gathered warriors, having just pillaged a small settlement and on their way back to Umor. One of the warriors wondered why the man was dressed in strange garb. Another raised his spear, his face showing disinterest as he readied to kill Okoi.

"Ke ka nung!" Don't do it! Binah Umor ordered, which shocked the gathered warriors, as they knew their binah never took prisoners unless a woman he liked.

Since the defeat at Idomi, the binah had followed the warriors for every raid, each drawing them closer to Yakpani. The warriors couldn't understand why they couldn't just raid their biggest enemy, especially now that binah went with them, making sure they won.

Binah Umor knew their silent questions but refused to answer them. Yakpani was protected, and he hadn't yet found out how to bridge the protection. So the only plan he had was to raid around it, hoping to draw them out while he waited to meet a certain woman with blue eyes. He was yet to know where she had come from.

Looking at the strangely garbed man before them, a warrior's aura surrounded him; an aura stronger than the fiercest of Umor warriors. Of course, his warriors couldn't see this—they saw a weak man not worthy of much.

Binah Umor saw power. He saw a man that had survived the trials of the gods. He saw purpose and a great destiny. Such a man couldn't be killed like a mere animal. Such a man required a ritual, one that would allow him to take over his sacred essence, which would increase his powers immeasurably.

The man before them had the touch of the gods. He was destined for greatness. Binah Umor was going to take that greatness, for the man wouldn't know what to do with such powers granted him freely from birth.

Binah Umor laughed, throwing his head backwards at the unexpected gift of the forest. He leaned forward and touched the man of destiny on his temple, sending him into deep slumber. He directed one of the warriors to carry him, and they resumed their return to Umor.

***

Could intense pain really slice through unconsciousness? Okoi answered the question himself when he gasped awake from his faint to realize he was tied up and hanging down horizontal over an unlit hearth. The tightly wound rope bit into his injured arm, the throbbing pain snapping him from his oblivion.

Terror engulfed his mind when he immediately realized what would happen to him when the fireplace was lit. He would become roasted meat, just like the other men. The stench of burning flesh drifted by, and he unfortunately inhaled it deep since he panted in fear.

Instantly, the stink roiled his stomach, causing nausea. He was ready to vomit bile since his stomach was empty. Bitter liquid dribbled from his cracked lips and dropped like a gummy strand to the hearth piled with dried firewood. He didn't even know how long he'd been unconscious.

They'd used heavy rope to tie him up from neck to knee against a wooden pole currently wedged in between the forked mouth of two heavy sticks buried in the ground. It was the usual manner animals were roasted universally — even the white men had roasted celebratory animals this way back at the plantation.

Okoi could barely move his neck, but it proved enough to see other similarly tied men in the clearing, but with a difference. The men were already dead, their skins currently bleeding oil over the sparking fire as they roasted, and no figurines surrounded their hearth.

He was robbed of breath when he noticed these differences. The hearth he hung over was unlit, he wasn't dead, and even though the sky was quickly turning dark, he could make out the painted skulls and figurines surrounding his area. Even though he knew nothing about the culture, he was sure he was sacrificial. Having gone on enough evangelical treks with Samuel Ajayi Crowther around rural Onitsha, he'd experienced the traditional religion enough to recognize a sacrificial area.

Despite the tightly wound rope, Okoi began twisting his body in an attempt to escape the hopeless situation. Of all the rotten luck he could have, he'd fallen into the hands of cannibals. He really was cursed and destined to die. Who could have cursed him? Had his mother known he'd been cursed? Why hadn't he been simply killed at birth instead of going through these challenges, coming out victorious and then finding himself in more difficult trials?

As tears of frustration dripped from his eyes onto the firewood, he accepted that this was the end; at least, he would finally be at peace.

Just then, loud drums sounded, and a cheer went up from a distance. The increasing clarity of the drums and the accompanying song alluded to the approaching crowd and certain death.

Though Okoi looked forward to finally having peace in a life that had only been turbulent thus far, his heart lurched to his throat and refused to go down. He was terrified and couldn't breathe. Unconsciously, his body struggled against the tightly wound rope. He might have consciously accepted defeat, but his spirit was that of a fighter. Even without his brain, currently inundated with terror, he struggled, fought for a way.

Without meaning to, his lips moved, whispering words he'd forgotten; words that had been meaningless when the white missionaries had taught them to the newly freed slaves. It was a prayer to the white God, and he had just gotten to the part that said 'but deliver us from evil' when the painted face of the priest bent into his sight.

"It is time," Binah Umor pronounced with a wide grin while drums and songs blasted around the clearing in the forest, close to his shrine.

Okoi didn't understand what he'd said, but sobbed and repeated that part of the prayer over and over as he knew he had come face to face with evil.

Binah Umor laughed even though he didn't understand the words of the destiny man and didn't care. He would get his power tonight, and Yakpani would fall in the morning.

The women danced around the banquet with trays of 'yedamblongh' which would be used to eat the roasted warriors. Binah Umor smiled. While Umor thought this was a celebration of victory and would feast on the other men, he would have the destiny man to himself, after he'd sucked out his essence.

Thumping his engraved staff to the beat of the drums, he laughed into the black sky, his eyes turning a murky hue as dark powers filled his veins. He flicked his wrist, and the hearth, piled with firewood under Okoi, exploded with cackling fire.

Terror snatched the prayer from Okoi's lips and left him with only terrified screams. This was a terrible way to die. He screamed while hearing the priest's chants above the drums and songs. He screamed until his voice went hoarse, the fire licking at the ropes which bound him. Heat slowly but surely permeated his skin, boiling his blood. Smoke burnt his eyes, and his screams stopped when the only air he could breathe was fiery heat.

***

Nnanke snapped awake with a terrified screech. Even though she couldn't see a reflection, she could feel the hum that meant her eyes gleamed blue fire. Her breath came in pants with the memory of her nightmare fresh on her mind.

The dark man and the handsome man had met. Her dream and nightmare had collided. But the nightmare had engulfed all.

Chapter Fourteen

There was a problem, both in the spirit and physical world, and I couldn't solve it.

Even I was happy when Onen snatched open the heavy drapes to Mmatami's inner room, not caring about propriety. I could hear his heart slamming against his chest in panic. For the last five minutes, he'd been listening to Mmatami's increasingly perturbed voice as she tried to bring Nkoyo back from the realm of the past to no avail.

I had heeded the old woman's call and returned, thinking Nkoyo would do the same. I'm shocked to find her stuck.

The sight Onen met robbed him of breath for a second. His wife was thrashing hysterically on the wooden seat, her strength so much, she flung the old woman meters away with a flick of her wrist.

Mmatami jumped back up spryly and returned, grasping Nkoyo's flailing hand and determinedly stated, "*Fuken!YanenWenwobol, fukeneeh!*" Come! Wife of the prince, come! Mmatami drew out the last word in frustration as Nkoyo continued to struggle, her lips moving as she garbled unknown words.

Onen was panting, his throat clogged up with fear as Mmatami turned worried eyes to him.

"*Oowentafuken.*" She refused to come, she reported unnecessarily.

"*Mbong onung?*" Onen asked why, his eyes flashing both fear and anger.

"*Nnyieeh.*" I don't know, she replied, helpless, her gnarled hand never leaving Nkoyo's wrist even though his wife's jerky movements shook her frail frame.

Not knowing what else to do, Onen went on his knees before Nkoyo. Her legs and knees thrashed and hit him, but he made no attempt to move away. Instead, he crowded her, calling out her name.

Then, determinedly, he dodged her flailing arm and lifted her from the seat. He walked a short distance on his knees, reached a corner of the room, and lowered himself onto the cracked mud floor, leaning his back on the wall.

Mmatami's hold on Nkoyo's hand had slipped, but the old woman followed him, muttering under her breath. Onen assumed she was probably saying incantations that would help bring Nkoyo back.

But that wasn't happening, even as he joined his voice and called her name. It appeared she was obviously still deep in the realm of the past, and her struggling meant she was refusing to come out of it — or she wanted to come out but was unable to. Either way, Onen didn't like it. He silently swore he wouldn't let her go into it again after now, traditions be damned.

"Sweetheart, please," he muttered in her ear, close to tears, his heart hammering against her restrained arm as his stronger arms had rounded her body and held her close to his chest.

Her jerky movements reduced with his closeness, Mmatami helpfully reported, but he barely heard this. It wasn't her stillness he wanted, it was her. And that began with her eyes opening—without it, without her, life was worthless.

He didn't say all this to the frail old woman, though. He bent his head and whispered his need into his wife's ear, his need of her.

Onen had no idea what prompted his actions, but after whispering for a minute, he raised his head from beside her drooped one and stared down at the glowing ring stuck on the centre of her forehead in the midst of dripping, yellow clay. In that moment, his wife looked like an ancient goddess, one who had her eyes tightly shut. He understood then that she fought the call to return, and he wondered what would have caused that.

Nkoyo's neck was propped up with his left hand, and his upwardly bent knee supported it. He only had to bend slightly to get close to her. His breath brushed her face, and while Mmatami murmured incantations at his elbow, he felt a strong pull to be closer.

The pull became magnetic when he drew towards her, as though he had no will of his own. For once in his life, he refused to rationalize a clearly unexplainable urge and went with it. Mmatami's voice seemed more distant—it became an echo as he drew near to Nkoyo's face. Before he knew what he was doing, Onen had his forehead pressed over the glowing ring on his wife's, and he was instantly sucked into the dark whirlpool of the past.

Mmatami gasped in shock and obvious panic back at her inner room, because, obviously, the prince had decided to join his wife in the realm of the past. The old woman had not just one, but two royals to bring back to the present. While she worried, Onen experienced the dizzying vortex through the eras that occurred when one consciously crossed that line.

I mean, it's a different situation to when he'd gone into the past through a dream after his wife had mistakenly placed her ring hand on his head. There had been no vortex then. But the prince had consciously — okay, not entirely, but he was awake, not asleep when he placed his forehead on the ring; so, of course, he experienced the violent suction into the past.

It was a feeling akin to one's soul being roughly sucked out of the body, which, technically, was what happened when one plunged into the past. Not for me, though, spirit that I am.

I'm cruising through the whirlwind, following the silently screaming prince as he was flung along like a rag doll in a tornado. I bet his physical body would be jerking violently back at Mmatami's inner room with groans and grunts as his soul got tossed through the waves of ages past.

I float along, my eyes taking in different eras that appear like snatches of images on the roiling blackness of the vortex. Soon enough, the prince is flung onto the forest ground, quite roughly. It looked like he'd just been spat out from the mouth of a roaring beast.

Onen landed, bumping against tree roots on the forest ground, his scream now vocal and no more muted, as we'd arrived at the right era. His body twirled, bumped, and stopped at his wife's feet.

I rolled my eyes sarcastically. Figures, this couple is perfect like that. I mean, he just happened to roll and stop at her feet, in a thick forest full of green plants, beside a cave that had a profusion of flowers all over it. A perfect movie moment, if you ask me.

"Onen!" Nkoyo gasped, leaving the tree she'd been grasping, obviously where she'd held herself in refusal to return to the present, and knelt before her recovering husband.

"Shit, babe, you refused to return," he grumbled, getting to his knees and hugging her tightly.

"So, you came?" she asked with an incredulous laugh.

"Don't you get it? I love you," he declared, his eyes portraying both his emotions and his worry for her.

Nkoyo's eyes and body practically melted at his declaration. "I love you, too, darling," she purred, her face moving towards his with pouted lips; they were going to kiss.

"Oh my God, you guys!" I exclaimed in exasperation, instantly breaking up the tender scene as they gasped and squeezed into each other's body in trepidation, their eyes bulging as they stared at my direction.

For a minute there, I was confused, because, usually, they shouldn't hear me or see me. I'm a spirit, after all. But then, I recalled they were in the spirit realm, and it made them spirits, too. So, they could both see and hear me. Crap.

I lowered myself from the night sky where I'd been floating, allowing my feet to touch the green forest floor delicately. I felt so regal in that moment and silently wished Trouble could see me now.

"Who is she?" Nkoyo asked in a shaky voice.

"I'm new here, Nk, why are you asking me?" Onen replied in shock, never taking his eyes from me.

"But she came with you through the black hole," she pointed out crankily, a smidgen of jealously in her tone.

Like seriously, who has time to cheat when they're passing through a freaking vortex? I rolled my eyes again.

But I don't blame the woman. I know what they were seeing—a petite woman with svelte curves, dark-complexioned with big, brown, cartoonish eyes, and pouty rosy lips, dressed in a short, see-through, white gown. Anybody would be jealous of my beauty.

To be fair, though, everybody got dressed in see-through white after passing through the vortex. And right now, I was jealous of Nkoyo. My goodness, despite the darkness of the night, I could still see the prince was hung between his legs. I had to force my eyes away from his see-through trousers as he slowly got to his feet, his wife tightly clasped against his body.

I wasn't just jealous of her husband's 'weapon' but of how her long gown draped provocatively over her voluptuous curves of prominent boobs, ass, and hips. I was jealous of her height, of her fair complexion that perfectly contrasted with her husband's dark skin.

Beside Nkoyo, I felt like a waif at the foot of an Amazon.

Mentally groaning, I wished Trouble was with me. His handsome, fair complexion, and broad shoulders would so kill this jealousy in me, for then, I would be with my own man.

Whatever, I mentally rolled my eyes again.

"I'm Gossip," I said, stepping closer but smiled giddily when they moved backwards in fear. Okay, this was fun. Now I had no reason to be jealous — they feared me.

"Gossip?" Nkoyo stammered, her eyes showing her disbelief. "As in gossip…the act?"

"Yes, as in that gossip," I snapped, folding my arms over my meagre chest. This is why I preferred to be called Kedei, but I don't tell her that.

The couple exchanged confused gazes and then returned them to me. "Is it just the name or are you —?"

I interrupt the prince insolently. "I'm it, you —" but then my insult is equally interrupted by a huge splash from the river.

All our heads snapped to find Nnanke with her hands raised over her head, one of it holding her staff, the inscriptions on the wood glowing blue while her voice echoed as wind drove waves on the surface of the river. The wind wiped branches of trees in the forest, flinging debris in circles as her voice rose in crescendo.

"What is she doing?!" Onen had to shout above the howl of the wind, snatches of lightning illuminating our faces.

"She's going after her dream man!" Nkoyo replied, excited, clinging onto her husband's arm as they watched, their eyes squinting to see through the wiping wind.

Onen smiled lovingly at her, pulling her close, immediately understanding why his wife had refused to return. He leaned down and kissed her tenderly…and, of course, I rolled my eyes again and turned to watch the past unfold.

***

Nnanke had woken up with fiercely burning eyes, and that had never happened before. In the past two *koke*—six market days—which amounted to twelve weeks in modern times, since she had been chosen by the spirits, she'd never experienced waking with burning eyes.

She wondered if it had anything to do with her nightmare engulfing her dream. She recalled with succinct clarity as the evil binah erupted fire under the bound body of her handsome man. The memory seemed to increase the sting in her eyes.

They burned so much, she could barely keep them open. Scrambling to her feet, she staggered out of her cave and stumbled down the path to the river of the spirits. Nnanke hoped that submerging her face in the water would heal the unexplainable ailment.

It didn't.

Rather than reduce the burn, her chest lit up, too. Breathlessly, she submerged in water up to her knees, choked, and murmured pained questions to the spirits but got no replies. Looking down, her reflection in the clear water, made clearer by a sliver of moon, showed her eyes glowing a sharp, fiery blue.

Her heart hammered as she wondered why this was so, but in the next instant, she had to cover her ears as an agonizing scream pierced her eardrums. It was of no use since the scream seemed to be in her head; a very manly scream…an exact sound like that of the burning, handsome man in her nightmare.

As though she'd always known, Nnanke suddenly became aware of where the abomination was taking place. Her spirit surged with a pressing urge she couldn't deny, one that prodded she immediately rescue the handsome man.

Nnanke flew from the water onto the bank as though a force had elevated her. Without pause, she raced to her cave, grabbed her staff, which started glowing through the scrawled inscriptions on it, and a tiny sack of dust she couldn't recall ever having.

The more her eyes and chest burned, the more her anger increased at the injustice of burning a man alive. A very tiny part of her mind reminded her to inform Binah Yakpani and Ekori about this action, slowing her momentum. Her chest hammered as she considered the smidgen of reason, but then, the man's screams echoed louder, burning her eyes more, and she discarded the idea and hurried back to the bank of the river.

Nnanke had never wanted to be anywhere in a hurry, but this night, she needed to get to the burning man. Standing on the bank of the spirit river, the sliver of moon seeming to illuminate more than its slim shape should, she raised her hands, her staff glowing in her right hand and the small sack dangling from the fingers of her left, and then she spoke words she ordinarily wouldn't.

Deep down, she knew she shouldn't be able to speak these words that weren't the local dialect. The earlier force that prodded speed and a pressing urge to save the handsome man was also responsible for pouring these strange words out of her lips.

The wind picked up as her voice increased, fingers of lightning lit the sky, and right before her eyes, a huge, transparent fish-like creature broke the surface of the violent river and then returned into it with a loud splash.

Naturally, Nnanke would have stopped her chants and stepped back in trepidation while she watched the strange, glowing fish in the water. But she didn't. The odd words only poured more from her lips. The wind wiped at trees harder, the anger in her chest increased, and a second, glowing fish appeared, swimming in circles with the first one.

The water creatures glowed the same fiery blue like her eyes. Were these her spirit guides? Before she could ponder more, branches with leaves from trees hanging over the spirit river began falling into the water, making loud splashes. Nnanke curiously felt no fear. Rather, she watched in exhilaration as the wind broke branches into the water and the fish swam around, corralling them and creating a drifting craft.

Both glowing fish grasped each end with their mouths and floated the leafy craft to where she stood. Without prod, she stepped on it, sat cross-legged, and was instantly drifted down the river so fast, she grasped a branch tightly to hold on.

The river of the spirits sloped into a narrower space. Here, the forest was thicker, and the moon couldn't be seen through the interlaced branches over the river. However, the glowing fish that floated her from under the craft illuminated the dark water as they sailed through so fast, the spirits she spied on the riverbank were mostly wispy blurs.

Despite the novel experience of taking a water ride with spirit guides, fury still burned in her chest. It was one she'd never experienced before, and with it, a violent wind followed behind her drifting craft as they approached Umor. She could feel the almost uncontrollable strength of the wind roiling behind her. She should have been scared—such volatile power should have terrified her, but it didn't, not with the equally volatile fury in her heart.

Nnanke squinted her glowing eyes as she faced the narrowing river, determined. She couldn't wait to unleash her fury on the people of Umor.

***

Binah Umor felt giddily pleased with himself as he continued to chant the incantation that would transfer the destiny man's divine essence to him. His pleasure had no bounds as the man began to inhale the heavy smoke from the fire and stronger lightning pierced the dark sky.

The howling wind picking up strength was a thing of joy to him even though the people were beginning to worry as branches cracked from trees and blew uncontrollably across the clearing.

Binah Umor assumed the incantations were working. He assumed the destiny man must have been more blessed than he'd thought. The more fiery the wind, the more power he would receive from the burning man.

Nnanke's heart broke as she cleared the heavy trees surrounding the clearing. Her gaze immediately traipsed through the charred remains of the other men to that of the handsome man of her dreams. Her heart broke because he wasn't screaming any more.

As though the wind were intrinsically connected to her emotions, the howling increased like it cried for the poor handsome creature. The strength of it didn't only crack branches but lifted the heavy braid of her long hair from her back, blowing it like a piece of rag caught on a tree in the gale.

Her eyes glowed over the dancing villagers until it focused on that of the evil binah as he rounded the unmoving body of the bound man, chanting and pouring things into the fire.

Was she too late?

That thought alone prodded her determined steps into the clearing. She didn't sing—she stamped her staff on the ground, and it stood by itself, without support, despite the strong wind. Nnanke loosened the string of the small sack, dipped her hand, and scooped some of the dust in it. Without hesitation, she lifted it into the wind, and it scattered among the villagers, causing them to fall into deep faints.

Binah Umor instantly felt the strain of new power. His black eyes looked up and immediately focused on the glowing blue eyes of the woman he'd been looking for. He smiled; he would kill her like a mere bug. He was the lord of violence, and she, the priestess of peace, could not compare with his powers. Apparently, she had come to rescue again.

However, he'd underestimated her—he hadn't expected a priestess of peace to be furious.

As the villagers dropped where they stood and the melody of their revelry abruptly ceased, she marched with the fury of the wind, flicking her wrist and sending a burst of air that instantly wiped off the fire under the destiny man.

Binah Umor blustered angrily, instantly forgetting to complete his incantation. He equally flicked his wrist, and the fire exploded from the embers, burning bright.

The smug grin was wiped off his face when the chubby priestess didn't miss a step. Rather, she pointed her glowing staff behind her as she approached and then forcefully dragged it forward as though it were suddenly heavy.

And it was, for when she pointed the staff at the bound man, the resulting wind that snapped off the cheery fire did so with a bubble of water. The water doused the fire, totally soaking up the embers and emitting heavy smoke from the hearth.

Binah Umor roared in fury. He couldn't understand where the bubble of water had come from, but he knew he wasn't going to lose to a damn woman. A priestess of peace, he silently sneered.

Nnanke saw his familiar dark eyes from her nightmares, made even more evil by the animosity he directed at her. She should've been petrified, but her natural self seemed to have been swallowed by a supernatural urge to save the handsome man, and so, she was defying all obstacles to do just that.

"You dare me, Priestess!" Binah Umor roared, taking several steps to block her approach towards the bound man.

"You perpetrate injustice, *otanabinah*," she spat righteously, calling him a wizard priest. "Step out of my path and preserve your pride," she threatened, her staff held tightly in her hand like a weapon as she stood with widespread legs a few feet from him.

A deep, belly laugh exploded from Binah Umor. He laughed so hard, his head flung backwards in enjoyment. He stamped his equally engraved staff on the ground as he tried to control his mirth. When his calm returned, his eyes were filled with derision as he stared at Nnanke.

He saw a short, plump girl, with unusually long hair and curiously coloured eyes. The white cotton woven wrapper wound over her chest and reached to the top of her knees, moulded over her impressive curves. Binah Umor licked his lips lasciviously while wondering what a mere girl could do to him. Maybe he wouldn't kill her; he would defeat her and make her his concubine, after sucking out her powers, of course.

"You feel that I am impressed with your child's trick? You feel that with your binah staff you can become high and mighty? Which village do you come from, and why were they stupid enough to choose a woman as their binah?" he spat his demeaning questions and chuckled as though the entire idea were ridiculous.

The strong wind howled and wiped around them in the clearing littered with fainted villagers and burnt men. Nnanke's eyes flicked worriedly to the handsome, unmoving man, not knowing if he was already dead. Her eyes immediately took in the skulls and figures surrounding the hearth he'd been bound over, and she knew what the evil binah had been about to do.

Angrily, she sent the skulls and figures smashing against the trunk of a huge tree with just a wave of her hand and watched in satisfaction as the objects landed in pieces on the ground.

Binah Umor waved his hand with force, and an obvious punch to her stomach drove her several feet backwards. Her heel hooked on the body of a fainted villager, and she fell gracelessly but immediately stood up and took a stance for war.

The wind wiped around in fierce gales, flapping their wrappers. That of Binah Umor flapped so much, Nnanke was privy to his nakedness underneath the cinch on his waist.

"That ritual took me so long to prepare," he barked. He moved towards her with the intent of finishing her off, but then momentarily looked back at the smashed figurines. He was so angry, he was confused as to what to do first, then he made his decision and faced Nnanke.

"Why do you insist on daring me when you are no match for me?" he shouted over the howl of the wind as he approached her.

"Because I fight for good and you are evil!" she shouted back, her hand tightening on her staff in readiness. Tendrils of her hair wiped wildly around her face, obstructing her view, but she squinted and waited, ever determined.

"Little girl, you have no idea what you have walked into." He smirked just before he swung out his staff, and Nnanke was unceremoniously lifted off the ground as though she were a mere puppet and he the puppeteer.

She was reminded of her mother's children when they played with insects. They would pick up an ant and watch as it squirmed its tiny feet in the air. She felt like the ant as she squirmed, twisting and turning in the midst of the stormy wind but unable to affect her present situation.

Nnanke panted. Terror finally pierced her armour of fury as she realized she was at the mercy of the evil binah. He could fling her wherever, even skewering her on a jagged edge of a branch.

"What do I do with you now, little girl?" Binah Umor asked, shouting above the howling wind and still managing to sound considerate in the situation.

Nnanke struggled against his invisible hold, gritting her teeth in her effort to escape, but she yelped in pain because Binah Umor tightened his hand then, and she felt like a sharp clamp had been affixed on her waist, holding her in place in the air.

"You want to save the man, a dead man?" he shouted, fury lacing his words.

Her heart skipped. No, she thought, still gritting her teeth against the pain of being held adrift. No, he couldn't be dead. The pain that pierced her heart at the thought was even more than the physical ache she was experiencing at Binah Umor's hands.

"Since you want the man," he continued his mocking rant. "Then go to him." With that, he forcefully shifted his staff at Okoi's bound form over the charred hearth.

Nnanke gasped, her stomach plummeting as she was flung like a rag doll through the wind. She had no control of her momentum, but she held on tightly to her staff. Her eyes shut in fear as her body neared the bound man. She gritted her teeth, folded her body in, and prepared for the painful landing.

Air was knocked out of her when she landed, the force whacking the sticks the man hung from, and both of them slid on the rough ground. Though her whole body ached immeasurably, Nnanke stumbled up to her knees, her hand never letting go of her staff. As she struggled to her shaky feet, she thought she heard a moan from the man. Her eyes snapped to him, and she could've sworn he moved but she couldn't be sure, though it was hope.

She knew she couldn't finish this battle today. Her aim from the onset had been to rescue her dream man, so that's what she was going to do. Defeating Binah Umor, who was yet to know where she had come from, could wait for another day. Her dream man needed saving and healing, she thought as she glimpsed the burns on his face.

"I will show you what is done to insolent children," Binah Umor shouted as he marched towards the weakened priestess. His staff slammed the ground as he walked, his wrapper flapping crazily in the wind, showing the length of his lean thighs.

Nnanke saw his approach. She looked at his face and saw the evil glaring at her through his dark eyes. He sneered at her, his teeth through the bushiness of his beard making him look like a dangerously wild animal. She saw his inimical intent in his determined stride and knew she wouldn't win this battle. She had to find a way to flee from the evil binah.

Nnanke maintained her half-kneeling posture of weakness to keep the approaching binah from guessing her aim. She knew from her little discussions with Binah Yapkani and Ekori that a binah was never to be naked at the site of his ritual, especially a powerful ritual like the one the evil binah had been performing on her dream man. Nakedness in this clearing would render the binah weak for several days.

She allowed him to reach her, standing victoriously over her lowered form.

"You think you can come into my land and attempt to steal the powers I intend to harness without consequences? Shame on you, Priestess," he said and spat on her lowered head. "Now, I have more powers to gather, and then I might just keep you for a few *koke* for my enjoyment," he declared and laughed, flinging back his head in the wind.

That was Nnanke's moment. She slid her staff under his flapping wrapper, enjoying his groan of pain as the glowing wood burned his skin on its way to hook the knotted waist.

Standing rapidly, before the binah could react, she landed a kick on his stomach, sending him backwards and effectively loosening his wrapper, which floated away in the wind.

She saw the initial fear in his eyes, but then it turned into mirth as he laughed mockingly at her. He stood proudly, with his feet apart. His right hand held his staff, planted on the ground while his left hand settled on his hip like the conqueror he felt he was.

The man was not ashamed of his genitals hanging in the open. He stood there with only dark wood figurines hanging from twines on his neck.

"I am beyond such constrictions, little girl." He laughed again, bending so far backwards in his mirth, it was too late when he realized the twines on his neck were breaking one after the other.

He felt the power that had been surging strongly through his veins dissipate. His laugh tapered off as he leaned forward, his eyes meeting the glowing ones of the priestess. She gave him a benign smile as she swirled her staff. His twines of figurines suspended in the air just as he'd earlier suspended her.

"Nobody is beyond constrictions, *otanabinah*," she declared and flung the twines as far as she could, the wind assisting in floating the clanking figurines away.

As her eyes had never left his, she saw them widen. The fear returned, then he turned and fled in pursuit of his figurines.

She would've loved to destroy the physical representation of his power source, but it required a specific spell to do so. One she would endeavour to learn when she got to her cave.

Nnanke turned to the still form of her dream man, still completely bound on a wooden pole. She didn't know how soon the evil binah would catch up with his floating figurines, but she didn't want to be there when he returned.

With the wind still wiping at everything, tendrils of her hair getting into her eyes, she took a deep breath, went on her knee before her dream man, and hefted him. After three tries, she finally had him on her shoulder as she'd seen the warriors at Yakpani do, when they returned with a wounded warrior from a battle.

She struggled to her feet, panting at the effort, and proceeded to move as fast as she could through the fainted bodies of the villagers scattered in the clearing and into the forest, towards the river and her drifting craft.

So many times, she stumbled and almost dropped her load. Her nose twitched from the smell of burned skin, but she persevered.

Nnanke gasped in relieved delight as she sighted her drifting craft, bobbing at the bank of the volatile river. The wind caused waves to rise and crash against the trees close to the bank, but her raft held. Her spirit guides held it, patiently waiting.

When she finally stumbled to the edge of the bank, she off-loaded the handsome man of her dreams on the craft. She had barely climbed on when her spirit guides took off up the river, returning the way they had come.

The return voyage wasn't smooth at all. The constructed raft struggled against the violence of the river and the extra weight of the man. He was so tall, his legs hung out, tunnelling along in the water as they sped towards home.

At some point, she feared they might be upturned into the dark water, so she had to climb over, lying spread on top of the man with her staff in between their bodies while her hands tightly held on the side of the tumbling raft.

The river calmed as they entered the protective boundary of Yakpani. The spirit guides floated them to the riverbank, close to the beaten path that would take her to her cave. With some effort, Nnanke dragged the unmoving man, her nails breaking as she grasped the hard rope that bound him and pulled until half his body draped on the riverbank.

She dropped, tired, on the bank, her legs still in the water while she panted. Her mind couldn't begin to encompass what had just happened. She looked up just in time to see her spirit guides swirl in the water, glowing beautifully, then they sank, their glow dimming as they swam lower, until the water was once again dark, with only the sliver of a moon reflecting on its calm surface.

Her staff had stopped glowing. Even the burn in her eyes was gone, though she could still feel the blister around her eyes. She scooted on the muddy ground, her cotton wrapper stained with dirt as she got close to the man.

Nnanke sobbed when she saw the extent of his burns. She could still recognize his handsome face, but his skin looked wrinkled. She tenderly touched his shoulder wrapped tightly with heavy rope and shook him, trying to wake him up, but she wasn't even sure he was breathing.

The pain that suffused her heart choked her breath.

"You can't die," she sobbed.

For the first time in her outlandish life, she felt alone. And it was a strange feeling since she'd never experienced it before, seeing as she lived in the forest on her own, with no other human present for miles.

Nevertheless, the thought of this man she'd never met leaving her hurt so much, she could barely breathe.

With nothing to lose, she grabbed her staff, pushed the heavy form of the man into the water, and waded in, floating him to the centre of the river. Just as she'd done the ritual to the fertility spirit to bless the women of Yakpani, she did so now, swimming around in the water while mentally calling out her prayers for healing and life for a man she didn't know.

At first, the spirits were silent, unlike the instant response she'd gotten when the women of Yakpani had waded into the river. Nnanke's head bobbed from under the surface. She stared at the floating man still bound to the wooden pole, and he actually looked peaceful—dead.

She had no idea what she would do with a dead body, and she refused to believe she'd just battled with an evil binah for this man to simply die. With determination, she swam under again. This time, she floated under the form of the man and slammed the edge of her staff into his back.

The reaction was instant. Her staff hummed and glowed brightly in the water, illuminating her wide smile and floating hair. One would've mistaken her in that moment for a water nymph.

Just as she'd done with the women of Yakpani, she swam away and climbed onto the bank, squeezing her soaked wrapper and wringing her thick braid before she sat on the low rock to wait.

Chapter Fifteen

Okoi woke up disoriented.

His eyelids were so heavy, they kept drooping despite his efforts to lift them. He blinked while his eyeballs rolled listless in his head.

He must have slept, because when he tried opening his eyes again, everything seemed so bright, he had to squint to get all the sharp colours into focus.

He was in a forest.

Shutting his eyes again, he mentally catalogued his physical being. His arms were bound to his body, but his neck wasn't, because he could breathe and turn freely. A vague memory of a nightmare gave him the feeling it shouldn't have been so. Even his legs were untied and right now buried in cold water—he had no idea why part of his body was in water.

His mind kept flashing snatches of images, some horrific and some quite calming.

Taking a deep breath, he tried to understand why he felt, literally, well. The last he could recall, he'd been through harrowing experiences in the forest. There was no feeling to aptly compare or to succinctly explain how he currently felt. Like he'd been soaked in hot water, washed thoroughly, and rinsed in cold water; a similar treatment usually given to the white man's bedspread back at the plantation.

Comparing himself to a washed bedspread might not be reasonable, because how could a human being be laundered? But it didn't stop him from feeling clean, brand new, and invigorated. He was filled with strength and ready to take on anything as opposed to the last time…

And suddenly, the entire sordid experience came pouring into his consciousness. After getting captured by the tribe of cannibals, he'd not been instantly roasted like the other dead men but had been tied up and hung over a hearth in readiness.

Okoi moaned in terror as he recalled the heat of the fire, the suffocating blanket of the billowing smoke, and the hopelessness of surviving that particular trial. He must've died and transcended to the world beyond. Probably why the colours were so bright and sharp, hurting his eyes.

He must've been on the way to the world beyond when he recalled a vague memory of floating on water with a very beautiful woman hovering over him. Okoi took another deep breath and tried to recall the face of the woman—she had skin like the white man, curly hair, and she had smelled like fruits.

The vague image made him think of the heaven the missionaries had spoken about. Maybe he'd been taken into the sky, but he could distinctively recall floating on a raft with a woman over him. He was glad he was dead and finally at peace, and he sincerely hoped the woman in his memory was his angel. After all, the white man had spoken of beautiful, ethereal beings allotted by God to guide and guard mere humans like him, especially dead humans. But if he was dead, why was he still bound? Did they fear he was a volatile spirit as he had died violently?

As he inhaled the flowery scent in the air, which reminded him of his vague angel, the worrying thoughts drifted away.

Okoi tried opening his eyes again, and it didn't hurt so much this time. He could see the sun peeking through the thick branches and leaves above him. Birds chirped cheerily in the trees, brightly coloured butterflies flitted from flower to flower. Indeed, paradise was as beautiful as the missionaries had described — for once, the white man hadn't lied.

However, the same thought occurred to him: if he was in paradise, why was he still bound? According to the missionaries, when one dies and gets to paradise, their soul is released and free to float about just like the angels. Okoi was very aware he was still partly bound like he'd been at the dark, evil clearing.

Curiously, he turned his body, which meant he used his free legs, wedged them at the edge of the water and pushed, flipping to the right. His eyes immediately settled on no other but his angel. He knew this because he would recognize that hair and skin anyway, and...

He swallowed with difficulty. His lower body instantly came to life as his eyes carefully took in the prodigious swell of her voluptuous breasts through the wrapper. He noticed the obvious smoothness of her skin that was like that of a white baby's and the thick softness of her hair, how the heavy braid drooped over her shoulder and how tendrils curled on her temple and nape, more beautiful than the most beautiful white woman he'd ever seen.

"Angel," he whispered.

At least, he'd hoped to whisper, but it unfortunately came out as a croak, a terrible sound caused by the dryness of his throat. It instantly woke the angel, putting fear in her...curiously coloured eyes. Her eyes were like the colour of the sky on a beautiful morning. He grinned at her.

***

Nnanke gasped the moment she woke and scooted backwards on her buttocks while her eyes stayed on the handsome man of her dreams. She wondered how he had gotten to the riverbank with his bound limbs. Nevertheless, she was glad to see the scars that had marred his skin the previous night had cleared.

Her brow furrowed at the sounds coming from his throat, and belatedly, she saw he was smiling while his eyes focused on a spot below her knees. Nnanke wondered what would capture his attention so and followed his dazed gaze, looking down. She gasped when she saw that he was staring fixedly at her secret place.

She scrambled to her feet in a feat of embarrassment more than anger and grabbed the small satchel of dust from her bosom, pinched a bit of dust from it, then blew it in his face.

With a hammering heart, she watched as the handsome man's head dropped easily. He fainted with a smile on his face.

***

When Okoi came awake again, he was glad to find a broken gourd filled with water placed conspicuously close to his head. With some effort, he twisted and manoeuvred his still bound body until he could slurp the deliciously cool water into his parched throat.

With his thirst partially quenched, he lifted his eyes a bit and found a bunch of ripe, red berries lying close. Crudely, he jostled his body again and was soon devouring the sweet, juicy fruit.

After feeding like an animal, he fell back and belched, chuckling at the satisfyingly loud sound.

"Now, I loosen these ropes," he muttered while twisting with some effort to get the ropes off.

"You're a man with no honour for...for looking at my...my..."

Okoi heard the irate female's voice stammering in a strange language that vaguely sounded like the cannibal tribe—he sincerely hoped it wasn't.

He immediately bent his heard awkwardly, rewarded with the upside-down sight of his angel. He couldn't sustain the position for long as his neck hurt. So, he used his legs again, crab-walking sideways until he faced her, leaning his back on the trunk of a tree not very far from the river. Apparently, the angry woman with the strange language had pulled him from the water. But why was she furious?

"Please, help loosen these ropes?" he asked in clear English and worried when his angel cocked her head to the side with a confused frown.

Okoi shook his head in disappointment. Even in paradise, he still had rotten luck as he'd ended up paired with an angel who spoke a different language, and somebody had clearly forgotten to release him.

His gaze left her lovely face to scan the thick forest with no other person in sight. He breathed another sigh of frustration before turning to the English-impaired angel, which was weird because the missionaries had explained angels understood all languages.

"Go find someone that understands English or we will go nowhere today," he grunted in frustration because he couldn't gesture with his bound hands. He really needed to get these ropes off.

Her brow furrowed more, and then suspicion entered her eyes.

"Are you abusing me in your strange tongue?" Nnanke snapped, because, when she'd dreamt about him, they'd communicated perfectly in *Lokạạ*, the Atam language.

"You should feel guilty for looking under my wrapper, in between my legs," she shouted angrily while spreading her legs more and pointing under her wrapper with an accusatory mien.

What is she saying? Okoi wondered, trying to follow her wild gestures that kept ending between her legs.

And just like that, his train of thought shifted from the impossibility of the situation as his eyes travelled over the length of the short woman, appreciating her obvious curves with inherent male interest. Without meaning to, it manifested physically, growing hard and taut as it strained the front of his slightly burnt cotton trousers.

Suffused in embarrassment, Okoi wondered why his body readily reacted to this strange woman when it had taken the white woman—and in fact, all the other women at the plantation he'd had carnal knowledge of—some effort to bring his interest alive.

He cleared his throat and tried to twist so he could hide his unrelenting erection from the angry woman, who kept making signs and speaking in her strange language.

Nnanke noticed the man trying to fold his knees and turn his body from her, but it was difficult with his restraints. She stopped ranting. Her inherent kind nature demanded that she help him, but then her eyes caught the bulge in his strange garb.

She gasped and instinctively wanted to turn away in fury, but she couldn't take her eyes away from the impressive protuberance. Her mother, Ibiang's first wife, who had picked her in the forest as a baby and nurtured her despite the whole village postulating that she had picked a witch, had explained what the straining bulge in a man's wrapper meant. Nnanke had caught her father sporting one when he entered his second wife's hut.

Uben, the warrior who'd been courageous enough to come for her hand in marriage, had also, suddenly, had that same bulge whenever in her presence. Her mother had explained that men had this when they liked a woman and wanted to make babies with her.

A shiver of dread and a tingling of intense pleasure suffused her body and settled warmly in between her legs, in her secret place. She was instantly reminded of the things he had done to her in the dream, and she whimpered, pressing her knees together to take away the sweet ache assailing her secret place. Her nipples became so hard, they felt like sharp stones trying to break out through her wrapper.

Okoi heard her whimper and looked up, catching the look of pure carnal lust on her face. Unconsciously, he replied with an animalistic growl, a sound he'd never made before, his manhood hardening to the point of bursting. If only he could loosen these ropes, he would show her so much pleasure...

But then, the woman rapidly pulled out a small sack from her breast, and he recalled what the substance in that sack had done to him last time. His eyes widened in alarm while he shook his head. "No, no, no! Do not do that. Please..."

Still, the woman blew the pinch of dust at him. Okoi swerved from the direction of the charm but couldn't escape far. He felt the instant dulling of his senses, the slow weakening of his bones, and the heaviness in his eyelids.

"Stop doing that," he slurred heavily before slumping against the tree.

***

Nnanke paced the clearing behind her cave as she wondered what to do with the handsome man. It had been two *koke*, and though she'd managed to go about her usual duties, she was terrified the spirits would reveal the man's presence to Binah Yakpani and Ekori, and this meant dire significance.

Nonetheless, even with devastating consequences looming, she couldn't think of letting the man go, which was why she'd refused to loosen his bind. Imagining waking up each morning and not seeing his smiling face the moment she stepped out of her cave made her want to cry in a heart-wrenching manner — quite a strange feeling for her.

If she hadn't saved him from the evil binah at Umor, she would've suspected he'd bewitched her. If he had such powers, he wouldn't have been caught in the first place and almost burnt to death.

Nnanke had supplicated, whispered praises and ritual sacrifices to the spirits to find out the purpose of the man. Yet, they remained silent on his behalf. However, they were loud and accepting of the praises and sacrifices from the villagers who came in gratitude for fertility in their homes.

It had been a shock to discover a sudden array of raw food baskets, mainly yam and garri, bound goats and chicken, and gourds of palm wine decorating the edge of the spirit forest. So, she had hastened to Binah Yakpani and Ekori, and they had giddily informed her that women were getting pregnant all over the village, so the people of Yakpani were showing their gratitude to the fertility spirit.

Nnanke hadn't known what to do with that much food, so she'd transported most of it to Binah Yakpani's hut. She had used some to prepare the spirits' meal which she'd flung into the spirit river and watched as it duly disappeared, meaning it had been accepted, and the little remaining had been taken to her cave.

She had never worried about her meals. When sacrifices were left at the periphery of the spirit forest, she did the usual, shared some with the binah, cooked for the spirits, and did the ritual flinging into the river and mostly survived on wild fruits.

However, since having the handsome man from her dreams in the forest with her, she had been plagued with the pressing urge to cook elaborate meals that would entice his palate. It was quite strange, the urge to cook for him, and despite his bound hands and the difficulty of eating the fruits she always left for him, he always had a smile for her after feeding.

Like he knew she was watching him from inside her cave and he always shouted one word, 'tankiɔ,' whenever he finished eating. Nnanke wondered if that was his name. Her heart palpitated every time she saw his smile, and she usually had the urge to reply whenever he spoke his strange language even though she didn't understand it.

The forest seemed to have accepted him. At night, the spirits welcomed him, too. She usually found wisps of feathery light cotton on his head in the early hours of the morning when she checked on him. The sight of that immense blessing from the spirits made her breathe easier. If they had accepted him, then he couldn't be detrimental to her.

Still, she worried.

Though not as much as when she'd discovered that manly bulge below his abdomen. She had thought with him here in the forest he would leave her dreams, but that wasn't the case—he plagued them even more. His smile was the same. He played with her and spoke *Lokaa* fluently. He enticed her. He cared for her so tenderly, it brought tears to her eyes. He held her to his massive muscular chest. He walked with her in the forest with his arm flung lovingly over her shoulders.

Then, still in the dream, he pressed his mouth on hers, a strange act, but then she accepted it because it suffused her body with warmth that made her shift closer to him. His touch burned her skin no matter how feathery. Oh, and then his mouth on her neck, breasts, stomach, and…

Nnanke stopped pacing as her breath hitched once again at the memory of the overwhelming sensations that had woken her up prematurely. Not yet day break, but it was a new day, a long time before the sun's rising. She was afraid to go back to sleep and experience the dream again. Yet, she was even more terrified that she longed for the man's touch. Not in the dream, but in real life; she was curious to find out if such intense sensations could actually be possible, especially since her own life, apart from serving the spirits, had been bland so far.

She couldn't have deep, personal conversations with spirits, and she'd longed for that all her life. Because she'd been born extremely different, her adopted mother had been the only one to bother about her despite her solemn attitude. Nobody had seen she was lonely in her difference, but she hadn't made it easy on people to know that. Rather, as a defence, she had embraced her uniqueness and had been glad the spirits had finally decided to come for her instead of the bothersome dreams she'd had as a child.

Drinking from the calabash close to where she'd been pacing, Nnanke decided to do something productive since she wasn't going to find sleep anymore. Determined, she marched from the back of her cave and without meaning to, her legs took her to where the man slept leaning on a tree. He looked uncomfortable with the rope still binding his arms to his body, and she knew how cold the night could get.

Guilt suffused her body, and with the slight brilliance of the moon, she worked on the tight knots until they loosened. She refused to pull the ropes so as not to disturb his sleep. Kneeling close to him, she studied his face and the powerful muscles of his body, and felt the familiar heat that usually came with his touch coursing through her.

It scared her. Instead of running, she reached out tentatively and touched his brow, noticing wisps of cotton in his hair, evidence of the spirits' favour. So why had he been abandoned to die by fire, she wondered in a small fit of anger. Sometimes, she really did not understand the gods.

She wondered where he'd been and how he'd come to be captured. She had the pressing urge to know everything about him as opposed to her previous passiveness in knowing about other people except spirits. Her indifference had been the reason she'd embraced living in the forest alone; people were generally foolish, and though she liked Binah Yakpani, sometimes, he could be just as foolish as the rest of the village despite his authority as the binah, as the leader.

Her hand drifted from his brow to the shell of his ear, and then down to the strength of his shoulder. She was entirely fascinated by him. She wanted to speak with him, know him, laugh with him. She was tired of hiding her smiles when he smiled at her, tired of wondering what he was saying when he spoke in his strange language. So, she made a decision.

Swiftly getting to her feet, she hurried into the denser part of the forest, feverishly plucking leaves and herbs and digging clay from the spirit river. Instead of returning to her cave, she sat in the forest, found a broken gourd, and began mixing and chanting the portion that would make *Tankio* understand *Lokąą* fluently. She had never cast the spell before, but she was desperate enough to try the incantation Binah Yakpani had described as a myth, mere folklore told by his father's father before they had left Akpa, the ancestral land.

When she stumbled out of the dense forest, tired after so many efforts to make the potion and not quite sure her end product would be effective, Nnanke was shocked to find *Tankio* missing.

The loosened ropes were exactly where she'd left him. Looking around, her heart tumbled. Had he decided to flee? The thought brought pinpricks of tears to her eyes, an odd phenomenon since she'd been told she hadn't cried even as a baby.

Tiredly, with tears blurring her sight, she stumbled down the beaten path to the spirit river, intending to throw her potion into it in anger. Nnanke had to suddenly lean on the trunk of the tree that shaded the low rock she usually sat on close to the river because her heart ached so much, it weakened her limbs.

Panting and sobbing as though her heart had shattered into several irretrievable pieces, she slowly dropped the broken gourd containing the potion and reduced herself onto her rock, folding over and wishing to become smaller in her grief.

Over the sound of her pounding heart and sad sobs, she heard a splash from the river that sounded heavier than the usual bird falling into the water. She looked up in alarm. The sight made her quickly wipe the tears from her eyes to see clearer.

Her heart soared when she saw him swimming in the river with a relaxed joy obvious on his face. Then, her heart lurched in fear because an ordinary man was swimming in the spirit river.

Nnanke got to her feet and rushed to the bank, calling out to him frantically. Binah Yakpani had said that before the forest and the river had been abandoned as the spirits' dwelling, many men had died just from drinking or bathing in it.

"Tankio! Tankio!" she called and hysterically waved, indicating he should come out of the river. "You cannot bathe in the river! Come out instantly!" she called, her heart hammering in her throat.

Okoi grinned when he saw his angel, his heart instantly more joyous than when he'd woken to find his bindings had been loosened. But then, the smile tapered off when he saw how perturbed she looked. Even at a distance, her eyes seemed swollen and red, like she'd been crying, and she frantically wanted him out of the water. He wondered if that was that had caused her tears.

Still, he hesitated, realizing he would be entirely naked and exposed if he heeded her call. But the tears were threatening to fall again. He hurriedly swam towards her, hesitating only a little before getting to his full height and stepped onto the bank.

The panic and threatening sob squelched in her throat as her eyes bugged over his naked form. Nnanke knew she should look away, but she couldn't. Words failed her. Not like he would've understood her, but it would've been right to show some angry reaction at his shamelessness.

Her mouth went instantly dry as her eyes scanned every hard plain and length of him. When she got to below his abdomen, she stopped and couldn't move. Right before her eyes, his manhood jerked with a life of its own and grew long, swollen, and hard. Her body was instantly attacked. It erupted with tingles that left her weak and her mouth dry like she'd chewed cotton, something she had tried once, unfortunately.

Okoi was embarrassed at his uncontrollable carnal desires. He couldn't understand how his manhood would get so hard and ready to copulate from just a look from his angel. He hoped the angels in paradise weren't as disciplined as white men. A reaction like this to one of the white women would have gotten him several hundreds of the whip on his bare back.

"Sorry," he whispered and hurried past her to his slightly charred cloths.

Nnanke followed his progress, getting an eyeful of his buttocks as he raced by her. Helplessly, she licked her lips as though savouring a delicious fruit. It was then she noticed he had washed his strange garbs, which were charred at the edges, and placed them on a fallen log that caught a patch of sunlight. She watched him pull on his clothes and turn to her, looking quite uncertain, especially with his slightly damp cloth plastered on the obvious bulge in between his thighs.

"Tankio, you should not have baths in the water. It belongs to the spirits," she explained, her eyes growing large with worry, because she had no idea what the consequences of his swim would be.

Okoi swallowed hard at the concern etched on her face, a different and encouraging look than what he'd been getting from her these past weeks. He really wished he could understand her, and with confusion etched on his face, he said, "I cannot speak your language."

"*Mmpue!*" Nnanke exclaimed in frustration, expressing her lack of understanding.

Then like a flash, she recalled her potion. With a wide grin, which shocked Okoi to no end, she raced off to her rock, grabbed the broken gourd, and returned with it.

He frowned in confusion when she dipped her finger into the gooey clay and marched determinedly towards him. He took a hesitant step back but stopped at the sight of her smile. His chest expanded in reaction. It felt like the sun had come out from behind a heavy cloud, making everything better.

Physically unmoving because of her beauty, she reached him, making him blink rapidly. Then she shoved her stained fingers into his mouth and stepped back to give him a speculative gaze, like she was waiting for something to happen.

Okoi gagged in disgust, using his teeth to scrape his tongue as he frowned at her.

"Why did you do that, woman?!" he sputtered in alarm as a bit of the tangy clay slipped down his throat.

She squealed in delight, shocking him into inaction. Again, he was stupefied as he watched the angel, the beauty and the joy of her happiness. Everything in his body quelled and rose again, and this time, it wasn't carnal but simply the purest joy in his heart for being in her presence.

"Tankio, you can speak *Lokaa!*" she exclaimed and danced with exuberance while grasping the broken gourd to her bountiful chest.

Two things smacked him into suddenly grinning and frowning at the same time. The angel wasn't insane—he could indeed speak the local tongue, though he knew not how and...why was she calling him 'thank you'?

Chapter Sixteen

In the days and nights that followed, Okoi and Nnanke got close.

He got to know why she had referred to him as 'thank you,' a phrase he'd always shouted out to her whenever he'd completed the fruity meals she'd left for him. No wonder she'd assumed it must have been his name. He related his ordeal as a slave at the white man's land and how they'd been released and brought back home. She sobbed over the hot brand scar on his back.

Okoi endeavoured to describe the ship that had brought them home, a large wooden vessel that floated on water. It surprisingly hadn't been difficult for his angel to understand, though she had explained how the floating craft made of tree branches which she'd used to rescue him had been made by spirit guides.

Everything she said smacked him as strange. Even though she had explained that he'd almost died but the spirits had saved him, he couldn't stop referring to the beautiful spirit forest as paradise, because it really was, especially with Nnanke in it.

How could he not, when at night, he could see luminescent creatures that jumped out and played at the river or floated around her beautiful cave. Everything about the woman was ethereal, making it difficult for him to stop staring into her eyes.

When she described her duties to the spirit and the sacrifice she had to make, he'd been entirely crestfallen. How could the spirits be so cruel as to take such a magnificent being for themselves?

Why was he the unluckiest man on the face of the earth? Sometimes, he felt it would've been better if he had truly died at the hands of the evil priest. Not subjected to dwell with the most beautiful woman he'd ever seen, only to remain friends, talking, laughing, and helping in her spirit work any way he was allowed to.

Nevertheless, he would look at her and shake his head. No, it was better that he'd been accorded an opportunity to step foot on his homeland and be in the presence of such supernatural beauty than be dead without this experience.

He had been entirely ecstatic when Nnanke had listened to his mother's story and had confirmed that, indeed, he was at the right place, though she didn't know where Lekanakpakpa, the ancestral land his mother spoke of, now called Akpa, was. But the stories told were of their tribe originating from there.

Okoi didn't mind—he would rather be here with Nnanke than at any ancestral land, and he told her so, enjoying her blatant delight and shy smile. Nobody would know him or recall his mother if he went there. From her story, it was possible his mother could have been from any of the other tribes to have moved from Akpa.

In all of this, he had to hide his unrelenting carnal desire from her. Several times, he had to run from her, pretending he had to urinate or excrete or fetch firewood, which meant he went into the dense part of the forest and tried to calm his ardour.

It was the same reason he refused to sleep with her inside her cave. Not when he rutted after her like an animal in heat. He was afraid that one night, he would lose control and do what would be detrimental to her life. He did not want that.

Even sleeping outside her cave proved a trial. All he had to do was recall her smile or something she'd said. He could remember how she went about her spirit duties, unconsciously bending over and rewarding him with a flash of her fat, fair thighs. Sometimes, he glimpsed her secret place when she sat grooming her toenails, or the shape of her prodigious buttocks in the air when she knelt to blow flames under her cooking pot, and he would immediately go so hard, he could use his erection to crack palm kernel.

Sometimes, it was the look he caught in her eyes, like she was feeling the heavy pull of carnal desire just like he was, and then she would quickly glance away. It was also the way she tenderly took care of him; a strange phenomenon. She always had roasted yam and bush meat, prepared with *yedamblongh* and chilled palm wine previously buried by the bank of the spirit river overnight for him.

Most times, he fought the pressing urge of touching her. The few times he had, especially the first time, he'd felt a fierce jolt when their skins met. He could only describe it as a force of lightning shooting through him, and the resulting pleasure coursing through his body had been so much, he wanted to do it again.

Okoi had done it again, but then, it always led to the embarrassingly rapid swell of his manhood.

He wanted to marry her in all the ways possible, be it like the white man or as culture demanded in Yakpani. He wanted to fill her belly with the cream of his manhood and watch it swell big and round with his children. He wanted to carry little, fair children she had birthed for him and live in the spirit forest with them until he died with her.

Okoi's heart twisted in pain, for no matter how he wished for these things with Nnanke, it would never happen, not if he wanted her alive and well. She was never to lay with a man, or be severely punished by the gods.

Even this terrible thought could not bring down the effect of his carnal craving. Several times, he had been tempted to grab his manhood in a fist and rub it until he spilled his manhood cream, at least to experience some relief. But he'd felt like he'd be cheating Nnanke if he did that. So most times, he slept with the painful hardness and woke with it, too.

Today was harder than most, he thought as he stared at the sprinkle of stars in the dark sky. His fingers nervously strummed on his stomach as he sought to think about his ordeal as a slave to reduce his desires, but nothing happened.

Past the middle of the night, and yet, he couldn't sleep. His whole body felt like ants and fireflies roamed beneath his skin. Okoi made a hasty decision and allowed his hand to creep towards his hardness, when he heard a rustle.

His fingers stopped moving. Holding his breath, he pretended to be asleep. He knew the sound came from Nnanke. She did this sometimes, always coming out to him whenever he couldn't sleep. He knew she meant well, but it made everything more difficult.

The rustle came again, and the scent of the flowers draping heavily over the mouth of her cave bloomed in the air. Okoi had no choice but to inhale deeply because that scent was Nnanke. Whenever she was close, her hair gave off the aroma of flowers and her skin smelled of fruits, which mostly made his mouth water — like now.

When he perceived her smell, he wanted to put his mouth in her secret place and lick her until she cried. He had hated the act when Eugenia had forced him to, but now, he wanted to do it to Nnanke so much, his mouth flooded with his greedy saliva.

"Okoi, *adowake?*" Nnanke whispered, wanting to know if he was asleep.

Her husky voice and close proximity caused his breath to hitch noisily, so he couldn't pretend to be asleep.

"Eh-eh," he replied in the Yakpani way of saying 'no,' sighing heavily, almost like a groan. He kept his eyes closed, gnashing his teeth and fisting his hands to desist from dragging her on top of him and tearing off her wrapper so that he could get his hands on her soft, naked skin.

Nnanke knelt close, her eyes taking in his whole, prone form, especially the upward bulge of his trousers. She noticed his closed eyes, hard jaw, and fisted hands. She knew what he was fighting, and it was a battle she had given up, the reason why she was outside.

She couldn't sleep. Her body had heated up to such fiery heights, even her palms were hot. She had lain in her cave, her thighs tightly pressed together as she battled the sweet ache and tingling she knew only Okoi could make go away. It had been that way for so long, but tonight, it felt as though she would die if she didn't feel his touch. She felt as though her breath would stop if she did not press her mouth on his own just as he had done in her dreams.

Her breasts had swollen in its binds, her nipples hard pebbles that caused a pleasant pain which coursed through her body and settled in the building ache between her thighs.

"Okoi," she whispered again and scooted close, her voice desperate.

"Please, go inside the cave," he pleaded, sounding equally desperate.

"I can't...I will die," she begged. Her fingers whispered across his collarbone, for she couldn't bear one more moment of not touching him.

Okoi's breathing became noticeably difficult. He wheezed as he tried to fight the overwhelming power prodding their carnal desires for each other. He flung his right arm over his eyes to keep them closed, because he had the pressing urge to see her face. He knew if that happened, if he saw the longing for him on her features, he wouldn't be able to control his ardour.

"You will die if I see you naked. I want to see you naked," he sobbed, still not opening his eyes. Now he understood what the missionary had been talking about when he explained love, the emotion one had towards one's wife. He really must love Nnanke. He would fight and deny himself what he most desired just so she would live.

"I have never felt like this before." She sobbed, too. "I feel so hot, it's like I'm being roasted from the inside. My secret place is so moist, it's like I'm sweating there. I can feel it dripping down my thighs."

Okoi groaned at the image of her innocent description of carnal longing. He had never thought his manhood could be harder than it had been, but he'd been wrong. Right then, it felt like if he did not push it into her, it would burst.

He choked on his rapid breath and scrambled to his knees, facing her painfully beautiful face.

"*Num mboke*." I'll die, she whispered while tears rolled down her round cheeks, her eyes soulfully pleading.

His naked chest heaved, as he'd discarded his shirt for the night was balmy.

"The spirits…"

"The spirits accepted you. It has been two *koke* since you bathed in the river, but nothing has happened to you. Every night I came out to look at you when you slept, tied up by the tree, I would see the welcome of the spirits on your head…"

"But you never told me this…"

"I did not understand what it really meant. I have been dreaming about you before I came to rescue you at Umor."

Okoi's eyes widened in shock.

"You said the spirits sent you," he pointed out, walking on his knees to be closer to her.

"When the spirits send me, they visit my dream and *speak* to me. None of them visited. I was dreaming about you and the evil binah, until I dreamt of him burning you over the fire. I don't know how I knew where you were, but the knowledge came to me. I don't know how I did some of the things I did that night. I just know that my eyes were burning so hot, just like my body now, and I knew that if I did not come for you, the pain would not stop."

Okoi couldn't speak through the choking hope in his heart. Could this true; was it possible? Everything she'd just said pointed to his deepest desire being conceivable.

When she got to her feet and closed the distance between them, he didn't move. Okoi was a tall man, so even though he knelt and she stood over him, his head still reached to her heaving bosom.

"There is something I have been hungering to do," she whispered as she stared into his raised eyes, his gaze squarely on her face.

"What?" he croaked, swallowing saliva that had dried up in his mouth at her proximity.

Her hands softly grabbed his face, and her head lowered until she placed her lips on his, mirroring what he had done to her in her dreams.

Okoi gasped and pulled back in shock, startling her in the process.

'Does it pain you?" she asked in alarm.

"How did you know that?" he asked, his chest beating with longing and the hot flash of jealousy. Had someone taught her to kiss, someone that had known the white man?

Nnanke saw the look in his eyes and wondered why the act that had pleasured her in her dream would anger him.

"You did it to me many times in my dreams," she replied.

Okoi was dizzy with the amount of pleasurable emotion slamming through his body.

"I…I did?" he croaked.

She nodded innocently, noticing his happy expression and smiling tentatively at him.

"So, will you put a baby in my stomach now?" she asked in an almost whisper.

"Jesus," he groaned, the exclamation leaving his mouth unconsciously. He had never understood why the plantation masters always exclaimed the name of God's son in some situations. Now, he knew.

"I don't know what that means." Nnanke frowned. Though Okoi had been teaching her small words in the white man's language, she hadn't heard this one before.

He couldn't answer her. He just wrapped his arms around her full, shapely waist and pulled her close. With no hesitation, he placed his mouth on hers and kissed her just like Eugenia had instructed him.

She tasted better than he had imagined. Her scent of fruits and flowers wafted into his nose, and he inhaled while his mouth fused hard on her. Nnanke's arms wrapped about his neck, and she pressed her body on his without thought.

He nibbled at her mouth, softly coaxing until she opened for him and he delved in, tangling with her innocent tongue while she moaned and surrendered to his expertise.

Okoi sought a better position by leaving his knees and sitting on the soft grass. He pulled Nnanke and made her sit astride his thighs. She gasped when the outline of his impossibly hard manhood pressed on her buttocks, making her shift restlessly, wanting what she didn't know or couldn't explain. She only knew the bulge held answers to the ache she was feeling.

With her legs astride, her wrapper lay agape, and the scent of her longing, the cream of her secret place, wafted into Okoi's nose, causing him to lose all control.

His hands shoved her wrapper higher up her hips, then he plunged his right hand in, his fingers brushing her inner thigh on their way to her secret place.

Just as she'd confessed, the whole area was completely drenched with her cream. He touched her soft, swollen folds and sighed, groaning in the next instant as his manhood threatened to explode when his finger slipped into her tight channel.

Nnanke cried out, not in pain but in pleasure unimaginable. Her waist unconsciously undulated, making his finger sink deeper into the hot recess of her woman cove.

It wasn't enough—he wanted more. Okoi withdrew his hand, ignoring her cry of protest to quickly loosen her wrapper, baring the beautiful sight of her bounteous breasts. The pale globes enticed him to bend his head and taste each delicious nipple, causing her to whimper her pleasure.

But that wasn't the prize he was going for. He left her breasts with a mental promise to return to them. Right then, he only wanted to taste one part of her, the one in between her thighs.

He placed small sucking kisses on her neck and assured her in a gruff but tender voice that he would take care of her. With her in his lap, he awkwardly spread her wrapper behind her and then tenderly eased her down on it. Her eyes met his, and he stopped breathing because they glowed a soft, blue light. She really was an angel.

Swallowing hard, he watched his dark hands trace lovingly over her fair skin. Then, he softly widened her thighs even though he wanted to plunge his face in her secret place. He went slowly, so as not to scare her.

The sight was more beautiful than he would have ever imagined. When his head began lowering, he felt the unconscious tightening of her thighs, her inherent propriety aiming to stop him. But he was stronger and determined; he wanted to taste her secret place more than he wanted to take his next breath.

She whimpered as he overpowered her and succeeded to lower his head there, breathing hot air on her as he inhaled her mouthwatering scent. Nnanke struggled because the act was strange and seemed unacceptable and unnatural. However, Okoi calmed her by the single brush of his finger on the lips of her fleshy cove.

He added more fingers and slowly widened the hairy, pliant flesh that continuously produced pearly cream he so wanted to lap up like a dog. He couldn't breathe as he saw her pleasure nub so rosy and swollen, looking a lot plumper than Eugenia's.

He extended his tongue and licked tentatively, shocked when Nnanke jerked, almost throwing him off her. He pressed his weight on her and went to work sucking, licking, laving, and chewing her lips and pleasure nub. She tasted sweet, like fruits, and he couldn't get enough. He had to bury both his nose and mouth in her while furiously lapping up the sweet cream gushing from her beautiful secret place.

Her cries echoed in the dark forest. Nnanke was sure if she died today, it would be from pleasure so intense, it felt like her whole body was on fire from inside. And she would die happy, she thought vaguely as her body began feeling as though she were floating. A surge built steadily from her womb, the force so intense, she cried out in fear. She knew she'd just thought of dying, but she hadn't expected it so soon.

What was happening to her? She had to let Okoi know, or else...were the spirits showing their displeasure already? Were they ironically going to kill her with pleasure?

She struggled to her elbows, her breath coming in pants, her body undulating of its own accord, even when she tried to stop it, because the movement seemed to be adding to the surge inside her.

"Okoi..." she gasped, trying helplessly to move her secret place away from his relentless tongue, but couldn't, because her limbs weren't functioning as they should.

"Please..." she begged, not entirely sure what she was begging for. The white strength of the pleasure building in her was scary, and she wanted to step back from it because she felt it would consume her. Yet, she wanted to reach for it, too. She might not fall from the edge of the cliff but fly from it, but she wasn't sure.

"Angel..." She vaguely heard Okoi call her the pet name he insisted on. "Angel..." he prodded, and she raised herself on her elbows again. Funny how she hadn't realized she'd fallen from them, and saw

Okoi's equally raised head between her legs while his fingers persisted to drive her insane, flick01ng continuously inside her core.

The sight of his head in between her legs and the knowledge that he had been buried in her secret place proved strangely erotic instead of shaming. She sobbed at the sight of him, her hips still moving of their own accord, to the rhythm his fingers set as they plunged and withdrew from her cove.

"Help me...please..." Her brow furrowed with worry, and Okoi smiled at her. If he was smiling, then nothing bad was happening to her.

And as though he could read her mind, he whispered, "Let go, Angel. Don't fight that feeling in you. I can feel your secret place tightening around my fingers, and I know what is happening, but you have been fighting it and holding back."

Nnanke shook her head, not agreeing. "I feel...I feel like I will fall and die..."

"You won't die, Angel. I'm here with you, and I promise, you are holding back from the best feeling you have ever experienced. Just let go," he coaxed.

He continued speaking to her, whispering sweet words and endearments that encouraged the fiery surge. She listened to him, letting go of control and bucked ceaselessly on the soft grass, screaming her first ever release. Her whole body jittered and shivered while Okoi covered her with his manly weight, his whiskers tickling her neck and face as he touched his mouth all over her.

Her breath returned to normal after a while. Opening her eyes took some effort, and she smiled when Okoi's handsome face came into focus. He smiled back. She could clearly feel his hot, throbbing, swollen bulge against her thigh, and despite feeling like she couldn't move her body, she experienced a quickening in her womb, which shot straight into her secret place.

Nnanke couldn't believe she was lying entirely naked, spread open under an equally naked man, without contemplating killing herself in shame. All she felt was a need for her secret place to be filled up by his heavy manhood.

With an inherent instinct present in every woman, she widened her legs and shifted to align her drenched entrance with his hardened length.

Okoi gasped and groaned as he rubbed his painfully engorged manhood on her warm entrance, drenched, pliant, and ready to receive him. Understanding that this was her first time, he held his ardour, reached between their bodies, and slid in his fingers again, tweaking and strumming her nub of pleasure until it enlarged once more against his fingers, readying her body for loving.

While she moaned aloud, making him pant in impatience to slide into her, he grabbed the burning length of his manhood and used the large, mushroom head to probe the soaked entrance of her delicious cove. He rubbed the bulbous head along her fleshy slit until the supple lips opened for him. Then he brushed the slit on the underside of his manhood's head on her swollen nub, groaning at the exquisite ecstasy that suffused his body. The wet, squishy sounds emanating from his act added eroticism that tightened his sacs and made him feel like he would expel his cream soon.

Not wanting that to happen, he levelled himself on his knees and carefully handled his manhood, shoving it into the real paradise. She was so tight. Her whimpers and unconscious raise of her hips to meet his drove him mad. He gritted his teeth to hold back the natural urge of plunging like a crazed dog, and tried to push in slowly.

Nnanke thrashed beneath him, not helping at all. Before he could grit out words that would calm her, she grabbed his neck and forcefully impaled herself on his shaft.

Both of them gasped for different reasons. Both their eyes widened — Nnanke in slight pain, and Okoi in shock she had done that. If he hadn't felt the block in her virgin channel, her impatience would've pointed to some experience.

His brow furrowed as he tried to breathe deep and hold back the surging explosion steadily building in his tightened sacs when she started moving her hips as she'd done earlier against his fingers. Sweat dripped from his temple as he frowned and shook his head at her. He didn't want this paradise to end soon; he wanted to be embedded in her forever.

"Angel, you are so tight..." he murmured as he joined her in moving but slowly.

She stopped undulating her hips.

"Is...is that bad?" she asked innocently, her eyes widening on his face in worry.

Okoi gasped out a strained laugh. "...Gods, no. Tight is very good." He began pumping with more force as the rising pleasure directed.

Tight was the best, he thought as he withdrew slowly and plunged in, feeling her wet, swollen nerves fisting his hard length so firmly, he just wanted to let go and shoot his seed into her, filling her with his cream. He had never felt this way with

Eugenia; it had always been a duty with her, a means of survival. With Nnanke, he wanted to impale her so much and all the time that she wouldn't be able to walk straight.

He wanted to mark his territory like an animal and announce to everyone that she was his, preferably with her belly swollen with his seed. The thought of planting his seed in her pushed him to the edge. He had lost count of how many times she'd flushed, drenching his shaft with her juices, moaning weakly into his ears, yet he kept going, wanting her to douse him again.

Laying on her and smiling because she tightened her hold around his neck, he kept plunging, his hips working furiously and enjoying the sounds their bodies made when they smacked together. Soon enough, he wasn't able to withdraw further, his basic aim prodding him to keep plunging. He pumped wildly, panting and moaning, knowing he was going to shoot his seed.

The pleasure was exquisite and unbearable, and yet, he wouldn't have done it differently. He pounded into her, until a scream erupted from his throat and he jerked and shivered, still pushing into the sweetest hole a man could ever find himself.

Okoi grabbed an equally sobbing Nnanke and kissed her so hard, she whimpered.

"I will die for you," he declared fervently, his eyes expressing his intense love for her.

She touched his face tenderly, her whole body feeling heavy and languid, like she could sleep for days.

"I would never let you die," she promised, smiling at him.

The explosion was more than they'd expected. Though gasping and panting, they held onto each other tightly, as though if they let go, the avalanche of emotions they'd created would overwhelm them.

It was simply magic — it was light, and he had to shut his eyes in the aftermath. Still, he experienced the burning brilliance of the climactic moment. They were tangled in each other, Okoi unable to withdraw from her, so he lay stuck in her, wrapped in her arms as they fell asleep.

In that era, a time where spirits reigned supreme for as long as could be recalled, another supreme power had been birthed in that forest — Love. Though inconceivable at the time, it was a power set to fatally compete with the spirits in the hearts of men. The spirits might have created this power, but then, men were known to complicate everything.

Chapter Seventeen

For some reasons I'm unable to explain, it has been nice to be back to anonymity, to the human world where no one sees me. The knowledge of a couple in the spirit world with the same intense love for each other as the prince and his wife left me feeling slightly inadequate. Please, bear with me as I recover.

I sat sulking in a corner as Onen stirred from a deep slumber but refused to move from the warm softness of his wife's body. Daylight peeked through the drapes in their room, but he didn't seem in a hurry to wake up fully. The memory of falling into the past a few days ago remained fresh on his mind. I couldn't blame him for that. Lord, it remained fresh on all our minds. Such intensity proved difficult to erase.

After joining Nkoyo in the realm of the past and weirdly enough with them seeing me for the first time, we watched with bated breath as Nnanke fought the evil priest. We were all anxious she wouldn't be able to defeat the atrocious man and actually applauded when she'd tricked him and rescued Okoi.

Nkoyo had tenderly teased Onen when he'd grumpily huffed at Nnanke leaving Okoi tied up for days. Of course, the entire time this happened, I kept rolling my eyes in exasperation. Seriously, how were there two pairs of lovey-dovey couples in one damn tale? They had gotten on my last nerve.

Things had gotten intense when it was obvious a power almost stronger than the spirits was pulling Okoi and Nnanke together. The night they finally gave in to their desires and the blatant sensual act had made Onen cough uncomfortably.

Even I had been unable to come up with any snide remarks, as I'd been doing the whole time. All of us in that time bubble had been left speechless at the intensity of the lovemaking from the past. Onen felt choked from all the love sparks created by the couple; he felt like he was watching himself with Nkoyo. Embarrassing for him, especially with me in attendance.

At that thought, he'd turned and caught me staring at him knowingly. Well, you didn't expect me to pretend I didn't know what he was thinking and what this episode of the past meant to him and his wife. Even though I turned away with a slight smile on my face, I could still feel his confusion at what my smile meant. Did it mean he'd met Nkoyo before? Were they watching their past selves? Because it really felt that way, he'd thought while looking down at his captivated wife. Well, they would figure it out, won't they?

At the last explosive climax, it was as though they'd all been roused from hypnotism. I had taken it upon myself to push and prod them into the dark hole, which took them back to the present.

When Onen woke up on Mmatami's inner room floor with his wife in his arms, his gaze swooped about, obviously looking for me, but I was nowhere to be seen. I heard him thinking that of course, I probably floated around them as a spirit without their knowledge. Well, look at Onen being all perceptive. Good for him.

Mmatami had sniffed at them, her eyes looking like she would've wanted to smack both of them, but she settled for announcing that with what had just happened, Nkoyo was to stay away from delving into the past for some months. She declared one didn't play with the past and spirits as though they were toys. Mmatami had angrily spat that there were consequences from playing with such power, and so Nkoyo had been temporarily banned from the past.

Nkoyo hadn't been happy at the decision, but she'd not had any strength to argue. Onen was secretly pleased about it, but hid his elation and took her home.

Well, as expected, it hadn't been a quiet night for them. Onen had enacted the love scene from the past and more throughout the night and the next few days. Christ, how virile could one man be?

Still, he sighed, his breath brushing tendrils of hair on his wife's nape. He wasn't satisfied. Just recalling what they'd done these few days after the debacle of the past got him hard.

For God's sake, can we move on already? Like, I'm done sulking, I'm ready for the tale to continue.

Of course, no one heard my pleas, not with what was about to happen. No nudge I sent their way could break up this morning's imminent romp, powerless in the face of their intense love and desire.

Belligerent, I decided I wasn't leaving either. I was tired of floating outside while they moaned in ecstasy. Christ, weren't they curious of what happens next in the tale? Am I the only one invested in this?

Slowly, Onen's hand glided over Nkoyo's silky nightwear, roaming her curves and ending under her bounteous breasts that had since increased in size because of the pregnancy. He recalled how Okoi had practically swallowed Nnanke's nipples and how ferociously he'd sucked them. His dick hardened more, and he pressed it into her soft buttocks, his hand sliding up to grab her breast.

As though aware of his dirty thoughts, Nkoyo's nipple was already hard before he got there. He squeezed the large breast and rolled the nipple between his thumb and forefinger. Onen was gratified to feel his wife nudge his erection with her arse while sighing and shifting on the bed sensuously.

His mouth lowered to her exposed neck and dropped tiny wet kisses there, his hand moving to the next breast to give it the same treatment. Then it lowered, gliding down the soft swell of her baby bump, arriving at her 'secret place' as referred to in the past.

Nkoyo, eyes still closed, widened her legs eagerly, and Onen wasted no time in placing his large hand over her silk-covered mound. She gasped when his finger slid into her, instantly dampening the nightwear.

"You're so wet, baby," he rumbled in her ear while his fingers worked her eager cunt. She gasped again, arching into his touch as he plunged into her pussy, her nightwear serving as a thin barrier.

She was unsatisfied with the arrangement, so she quickly pulled her nightgown upward, exposing fair thighs and a dripping cove, then she grabbed her husband's wrist and brought his fingers back to her soaking centre.

"You make me so wet, baby," she gasped as Onen flicked her swollen clit persistently. The back and forth of his finger over her hardened nub of pleasure built a delicious ache which she eagerly reached for, knowing the resulting crash would be so worth the keening rise of pleasure.

"I can feel you tightening, baby, are you about to come for me? Is my royal finger in your sweet cunt making you want to explode? Oh, princess, your cunt cream is drenching my hand, and I love it. Come for me, baby, come for your prince," he coaxed in her ear, biting the lobe and swirling his tongue over the sting of his bite.

Nkoyo's hips moved unrelentingly against his plunging finger. His dirty words in her ear drove her to the brink and over the edge in seconds. She climaxed with a gasp of his name. While she was yet to return from the high of such exquisite pleasure, her darling husband turned her over, spread her legs, and plunged into her swollen channel.

"Oh, yes, baby. I love your sweet, wet pussy. My pussy, princess, tell me," he demanded as his hips smacked into hers, creating another level of pleasure that got her whimpering.

"Yours, darling, my pussy is all yours to fuck anytime you want," she said, her hands grabbing her big breasts and squeezing, making sure her hardened nipples were engraved on her silky nightgown for her husband to see.

And he saw, growling as he stared, his hips pounding into her, relentless. His right hand left the place beside her head and grabbed her nightgown, tearing it in the process as he hurried to see her breasts and the beautiful brown nipples he wanted to suck.

"Yes," he growled and latched onto the large tips, sucking them one after the other, so hard it was almost painful.

His roughness added to the eroticism of the moment. It made her raise her thighs, almost to her chest, exposing her cove more. She stared as he looked down, watching the engorged length of his shaft withdraw and disappear into her. He gasped at the sight, his eyes clouding over in passion while his back-and-forth movements became rapid.

"I wish you could see it, baby, it's so beautiful. You're beautiful," he murmured and kissed her belly. "Our baby will be beautiful," he added, smiling lovingly at her.

Nkoyo gasped in obvious pleasure. "Describe it to me," she requested, her eyes soft on his, and he grinned.

"When I slide my cock out of your cunt," he began, doing exactly what he said. "It is covered with the milky cream from your pussy. My big cock is so hard and glistening with your wetness, and all I want to do is plunge it back into your sweet, hot pussy..."

"Oh, God, baby," Nkoyo moaned, feeling the keening rise of her pleasure at his dirty words. "I love your long, big, hard dick," she gasped, moving as fast as he was, meeting him halfway and enjoying the white tingles coursing through her body.

Onen went crazy at her words and plunged even deeper but not withdrawing as much as the building pleasure increased.

"I'm going to come so hard, baby," he growled in her ear as the rapture intensified.

"Yes…yes," she gasped and climaxed so fast, she had to shut her eyes to stop the spinning of the room.

"Oh, Nk, your come is so hot on my dick," he declared and groaned as he tensed, shuddering, yet he kept pounding into her through the exquisite orgasm that engulfed his body. "I love you so much, Nk," he murmured as his body finally stopped moving but remained buried in her dripping cove.

"I love you, too, my prince," she murmured back, holding him close.

He refused to stay on her body for long, conscious of his weight and the fact that she was carrying his baby. When he lay beside her on the bed, he drew her close and cuddled. They fell asleep.

Well, don't look at me. Since we returned from the past, I don't know what has gotten into them. They have become more risqué in their lovemaking, and loud. They were married, for heaven's sake, that should count for something. I mean, there should be some propriety to this lovemaking for married people, right?

Whatever, it's not like I'm married. What do I know? I'm only here for the tale.

Few minutes later, the couple were awakened by Onen's ringing phone.

The ring tone signalled a call from his father. He couldn't ignore it, even though he wanted to stay wrapped round his wife all day. Still holding her close, he reached for his phone, sighed, and picked the call.

We were moving along, finally.

***

Having shamelessly eavesdropped to their phone call—I mean, that's what I'm here for—I'd followed Onen as he hurried over to the palace to join the important meeting held in the throne room.

His father had told him the factions involved in the discord had finally agreed to meet at a middle ground, which was the palace. Onen was uncomfortable with the impromptu nature of the meeting. He felt like his father had been blindsided into a meeting he hadn't prepared for but had to attend as it was being held at the palace. Additionally, he had to agree to the impromptu meeting because he was the one advocating for peace among the warring clans.

The entire set up had sent his dad into a frenzy of gathering chiefs and elders who'd had previous engagements and weren't prepared for the drama between the clans. His mother, the queen, should've been the one sitting by his father, but she was out of town for royal business as were many other influential chiefs and elders. The ones his father could reach were absolutely of no help as they seemed overwhelmed with the almost violent situation.

Thirty minutes into the meeting, Onen realized the entire thing was a farce, as both parties didn't seem about to relent on their perceived grievances. Neither party wanted peace, no matter how his father coaxed or how diplomatically he tried to solve the issue.

He got the impression both clans wished for nothing but war on account of the land with rumours of oil. He couldn't understand it. His dad had offered to divide the land equally between the clans, raising a fence to avoid encroachment. Someone from the Umor clan had declared that the side given to the Yakpani clan could be the side with oil — rumoured oil. Same person had then dared to accuse the king of wanting the land for Yakpani as it was the royal town and would greatly benefit from the oil.

Onen had to bite his tongue hard to keep from retorting. How could the man suggest such a thing of his father who was the epitome of integrity and had been of no reproach in all the twenty-five years he had ruled?

However, it wasn't his place to speak, at least not without permission. His mother would've been perfect for this meeting. He'd never seen a woman capable of damning the consequences in her quest to be frank. Her words, always spoken with poise and grace, gave the receiver no chance to be angry or offended.

As the meeting progressed — or as Onen silently thought, digressed into a slanging match — he began to suspect there was more at work here than just communal disagreement. He blamed his suspicion on Nkoyo, Mmatami, and the whole falling into the past debacle. Now, he was seeing diabolic manipulations everywhere.

Despite his derisiveness at suspecting evil powers at work, he couldn't shake the cloying feeling clogging his jamming nerves. As he was mostly at that meeting for emotional support, he had the chance to sit back and watch everybody's reactions.

Generally, the men from both clans, eight each on both sides, all seemed riled up and ready to spill blood, except one. Chief Uken, from the Umor clan. He wasn't riled up, barely spoke, but his expression was of someone who knew something the others didn't, and Onen didn't like that at all.

At one point, when the discord was getting overheated and his father was barely heard in the resulting uproar, their eyes had met, and a cold shiver of dread had travelled down Onen's spine. Chief Uken's eyes, though smiling, which was odd in the midst of the hot argument, were dark, and it instantly reminded him of the evil priest who had almost murdered Okoi in the visions of the past.

Onen looked away after a minute but didn't miss the superior smile on the Chief's lips. His heart hammered at the debilitating possibilities that could occur if his suspicion was right. If Chief Uken was some sort of reincarnation of the evil priest, then the situation was more than just land dispute.

He looked at his father and saw the strain on his face. He was tired, and his age showed. Silver hair had popped out blatantly on his head and beard while frustration dug deep grooves on his face.

It wasn't only his father he had to save, it was the whole kingdom from the power of darkness. The problem was how to go about it. Would anybody even believe his suspicion? He wouldn't believe himself if he hadn't been recently subjected to the knowledge of such dark forces and the havoc they could cause. Would his father believe him? Even if he did, would the chiefs and elders? Maybe, if by some miracle they did, what would be the solution? As he'd been the one to detect the problem, they would expect a solution from him, and he had nothing to give them, absolutely nothing.

The crack in his father's tired voice as the king shouted above the din in the throne room pierced his pondering, instantly snaring his attention. The uproar of accusations, counter-accusations, and name-calling continued as though the king hadn't just shouted himself hoarse.

Onen was about to join his voice to his father's authority when Chief Uken, still calmly seated on the plush leather seat, a standard furniture in the throne room, hit his gold engraved walking stick three times on the tiled floor and said, "*Kọmạạ*." Stop. He did this without even raising his voice.

The room went as silent as a graveyard. This was the reaction that should've occurred when the king had raised his voice, but it hadn't. Uken's authority felt like that of a king.

Goosebumps spread rapidly like rashes all over Onen's back and arms. His limbs felt numb, and they prickled with dread at the blatant show of power. He'd already confirmed his suspicion before his gaze clashed with the Chief's eyes again and the darkness in them slowly receded.

He'd been held spellbound until the Chief's eyes cleared to their normal milky hue again. He'd then quickly looked to his father to check if he had seen it, but the king's head was bowed. He appeared defeated while his sparse council of chiefs and elders cowered in their seats.

Onen noticed he was the only person not affected by Chief Uken's dark influence. The evil man knew it, showing it by the slight raise of his brow before he dismissed him by turning to address the assembly, as though Onen wasn't worth his bother.

Chief Uken was tall for his age, which Onen placed at early fifties. He was dark in complexion as most Atam people were, his beard unfashionably long and untidy, and that, apart from his dark eyes, was extra conviction he was somehow connected to the evil priest of the past whose main aim had been to rule everybody.

A dreadful thought occurred to Onen — was Uken aiming for the throne? He had to swallow with difficulty, and as a human, he silently wished he was wrong about that particular summation.

Suddenly, he wished Nkoyo had not been banned from visiting the past, at least, for a couple of months for the baby's sake. He suspected the solution to their present dilemma would be found there. But how to get Mmatami to allow them return to the past was the challenge. As small and as frail as the old woman was, her anger was a force to reckon with. He swore his teeth had chattered in the face of her fury.

Dressed in white jumpers and matching trousers, leather slippers of the same hue, a multi-coloured towel draped on his left shoulder, an obvious sign of his chieftainship in Atam and the black, modern-looking and shiny walking stick with gold engravings, Chief Uken made a captivating picture as he lazily got to his feet.

How was it his father and his council of chiefs weren't seeing the wonder unfolding right before their eyes? The Yakpani clan seemed in obeisance to Chief Uken, an abomination, since he was clearly of the opposing party. Naturally, the Yakpani party shouldn't even want to hear him out, but, as Onen glanced at them, they looked up to him, almost adoringly. He concluded beyond reasonable doubt that the man was diabolically manipulating the whole situation—he only had to wait for the Chief's punch line, which he felt was about to be revealed.

Chief Uken bowed, though it was more like inclining his head, at King Liman who sat wearily slumped on his throne. The small smile on the Chief's face made Onen think he was silently mocking his father.

"*Oboool*," he hailed, dragging the two-syllable word, which literally meant King. "*Obol Lupon*." King of the kingdom, he hailed again, shaking his walking stick, which should have been a sign of obeisance but he managed to make it look mocking.

Onen took deep breaths and continued to bite his tongue to keep from reacting.

"*Nkurke*, I've seen the effort you have expended in your *peaceful* rule." He sneered the 'peaceful' but quickly moved from it. "We have all seen, and we appreciate it," he said, stomping his walking stick on the floor before him, in between his legs, and all gathered, even his father, nodded in agreement.

Onen's anger increased by the second.

"*Obol, sakani*," he thanked and stomped his glossy walking stick again. It made the act look like an innocent nervous tick, but Onen knew better.

"Hmm," Uken grunted, looking deep in thought. Of course, he stomped his accessory on the tiled floor again. "But, *Nnjena, ooyi* – yet, it isn't good enough," he proclaimed, causing Onen's immediate start.

His eyes rushed to his dad to see how he was reacting to the insult. His father just looked pensive.

What was the chief trying to insinuate? His father had always done the best for Atam throughout his whole reign. He could recall when he'd been a child and the kingdom had needed a lot of changes. His father had sacrificed time with his family to physically join the work of rebuilding certain communities that had been destroyed because of a communal clash.

In his reign, his father had drastically reduced the often occurrence of communal clashes in Atam. Yet, this obviously evil man had the effrontery to declare that his father, the king of Atam's rule, wasn't good enough.

"So as not to keep you wondering the direction of my speech," Uken commented, sounding magnanimous that he was going straight to the point. "I believe, *Obol Lupon*, Liman Ikpi Egu, that you should abdicate the throne. I believe that you should step down and grant another family, from another community, the chance to rule Atam. I believe that if I were chosen, Atam would be a better place with all its natural and material resources made available, equally, to everybody. I believe I have a stronger will which Atam people need in a ruler."

Silence reigned after his obnoxious declaration. Onen was seething at this point, but he chanced a gaze at the disputing clans and saw both parties with expressions of agreement. Despite knowing Uken was diabolically manipulating the situation, it still shocked him that the Yakpani clan wasn't reacting violently to his speech of disgracefully bringing down their king. How extremely unlike them.

The available council of chiefs looked everywhere else but at their king, and they didn't look like they would be angry any time soon. Onen's fury increased at this thought; it felt like his chest expanded with the rage belonging to everyone in that throne room, who should have been incensed on their king's behalf.

Finally, his gaze swivelled to his father's face. It was as though the king hadn't really heard what Uken had just said. The obnoxious Chief had spoken treason; he'd uttered words that deserved death as punishment. Yet, King Liman didn't react. To Onen's shock, he looked like he was actually contemplating Uken's words and seeing the validity of it.

Onen growled, furious, and the threatening sound, resembling that of a lion in this quiet room, was directed at Uken with a thought: over his dead body would he allow his father to be disgracefully dethroned.

So shall your wish be, he heard clearly in his mind while watching Uken smile evilly at him.

It was the last straw for the prince, and he attacked without warning.

Though angry, the speed Onen accrued in his attack on Uken's person had more backing than his anger alone. He was prodded by the will of kings, the urge to protect the sanctity of the royal family and the spirits protecting Atam from evil.

Onen was tall and muscular, and his ordinary fist usually packed a mean punch. But possessed by the protective spirits of Atam royals, his punches on Uken proved devastating. He gave the man no chance to stomp his walking stick on the ground. His long arm kept holding up Uken's wrist with the walking stick while simultaneously pummelling him with his right fist.

It took less than a minute before real pandemonium broke out in the throne room. But in that slight time, Onen had done damage to Uken's impeccable looks. By the time the chief had managed to land one hit on Onen's chin with the golden head of his walking stick, instantly weakening the prince, Uken was left looking like he'd been attacked by a wild animal. The chief's jumper was torn in places, his eyes red with both fury and the effect of Onen's punches on his face. He struggled to right himself into a dignified pose while the men held back the prince.

Then, without warning, Onen keeled over, dropping heavily on the ground in dead faint.

Chapter Eighteen

I cannot explain the panic that engulfed the king when his son dropped to the ground. However, I do know it was enough to swipe his mind of Chief Uken's evil manipulation.

"*Mbong binahlopon, okow?*" Where did the priest of the kingdom go, Mmatami grumbled after she'd completed a small ritual over Onen's still figure on his father's giant bed.

The guards had moved the prince there under the command of the king while other guards cleared out the palace of the disputing clans. At his wits end, King Liman had sent a car for Mmatami. His son hadn't fainted of natural causes. I mean, despite being under a spell, he had seen everything play out. His buff, healthy son could not have fainted from simply being hit by a staff.

Though the priest of the kingdom wasn't around, Liman was glad Mmatami was present to help counter the spell Uken had obviously put on Onen.

He was furious on his son's behalf just as he'd been furious when Uken had been talking. He was a king, therefore immune to Uken's diabolic machinations, but pretended otherwise. He had seen

Onen's fury rise by the second, and in that time, he'd wished for telepathic capabilities to communicate to him that he was unaffected by the man's manipulations.

King Liman had been powerless to stop Onen when he'd finally flown off the handle, unable to control his temper a second longer. He couldn't blame his son—he'd only been protecting him and the kingdom, and he loved him ferociously for that. He would make a great king, Liman mentally reaffirmed while he watched the still form of the physically gallant prince and wished the situation in the throne room had turned out differently.

Now, he knew his throne was in danger, the imminent threat of a communal clash just one of the strategies in place to force him out of power. It was pure blackmail. They knew he'd always preached peace and throughout his rule had endeavoured to maintain peace in Atam, so they threatened said peace in a bid to persuade him to step down as king.

However, they didn't know him enough. That he angled for peace didn't mean he was inept in fighting a war. He was of the royal family, from a clan of warriors with the history of kingship, put there by a long line of royal ancestors. As an EguOkoi, he was born ferocious and possessed the innate will to protect Atam and keep it safe from evil like Chief Uken, who sought to destroy it.

"I asked a question, Liman," Mmatami snapped from her position on the other side of the big bed, leaning heavily on her staff, which, weirdly enough, Liman noticed, was taller than her.

"The priest and the Queen are representing the kingdom at a royal gathering at Ikom," he replied with a tired sigh. He had never faced such strong opposition before.

Being a royal meant you weren't opposed unless you were inept at your job as king or had committed an abomination that required one to step down so as not to inadvertently curse the kingdom.

"When will they return?" the old woman, who didn't care for protocol, asked.

"The event is the entire week, and Atam has a big role to play in the whole thing. It was the reason I had to send the priest with my wife since I couldn't leave the kingdom in this perilous time."

"Atam will have no role to play at all if the binah doesn't return in this perilous time. He should never have left the kingdom defenceless against greed," Mmatami snapped quite angrily.

Liman agreed with the old woman. Uken was indeed greedy. He would call his wife and apprise her of what happened here and then allow her to make the decision to return. He knew she'd leave the royal event instantly.

"Will my son recover; will he be fine?" he asked, his eyes boring into the rheumy ones of Mmatami.

"He will recover before nightfall. He is fine. For now," she added ominously.

***

You know me—Gossip. The one spirit with a front row seat wherever drama unfolds. I found myself the perfect perch on the armrest of King Liman's throne. The most powerful seat in the kingdom, and I was on it, beside the most powerful man in the kingdom, not that he knew it.

While the shouting had been going on, just like the wise prince, I had been observing everybody's reactions. And I'd agreed with Onen's summation that Chief Uken was one weird man. Onen thought he was related to Binah Umor of the very ancient past, which made me scoff. Uken being related to the evil priest of the past was too preposterous. I mean, the prince was taking the spirit thing too far sha.

But his preposterous assumption didn't make Uken any less eccentric, and so, I'd followed him and his entourage as they drove out of the palace after Uken had caused the prince's unconsciousness. I needed to know how he'd done it.

Having seen the picture of their destination, I zapped over there and proceeded to snoop—no, look around. I'd be snooping if I were human and visible. But as a spirit, I confidently looked around the crumbling meeting hall at Umor.

An authoritative voice from behind the meeting hall got my attention, and I floated over there and was shocked to see Eja. He was the worker at the mill that had been absent for more than a week; the same one the prince has been worried about and had visited his home to find out he had run away.

"I don't want to do again. Prince Onen is a good man, and I would not be able to live with the guilt if I betray him this way," Eja snapped, but I could clearly see he was afraid.

What had the young man gotten himself into; what was he doing at Umor in the first place?

So many questions, but who to answer, I thought.

The tall, dark man with Eja, the owner of the authoritative voice, barked out a laugh that had nothing to do with genuine mirth. You know the kind of laugh that sent chills of apprehension down a person's spine. I wasn't surprised that Uken's associate possessed such a laugh; Uken himself looked like someone that would laugh as such…they probably practiced the cackle together.

I snickered at my private joke while sitting primly on the termite-gorged windowsill.

"You're a disgrace to Umor." The man sneered at the younger man who seemed like he would run off any moment.

"I was born in Yakpani, and the prince has been good to me," he declared while I stared, fascinated by the rapid tick of his pulse at the base of his neck.

The guy was more than scared—he was terrified.

The man scoffed. "Good to you? You work in his mill—"

"Just tell Chief Uken that I don't want his money again. I will not reveal your plans, but I don't want to be part of it any longer," Eja stated and turned to jog away, but the strangest thing happened.

His legs moved as though jogging, but he remained in place. My eyes widened in consternation while Eja's widened in terror, and in a second, Uken showed himself, walking out from the meeting hall, into the clearing at the back.

"And you think it would be that easy to walk away? How were you planning to repay the money for your mother's costly medications?" Uken asked calmly, his walking stick slightly raised.

I guess that's what kept the terrified boy in place.

Soon enough, the seven men that had followed him to the Atam palace trickled into the meeting hall with some other prestigious men of the Umor community. They were about to have a clandestine meeting there.

"Chief Uken, what is the matter?" one of the recent arrivals asked.

"The boy is withdrawing his support for our campaign," he replied, looking quite prestigious despite the damage Onen had wrecked on his clothes. He didn't seem bothered by it, though, and the men he'd garnered didn't respect him less for it.

"Ah, Eja, *mbong*?" the old man asked 'what,' while shaking his head in confusion at the boy.

"He is a stupid boy," another announced and spat on the broken cement floor of the meeting hall.

"Please, Chief Uken, I promise, I will not say anything to anybody. I just don't want to hurt the prince, it is an abomination," he cried.

"Stop behaving like a woman! You're protected," one of the chiefs snapped at the whimpering boy. "Have you forgotten that you are from Umor and was only born at Yakpani? The prince is from Yakpani, and the people of Yakpani, through time, never liked Umor people. They were always stealing what belonged to us. Is this the kind of people you want to rule you?!"

I could see the chief actually believed the rubbish that had left his mouth, and the other men in this conspiracy did, too. Uken looked at them with pride gleaming from his eyes, like he was happy his children were following his instructions to the letter.

"Don't get so angry, Enang. The boy is useful, whether willing or not." And with that proclamation, he flicked his wrist, sharply moving the hand holding the staff and sent Eja flying, his momentum stopped by the wall of the meeting hall.

The gathered men applauded the act with enthusiastic claps, and Uken moved among them like a king, giving instructions over his shoulder for the boy to be stowed in the boot of his car.

The man that had been with Eja earlier nodded and carried out Uken's instruction. Apparently, he was his henchman.

"How will the boy help when he is not willing?" one of the men surrounding Uken asked.

Many of them nodded, acknowledging the question as viable. "Yes, since the plan had been to send him out as a bait to lure the prince," another expounded, causing more nods among the gathered.

Uken looked at them with a magnanimous smile. "Gentlemen, don't you trust me anymore? If I'm to be your king, then I demand your trust."

"We trust you explicitly," the oldest chief announced. "How can we not trust the man which will bring back our birthright and secure the kingship in Umor, once and for all?"

The men nodded in agreement, murmuring their support as Uken raised his hand to silence them. Silence did reign.

"Then, I will suggest that you return home until the next meeting. By then, I will have a better plan to share with you, my loyal subjects."

Without objections from any of them, the group dispersed, and I followed Uken to his car. I flew in behind his henchman who doubled as his driver and was shocked at the next thing that happened.

King Liman had mistaken Mmatami's mention of greed as the verb version.

The moment Uken entered the back of his car, his body seemed to detach into two different ones before my eyes. The driver didn't see this — he only flicked a concerned gaze to Uken who fell listlessly to the side. In fact, he was unconscious.

I heard the henchman mutter that his boss worked too hard.

Apparently, he wasn't seeing what I was seeing. How could he? I was gazing into the rheumy eyes of one of the most ancient spirits of all time. I was staring at Greed in all his tattered glory.

"Little Gossip," he said with a calm smile that was pure evil.

His voice grated on my nerves, and his eyes gleamed a shiny black hue that matched the tattered robe draped over his stooped shoulders.

He was the picture of a tall, old man, bony and stooped with age, with a beard so long, the twisted tips grazed his lean chest. If he were human, I'm very sure he would stink.

"Don't call me little," I muttered, but dared not snap at the ancient spirit, not if I wanted to maintain my pretty face.

I'm old, but compared to Greed, I was a child in the spirit world. So all the snappish retorts that filled my throat, tickling my tongue to vomit them, were forcefully shoved down into my belly, and Greed cackled at that.

Yes, I said cackled. I would call him a witch if he weren't so clearly male.

"Did you know how hot it is to stay stuffed in a human's body?" he griped, frowning at Uken's slumped form with clear disdain in his eyes.

"Well, that body was created for just his soul, not his soul and you," I retorted and then bit my tongue in consternation. I'd not been able to help it—I just blurted that out.

Thank God the ancient spirit chose to cackle again, and I sighed with relief.

"Ah, yes," he sighed, and I settled for kneeling on the front passenger seat, facing him instead of hovering. "God had certainly created layers of protection for them. But do they appreciate it?" He sneered, glancing angrily at Uken again.

I wasn't sure if I should inform him that it wasn't our place to judge, despite our immortal state. I chose to keep quiet, a rare occurrence for an innate opinionated tattler like myself.

"No. They. Don't!" he answered himself, quite vehemently. As though the ignorance of man's favour in God's eyes has been a thorn in his flesh for eternity…which could be true.

"But why Atam?" I ventured to ask with a frown. I mean, the old guy has coveted his inimical intentions for Atam for as far back as their existence and has succeeded in some, over time.

Greed was so old, he was almost a fossil, but I wasn't taken with his frail looks. The ancient spirit could be as sprite as a fairy whenever he deemed fit. I sighed as he ponderously turned his gaze towards the fast blur of the road as though he had a crick in his neck. I'd seriously thought he wouldn't answer the question.

It'd been a stupid one anyway, because Greed wasn't just plaguing Atam kingdom, he was plaguing humanity. His dark eyes stared bleakly at the scenario. He looked so tired that I wondered, just for a second, if he regretted most of the things he'd done, but his reply wiped that thought from my mind.

"Why not? They certainly are wealthy enough in natural, material, and human resources."

"So, their blessing is their curse?" Was the ancient spirit senile? Could spirits be senile?

"Little girl, I go where the call is intense." He smirked, his expression showing he knew something I didn't.

So, I overlooked the fact that he called me 'little' again, not that I could do anything about it, really. However, instead of arguing the futile point, I hung on that seat and looked eager to learn. I'm Gossip, after all—juicy tales are my forte.

"World wars stemmed from my machinations. Coveting, the need to possess another's possession. Knowledge, the need to become higher and more than peers, to be seen as an authority in a field. Power, the need to rule over destinies and play God. Humanity's problems have greed as the deep-seated instigator of chaos."

"But the king is peaceful!" I cried indignantly. One would think King Liman was my father.

"Like I said, I go where the need for me is intense. Some people in Umor feel they are entitled to the Atam throne rather than the royal family. They also feel the palace should be at Umor…"

"But that is so inconsequential." I shook my head in shock. What is wrong with humans?

Greed cackled as though I'd told a joke. "People have killed for less. This is actually a big deal. And they really want that piece of land, too."

"You said some people are doing this, not the whole community, so why not ignore them?" I pleaded.

"And die of boredom?" he asked, incredulous.

If this didn't involve human lives, I would've laughed at his disbelieving expression. He looked as though he couldn't fathom not infecting humans with his filth.

"I enjoy my job," he enthused, grinning and flashing teeth browned so much, it almost matched his dark skin. "Plus, I just abhor Love. I'd do anything to stop its spread."

"Why?" Now I had the sceptical look; I couldn't fathom why he would hate Love. Everybody liked the plump, mischievous spirit.

Greed sneered at no one in particular, his long beard quivering with his hate. I got the impression he would squish Love if he encountered the jovial spirit.

"That spirit destroys well laid out plans, and the physical manifestation of it is so nauseating and senseless. I mean, that fat fuck prods humans to sacrifice for each other; who does that?!" he griped quite angrily. "Who gives humans added power that makes them gods with the ability to repel their basic instincts?"

I will laugh about this conversation later, especially that last sentence, since Greed was one of such basic instincts. But right now, I had to plead for lives. If that community clash happened, innocent people would suffer.

However, just as I took a deep breath to launch my campaign, the ancient spirit turned to me, his dark, emotionless eyes boring into my mind, seeing all in my heart in that one, intense glance.

"What a pity," he muttered in disgust. "You are like Eja who suddenly found his lost conscience. It is a disgrace that you think like the humans now," he said and shook his head. "Such potential, I could have used your talents."

He said it so regretfully, I felt sorry for myself, and without so much as a warning, he flicked his wrist and I found myself on the road, staring at the brake lights of the speeding car.

The old fart had ejected me like one flinging out a used condom. He could have killed me, I thought in alarm. Then shame suffused me — I indeed was thinking like a human.

But that lasted only a second, not when there were tales to be gathered.

Chapter Nineteen

I cannot imagine what Nkoyo must have gone through while waiting for Onen. When she finally gave in to her anxiety, driving to the Atam palace in search of her husband who hadn't answered his phone, she wished she'd been wrong about the gripping feeling that had seized her at home.

One minute she'd been happily browsing on her smart phone, and suddenly, she felt like someone had punched her in the gut. The force of it made her fall backwards, leaning on the chair she'd been sitting on while breathing heavily.

She had immediately known all wasn't well with Onen. Nkoyo had no idea how she knew, but it had been a cloying feeling that wouldn't leave. So she'd called. If she'd left without calling first, he would've barked at her about safety for herself and the baby, of course.

After several calls with no answer, her trepidation increased. So intense, it made her breathless and anxious and developed in her a pressing need to see him.

She'd been aware of the impromptu meeting and had suppressed the niggling doubt in the pit of her stomach that it was an ambush. Yet, she hadn't wanted to discourage him.

Due to that strong conviction, she had hurried over, faced then with her weakened husband perched on mounds of fluffy pillows on his parents' bed. It was a sight she never wanted to see again; not her super man. She saw him as untouchable and indomitable—it broke her heart immensely to have found him sitting that way.

Trust the prince to glimpse the worry on his wife's face right away. I wasn't surprised he instantly plunged into assuring her he was fine.

He has been fine for the past three weeks as Nkoyo hovered over him protectively.

She'd been told what a certain Chief Uken had said and done. Not that Onen hadn't recovered from the bout of weakness that had caused his unconsciousness—he had. However, Nkoyo simply didn't want to have him out of her sight for long.

Onen enjoyed the tender loving care his wife smothered him with. He'd even graciously agreed to attend work three times a week these past weeks. Nkoyo was scared, and she dreaded the topic of how he'd been made unconscious by Uken's staff.

He knew this because she had blatantly changed the subject every time he'd tried to share what he'd felt in that moment and his suspicions about the man. Having tried to talk to her and allay her fears, he'd given up and kept his suspicions to himself, silently hoping he'd been wrong, yet knowing he wasn't.

Several times, I knew Onen wanted to drop by Mmatami's house to see the woman and discuss his worry, but something kept holding him back. He didn't know how to explain it. Me neither. Every time he made plans to stop by on his way from work, he'd either forget or he would have a pressing urge to get home and he'd blip taking the diversion to her house.

After more than two weeks, the ominousness caused by the throne room situation faded away. His mother, who'd hovered over him almost as much as Nkoyo, had stopped calling more than four times a day, only limiting it to one call now, probably by his father's prodding.

Instead of dwelling on the crisis facing the kingdom, I was glad Onen focused on his wife's rapidly swelling belly. She was in the middle of her sixth month, but her stomach seemed suddenly so large, it constantly fascinated him how it had gotten that way.

According to the length of her nightmares before they'd discovered the cause, she had been pregnant for over three months, and her stomach in that time hadn't changed. Then, almost overnight, it began growing so rapidly, he felt like if he blinked, he'd miss something.

He loved his wife, more so now that she waddled around the house with her giant girth, bullying him into accepting her demands. Onen was weak for her; he couldn't seem to be able to refuse any of her ridiculous demands, like going to work only three times a week.

Though, after a particularly satisfying bout of lovemaking, especially now that she was always horny, he had explained that the mill was at the height of production and therefore all hands, even princely ones, were needed to meet demands.

She had pouted adorably but had agreed. He'd start work fully in the next week. He sighed as he held Nkoyo close, enjoying the warm firmness of her baby bump prodding his side. He leaned down and kissed her temple, his large hand rubbing the smooth belly, and just like clockwork, his child rumbled and swirled against his hand.

It had been the most exhilarating experience the first time he'd felt his child move in Nkoyo's belly. From that day till date, the baby swirled for him whenever he touched his wife's protruding stomach. As though they were having their own silent conversation.

He couldn't help the grin that split his face or the surge of love that filled his heart for the baby. They had decided against an ultrasound—they wanted to be surprised.

The movement of the baby was so strong and forceful, he worried it would wake Nkoyo, so he whispered his love to the baby, pulled his wife closer, and fell asleep.

***

For the first two weeks after the throne room saga, nothing had been heard from Uken and his minions. In fact, it had begun feeling like the debacle had never occurred.

However, that would've been too good to be true. The third week started with rumours buzzing in the village about an imminent communal clash, and those rumours were heavier at the mill, which was the central work hub of Yakpani, the royal community.

By the fourth week, when Onen had resumed work full-time, he had an earful of what was happening in town, the most disturbing being the slow migration of people from Yakpani.

I worried for the kingdom. Greed wasn't a spirit to be toyed with, but who could I tell?

Through time, Yakpani had remained the royal community, the town housing the palace of Atam kingdom. In that vein, the town had remained a haven for Atam. Clashes shouldn't happen in Yakpani—it was an abomination. But Uken had apparently managed to put fear in the residents' mind and had succeeded in making the king look like an incompetent ruler. How do I tell the prince that Uken was simply a tool manipulated by an ancient spirit?

The heavy possibility of a clash between the two biggest communities of Atam kingdom made the people doubt his father. Yet, Onen held on to Liman's advice of maintaining appearances. If Uken thought he would rattle them or blackmail his father into abdicating the throne, then the greedy chief had another think coming.

In preparation for any violence that might occur, his father had contacted the army barracks situated between Atam kingdom and Efik kingdom to be on standby. The army would swoop in and curb the violence, since all King Liman thought about was the safety of his subjects.

A knock broke through Onen's thoughts.

"My prince..." the older foreman heaved, and Onen instantly knew something was amiss when he stared at the man's wild eyes.

"What...what happened?" he asked, getting to his feet and moving from his desk, ready to help any way he could.

"We heard word about Eja. He has been found," he announced.

Onen's heart leaped in joy, for despite his own personal crisis, he'd not stopped worrying about Eja and hadn't stopped asking questions to, at least, know his way about for his ill mother's sake. But the foreman didn't look happy at the news—his expression caused niggling dread in the pit of his stomach. Was the boy all right?

"A hunter that knows him and his family and was aware he'd been missing—"

"Where is this hunter?" Onen asked briskly and moved to the door.

"Downstairs, my prince," the foreman answered and followed him down the iron stairs and through the deafening noise of the factory floor.

Onen glimpsed a thin, blatantly nervous-looking man with a locally made rifle hanging down his shoulder. The hunter straightened the moment he noticed the prince of Atam kingdom striding towards him.

"You have news of Eja," he prodded, and the hunter's mouth hung open in awe but he nodded his reply. "Tell me," Onen commanded.

It took a while for the hunter to get over his awe of speaking to royalty to relay what he'd seen without stammering.

So, the gist of the matter was that the hunter, while inspecting his traps in the forest bordering Umor and Yakpani, part of the land in dispute, had seen men torturing Eja. He described how he'd hidden behind the trunk of a large tree to watch the men tie up Eja and proceed to beat him up. He mentioned that just before he ran away, he'd heard one of the men announce that he would kill Eja.

Onen exploded into action. When he handpicked some burly mill workers to go with him, they followed him without question, grabbing factory equipment that could double as weapons. They had all heard of what happened to Eja—they knew of his sick mother, and they were aware that the prince had been making enquiries about the boy. It was probably why the hunter had been directed to the mill immediately.

I groaned and followed, sending a nagging thought to bother Onen: why had the hunter been in a part of the land under dispute? Most people were fleeing the community because of the imminent clash hanging in the air, but the hunter had been in that dreaded land, checking his trap as though he owned it. Something wasn't right.

Yes, something was definitely not right, I concurred.

However, curse on Onen and his innate responsibility. Curse his selflessness that led him to be more worried for Eja. The prince ignored the bad feeling and instead hoped he'd be able to get there before terrible damage was done to the young man.

Just so he would assuage the worry cluttering his mind, he called out a young boy just minutes before he drove off with the four men he'd picked in addition to himself and the foreman, asking him to take a message to the palace.

Thank God, I thought with a relieved sigh. Whatever happened in that forest, at least, Onen had a chance.

When the boy understood the message and took off running, Onen revved his Forerunner Jeep and zoomed off towards the land in dispute with the hunter in tow to show them the particular part he'd seen Eja.

***

The ancient spirit of Greed had been right to summate that I now thought like the humans. Perhaps I'd been with them too long. However, I was now immersed in this tale and wanted Good to win.

While the young boy rushed to the palace and Onen to the forest, I flew back to the prince's house. I met Nkoyo in their bedroom.

As I paced the giant space, wondering what or how to get her to do something in a bid to help the unfurling, dangerous situation, Nkoyo sighed and thrust her arms forward to ease the throbbing ache caused by hours of loosening her long braids. She arched her back and mentally celebrated the lone braid that remained to be loosened. She couldn't wait to comb out the dreadlocked curls of her naturally long hair and wash it with the new shampoo and conditioner set she'd wanted to try out.

She leaned back on the massive bed, a pillow wedged comfortably under her, and sighed with relief. Closing her eyes a little, she relaxed her shoulders, glorying in the fact that she had just one more braid and she'd be free.

Onen would throw a fit if he discovered she'd not called her hairdresser as she'd promised. Nkoyo had needed help, but at the last minute, she'd decided to loosen the long, big braids herself.

Sighing heavily again, she rubbed her massive stomach tenderly, smiling as she recalled how Onen did it and the answering swirl of their child in her womb whenever he touched her.

"Get up, Nkoyo, stop being lazy," she admonished herself and then struggled into a sitting position and grabbed the last braid.

It was the exact message I needed to impress on her, yet, I had no way of doing it.

She was halfway done with the braid when she was suddenly attacked with anxious jitters so intense, the slim comb with a pointy bottom fell out of her hand, tumbling to the tiled floor. I stopped my pacing. What now, I wondered, for once, dread slithering through my mind.

Nkoyo knew her delivery date, and she still had months to go, so it couldn't be the first signs of labour. Could it be hunger? Because she'd been eating quite voraciously of recent, and most times was ashamed of her blatant longing, especially when Onen teased her about her eyes following the progress of his spoon from the plate to his mouth. He would laugh at her painfully shy expression and then would proceed to tenderly feed her whatever he'd been eating.

Thinking of her husband calmed the jitters. Her eyes glared at the comb on the floor as though her eyes would elevate it since she couldn't bend to get it. With an exasperated huff, she decided to finish the braid with her fingers.

Instead of relief at finally completing the task, she was again inundated with nervous jitters. Her heart palpitated in a disturbing manner. It couldn't be hunger, she thought as her eyes caught the plate of biscuits she'd just devoured lying empty beside her hip on the bed.

She'd been having slivers of dread flutter in the pit of her stomach for weeks. Onen had described it as the aftermath of her trepidation following the throne room saga. Nkoyo had wholeheartedly accepted the explanation because she couldn't stand thinking that something bad could happen to her husband again.

I wish she had listened to those dread flutters. Perhaps she would've proactively found some sort of solution.

Yet, in this moment, she was recalling the unconscious need she'd begun having about knowing what had happened to Nnanke and her newfound love in Okoi. She had a secret even Onen didn't know about.

Apparently, I didn't know this secret either.

While Mmatami had been berating both of them for misusing powers they knew nothing about and had announced she was banned from viewing the past for some time, she had reached out in the dark, and her hand had touched a small covered container.

Nkoyo hadn't known what she'd been touching as it had been night when she and Onen had finally awakened from the past, but she'd been pushed to carry it, and she had.

After days of feeling guilty and wondering how she could return the small plastic container without punishment, Nkoyo had finally scrounged up the courage to look inside and had found the yellow clay substance Mmatami usually dipped her ring into before placing it on her forehead and sending her off to visions of the past.

She didn't deceive herself that she wanted to return the small container any longer. The yellow clay was her chance to go into the past despite the old woman's warnings. To Nkoyo, Mmatami was like a killjoy teacher who didn't want her, the student, to satisfy her curious mind.

With her heart thumping and her eyes riveted on the door of her giant wardrobe where the small container was hidden, she slowly got to her feet and moved towards it.

I have no idea if this is bad. However, it was something to do, right? Would going into the past help Onen and save Atam kingdom?

Besides, looking at Nkoyo now, she walked like someone under hypnotism. I noticed her fixed, unblinking gaze as she brought out the container from a drawer and returned to sit on the bed.

Of course, I looked around, trying to feel what other spirit was in the room. Something was prodding her to do this. I didn't even care anymore. Whatever was poking her, I only hoped it turned out all right for everyone.

Her hands shook as she acknowledged the possible danger of what she was about to do, yet, it didn't stop her from opening the container. She pulled off her currently humming vintage ring, which had started glowing a bright blue, and dropped it into the yellow clay.

As though she were seeing a movie in her head, she recalled the usual preparations Mmatami did before putting the ring on the centre of her forehead. Nkoyo did them exactly.

She dipped her finger into the container, used her handheld mirror in making the necessary dots on her forehead. With shuddering breaths, which she took to calm her thundering heart, she pulled out the humming ring currently flashing a hot sapphire through the muck of the yellow clay, lay down on the bed with her legs dangling on the side, and without much thought, placed the ring approximately in the centre of her forehead.

Hearing her thoughts, I knew it wasn't the usual feeling of falling into a blackhole and twirling around through time until she got to the right place in the past.

This was a zap!

One second, she was breathing in deeply, preparing to fall into the void—the next, she was opening her eyes to the dark, murky shine of Binah Umor's eyes.

Oh, shit!

Chapter Twenty

It had taken two *koke* for Binah Umor to recover his powers. In that time, his concubines, women he'd taken from their husbands in Umor and other communities, fluttered around him doing his bidding.

The village had woken up from their induced faint and hadn't remembered what had happened. They'd jovially returned to feasting on the other bodies. Binah Umor had actually been grateful they'd not been awake to witness his defeat at the hands of a young girl.

In atonement for his failure, the dark forces demanded an unfailing sacrifice on every *koke*. Binah Umor spent long months on his penance while silently plotting his revenge.

When he'd found where she'd been hiding, all because of the man she'd rescued, Binah Umor had laughed so loud, his women cowered in their huts in terror.

He'd simply used the hairs from the destiny man's private parts, hairs that had been part of the ritual she had interrupted, to cast a revealing spell. It would only have revealed where the man was, but because he had copulated with the priestess, the spell had also revealed her location. Though they were at the same place, he knew the forest was the sacred dwelling of the spirits at Yakpani, and he would never have been able to penetrate it. However, with the priestess having lost her sacred virginity, everything lay bare before him.

Nevertheless, he still couldn't bridge the invisible boundary surrounding Yakpani by himself, so he went hunting. As the dark forces were happy with him for his continuous sacrifices, he struck good fortune on his first try.

The spirits gave him Uben, a warrior who stood guard at the boundary of Yakpani. The people of Yakpani had always been tricky, which reflected in the name of their village and also why they still had warriors standing guard at the boundary even though the village was invisibly protected.

Their trickery was their undoing, for then, Binah Umor had been able to get himself a subject he could control. With simple manoeuvres, while hiding in the forest beyond the boundary, he'd sent a rat, poisoned with a controlling spell, to the warrior and watched as he jumped around, screaming in pain.

"*Oowoye! Oowoye! Oowoye!*" Uben had screamed the traditional exclamation of pain while jumping around, and other warriors had run out with spears in alert, ready to kill the perceived threat.

Uben told them he'd been bitten by a huge rat, but then lost consciousness.

He'd been taken to Binah Yakpani, of course, but he'd not been able to detect anything out of the ordinary, especially after the warrior had regained consciousness, looking and feeling as strong as always.

With the warrior's blood Binah Umor had extracted from the rat's intestines, he'd been able to make a revealing spell and could see everything Uben saw, which made it easier to create a compelling incantation that allowed him to wholly control the warrior's mind.

The warrior's wife had still been worried and had asked that the priestess be called to make sure her husband was fine. But both her husband and Binah Yakpani had shouted her down. It was a curious attitude for a priest to hate a priestess chosen by the gods, so he had investigated more.

He'd found that Binah Yakpani had begun being envious of the great powers given to the young priestess by the spirits and had recently started showing his anger towards her as she was rarely seen in the village. She would disappear for several *koke*, and when she came to his hut, she was always covered from the shoulders and wouldn't stay long.

Binah Yakpani interpreted it as arrogance because of the power she wielded. He refused to change this summation even after his friend, Binah Ekori, had reasoned otherwise.

It was then he also discovered how lucky he'd been in finding the warrior who still harboured tender thoughts towards the priestess, the woman he'd wanted to marry before the gods chose her. It proved quite easy then to amplify his jealousy and send him into the spirit forest, to spy on the priestess and her lover.

***

"My husband, my husband," the warrior's wife called, trying to get his attention in a bid to coax him to eat his dinner.

"*Komąąketonga!*" Stop talking, he barked in reply, splashing saliva in his vehemence like a rabid dog.

His sobbing wife scurried from his presence while worrying about him. Since a rat in the forest had bitten him, he'd not been the same again. Sometimes, he was his usual jovial self, but most of the time, he was overcome with anger so intense, he would violently fling whatever was in his way.

Then, he would march out of the house, muttering to himself, and return late in the night, when the spirits were about. She knew her husband was sick and she worried for him, but she didn't know what to do. The binah had forbid her from mentioning Nnanke, but she knew the woman would be able to cure his illness.

However, as a good wife, she'd never disobey her husband — talk more of the binah of the village who was like the king.

Uben did not feel any guilt for shouting at his wife. The woman was a pest, always needing his attention. He pushed the small calabash of food away, almost toppling the bowl in his anger.

He couldn't stop thinking about what he had seen in the spirit forest. As a child and while he'd grown up to be accepted into the warrior fold with his age mates, he'd been told no one but the spirits' chosen could enter the forest. Yet, he'd been surprised to find himself there and couldn't recall how he'd gotten there. Uben had been afraid and had immediately wanted to race out of the forest, but a longing to see Nnanke had seized him.

A longing that overwhelmed the terror of the forbidden forest and prodded his feet forward. He heard a tingling giggle not so far from where he stood and knew he was close to seeing the only woman that made his manhood stand without touching him.

Uben had hurried towards the joyful sound and had almost burst into the flowery clearing when he clearly heard a man's voice and stopped in his tracks. Quietly, he had approached, stepping on the soft moss on the forest floor instead of the dead leaves that would rustle and expose his presence.

The sight he came upon had twisted his heart so painfully, he'd had to bend from the hip to breathe without making a sound.

His beautiful Nnanke, a woman who had always carried herself above everybody and the virgin chosen by the gods to serve the spirits, was laid bare and spread on the fine flowery moss, naked, while a man he couldn't recognize heartily plunged his large and long shaft into her secret place. It was clear they both enjoyed the act of copulation, and it hadn't been the first time because he could see the protrusion of Nnanke's belly.

The virgin priestess hadn't just lost her virginity and purity, she was pregnant.

It was an abomination!

Shutting his eyes had been useless since he'd not been able to keep it that way for long, not with the arousing sounds Nnanke was making. Despite his fury at the sacrilege before him, Uben could feel his manhood raise the front of his wrapper like firewood, and he knew if given the chance, he would have committed the forbidden act without a second thought.

He should've been the only one to see her secret place if only she'd agreed to marry him. He should've had her all to himself, not the talkative wife he'd been forced to marry. And definitely not the strange man giving her carnal pleasure. Who was he anyway; where did he come from? How had he entered Yakpani with nobody's knowledge?

After retreating from the horrible sight, he had found his way back to his hut.

However, he had returned to the forest three more times, and strangely, he'd always caught them in the act of shameless copulation, during the day time. It seemed like the only thing they did throughout the day. No wonder Binah Yakpani had been complaining about the laziness Nnanke had been displaying of recent.

Uben was left with the decision to tell Binah Yakpani. The rules were clear—Nnanke wasn't to be touched by a man, but she was living with a man in the forest of the spirits. He couldn't keep quiet about it. The abomination had to be cleansed, or else the village would suffer for it.

With that decision made, the unexplainable fury that had engulfed his heart for days and made his eyes hurt like there was sand in it reduced, and he could sleep peacefully for the first time in a while.

But not for long.

Binah Umor bothered his dream with the request to come to the Yakpani border and invite him in. This was the only way the binah could bridge the invisible Yakpani protection. The son of the soil had to invite him freely and willingly into the land and at the hour when night gives way to morning.

Uben walked from his hut into the forest with his eyes closed, still asleep and communicating with the innocuous-looking old man in his dream who only needed a place to stay for the night.

"Old man, you are weary from your journey, come into Yakpani, I welcome you," Uben said to Binah Umor at the side of the boundary warriors didn't guard.

"Thank you, my son." Binah Umor sneered and stepped freely across the invisible protection.

The wooden carvings dangling from his neck swayed precariously as he passed the barrier, but held. If the strings had cut from his neck, it would mean he'd been caught. He breathed with satisfaction and tightly cinched his wrapper that held some herbs and already prepared spells.

As he followed the compelled warrior through the forest, back to his hut, he would've loved to cackle in glee at the success of his machinations. However, he had to remain quiet and unseen by the spirits of Yakpani, until he'd conquered the people.

Binah Umor preened without shame behind the stumbling warrior and walked arrogantly through the sleeping village, smiling in satisfaction that he would soon rule them. He saw spirits that protected the land hovering and fluttering over huts, so he quickly ducked behind the warrior and made sure he walked in his shadow. The spirits would only recognize the presence of its own.

***

While Binah Umor settled comfortably in Uben's hut, Nnanke rolled from the warmth of Okoi's arms and struggled to her knees in her cave. Okoi scrambled to his feet and helped her stand.

It had become increasingly difficult for her to do some things as her pregnancy progressed. Okoi's heart bloomed with happiness as he had watched her belly swell with his seed. He believed it was possible to live with her in the forest, with their children until they grew old.

"It is time," she murmured as he held her in his arms from the back, as her stomach was too big for him to hold her from the front.

He was reluctant to let her go, but she had a special ritual she had to perform in the time when the spirits floated over the river.

As a pregnant priestess, she had to present herself and her child to the *ase*, goddess of fertility. Okoi feared for her safety. He feared the goddess might reject her, especially because of the rule they had broken. Nnanke was meant to remain a virgin.

Apart from feeling intense happiness at being with her and the freedom of sliding into her ready secret place whenever the power of the mood seized them, he was terrified for her.

There were times she'd had to answer summons and go into the village to see the binah. Okoi had no idea how no one had noticed she was pregnant, as the only protection she'd had was the extra wrapper she had taken to cover her from her shoulders, draped loosely over her body. He'd still been able to notice the swell of her stomach.

He would pace the clearing behind their cave in worry for the duration she was gone, his heart hammering in fear that this time, someone would surely notice. But then, he would hear a twig break under her feet, and he would hurry to her, hugging and lifting her into his arms and back to the cave where he would proceed to confirm to himself that she belonged to him.

Okoi had learnt to count the months of pregnancy from the old man that'd been the quasi doctor back at the white man's land. His memories of being a slave were fading in the face of his joy at living with his angel in their paradise. Nnanke had only three *koke* left before the baby dropped from her womb.

He reached out his hand and rubbed the firm swell of her stomach. She sighed and leaned back more in his arms.

"Don't go," he pleaded, as he normally did whenever she had to go to Binah Yakpani's hut, though this was different. She had to sink beneath the river to visit the goddess of fertility.

Nnanke was sorely tempted not to go as usual whenever he pleaded. The strength of his voice, even though his words were whispered, always caused an intense surge of feelings in her chest. With her heart perpetually swollen with happiness, she always had the urge to do anything for Okoi. As he always proclaimed, especially after their copulation, she would indeed die for him.

A strong feeling in her heart, it indeed proved terrifying the things she could do for Okoi. For him, she had considered stopping her services for the gods. In her heart, Okoi came first before the spirits. But she knew how powerful the spirits could be when they were angry, and despite having broken the instruction of remaining a virgin, they had not shown their anger.

In fact, it had felt as though more power had been given to her. She could feel it swirl beneath her skin whenever she performed rituals or had to go into the village to help Binah Yakpani with healing. The ancient prophesy had said she would remain a virgin; had Binah Yakpani lied? She had also sensed binah's resentment towards her, but she couldn't do anything about it, not if she wanted to keep her pregnancy secret.

Men didn't have the power or whim to deviate from the rules of the gods, and so, she knew she faced more danger with men than with the spirits.

The goddess had visited her dream and had requested she come down to her. That had happened for the past four *koke*. Even though she was constantly given instructions on what to do for the village, the goddess continually reminded her to sink down the river to visit her.

Nnanke had been scared—courage had failed her, and she'd considered not going. But she couldn't avoid the spirits, she was connected to them. If the goddess wanted her to sink down the river, she would do it forcefully if Nnanke refused. She wanted to protect the child in her womb and so, she was summoning courage to do it herself.

With a deep breath, she turned in his arms and faced him. Her hand stroked his bearded jaw tenderly.

"I would die for you," she whispered and then felt the rapid beat of his heart beneath her hand at her words. It was the first time she was saying that, as opposed to her usual reply of 'I would never let you die.'

Tears dripped down Okoi's face at the strange, intense feeling engulfing his heart at her words. He squeezed her to him, not minding the nudge of her firm stomach against his abdomen.

"I would never let you die," he whispered fiercely. "I would never let you die." His arms tightened about her.

He knew she had to do this. He knew she had to sink beneath the river, and he knew his declared promise was useless when it concerned the spirits. If they harmed her, he would be powerless to save her. With men, he would have fought to the death to protect her and their child.

Okoi was determined, though. If by nightfall she hadn't emerged, he would dive beneath the water until he found her. He would perform all the ritual sacrifices he had watched her perform until the spirits released her. He would do anything.

"Let me help you rub the *ekọọ*," he suggested, referring to the traditional yellow clay Nnanke rubbed every time she performed rituals for the spirits.

Slowly, she stepped from his arms and walked outside the cave. She dropped her wrapper, standing naked under the full moon as Okoi took a while to come outside because he was getting the broken gourd of *ekọọ*.

Nnanke knew when he stepped out and saw her because he gasped. She could see in his eyes how much he liked her and everything about her. She'd been worried when she had begun getting big and feeling ugly, but Okoi's shaft had never stopped growing as hard as firewood whenever he was near her. As though he had heard her thoughts then, he'd expressed how beautiful she became everyday as her pregnancy progressed.

She stared back at him, noticing the raising of his wrapper and the answering pool of warmth between her legs. But they didn't have time for that. She had to sink beneath the water now that the spirits had come out to play.

Okoi couldn't take his gaze off her. She stood there in their flowered clearing, under the moon, her hair streaming down her back, her breasts swollen with succour for their child growing in her protruding belly. Her skin looked soft and smooth like fresh goat milk. He could see the dark triangle of curls in between her legs and the longing which scented the air as it dripped down her thighs.

She could've been a goddess as she stood there, her eyes glowing a warm blue as it usually did when she wanted him. But they didn't have time for that — he understood the timing involved in working with the spirits.

So, Okoi swallowed hard, his heart beating like the kingship drums on the harvest festival celebration. He ignored his engorged manhood and proceeded to design Nnanke's skin with the *ekoo*.

He used a soft, slim branch from one of the flowers and drew small thin lines, circles, and other elaborate figures on her skin. The markings on her body seemed to glow in the moon. By the time she picked up her glowing staff, her mouth moving with words of praise mixed with requests to the spirits to be accepted and welcomed, Okoi knew she was no more the Nnanke that enjoyed his touch.

She was more; she was another being, prepared and ready to be accepted into the world of spirits.

He followed her as they'd earlier agreed, down the narrow path, and stopped at the river bank while she proceeded. His heart felt as though it was lodged in his throat as he watched her glide into the river until she got to the centre where the water stopped at her neck.

With the brightness of the moon, the river was clear, and he could see beneath it. He could see the markings on her skin—the water hadn't washed it off.

Nnanke swirled in the centre of the water, causing ripples as her voice rose in adulation of the spirits. And for the first time in Okoi's life, he saw what she had described as spirit guides glide up from the darker depths of the water, their blue glow, so much like Nnanke's eyes, lighting their ascension.

The pair of creatures looked like huge fish but not a type he'd ever seen before. Their scales were designed with elaborate markings that looked as hard as shells, their eyes giant circles with a dot of yellow glow in the centre; one that matched the now glowing *ekọọ* markings on Nnanke's skin.

They swirled around her and glowed brighter as her voice increased, echoing in the calm hour. The water shone blue, and the vicinity around the river illuminated not just with the radiance of the moon but a mixture of blue and silver. Then, as though the spirit guides were wrapped round her, they, with Nnanke, began sinking beneath the glowing water.

Okoi's heart threatened to lurch out of his throat as he moved close to the edge as far as he could go to see her descent, his face equally illuminated with the blue glow from the surface. He couldn't touch foot in the water. Nnanke had warned him seriously against it as though she had known he would have the overwhelming urge to go after her as she sank deeper and deeper beneath the river into the darker depths.

Soon, Okoi could only see the blue glow on the bodies of the creatures lighting their descent. Moments later, that dimmed until it disappeared.

He hadn't realized how charged the forest had become. Gusts of wind shook the branches of the trees. The river swelled with waves, and the night hummed with the power of spirits. He hadn't realized all these until the blue light disappeared beneath the water and with it, his angel, his woman, his life.

He would kill himself if she didn't return to him.

The power that had cackled through the forest as Nnanke swirled in the water had calmed. The wind had returned to being a soft breeze, the river a cool transparent ripple, and the leaves on trees flickered lazily under the moon. Yet, Okoi's nerves still felt tight and strummed with anxiety as he settled on Nnanke's favourite low rock by the river to wait.

***

The sun had risen to the centre of the sky, blanketing the forest with its hot brilliance. However, Okoi didn't feel it, not when he was anxiously watching the glittering river for an appearance of Nnanke. It was also because he sat under the shade of a tree whose leafy branches spread out beyond the bank of the river.

He hadn't left the spot except to urinate against a tree and take a sip of water. He hadn't tasted food; he couldn't. His nerves were frayed from intense anxiety. Was she okay? Would she return during the day or at night? What she scared?

As her pregnancy had progressed, she'd become increasingly tired, and he worried for her. It made no sense that she had to sink to the bottom of the river to see the goddess. Why hadn't the goddess come to her as usual? He struggled to understand the justification of Nnanke's act, even though she'd told him it was to ask forgiveness for having broken a salient rule, to beg that Yakpani be not punished for her sins — their sins — and to secure protection for their child.

Maybe it had just been a ploy to lure her into being punished?

Such thoughts wove through his mind all day. He dared not eat anything, lest he vomit it from nervousness. However, if he'd eaten, maybe he'd have had the strength to defend himself.

Everything happened in a blur.

One moment, he sat brooding by the river. The next, he heard a rustle, which could've been a rodent scrambling in the bushes. But then, a twig broke under the weight of an unmistakable human tread, and Okoi turned. His temple became violently acquainted with the heavy base of a sturdy branch.

There was no opportunity to identify his assailant, not when another hit landed on the back of his skull as he moaned on the ground. Okoi struggled with the darkness that battled to take over his mind and lost.

Chapter Twenty-One

So many things are happening at the same time. Thankfully, I'm able to zap through these scenes. I'm worried, no doubt. However, I'm committed to bringing you all the details.

With Nkoyo in the past, and certain trouble brewed there, I thought it wise to be in the present. I mean, the past has already happened, right? It's not like we can affect any changes there. So here I am in the Atam palace.

The king and queen stared, perplexed, at the heaving mill worker. It was obvious the young man had hurried to the palace as fast as he could. Beyond that, they couldn't understand how he'd forgotten where the prince had said he'd gone.

Crap, Greed was working overtime on messing up everything.

From what was said, the boy could clearly recall the prince had sent him over to call in the army troops on standby. However, the poor boy couldn't remember the location Onen had mentioned he was going to rescue a certain Eja, another mill worker.

Understandably, King Liman was angry at his son for taking such reckless decisions in this perilous time. He knew that as a prince, he cared for his people, but it was as though Onen was unaware of the dangers lurking in wait for the royal family. I knew the king was conscious of the diabolical machinations at work in Atam, so he expected his son to have been careful.

In a bid to reduce panic in the kingdom, especially in the royal community, he'd desisted from sending in the full force of army troops. I wish he had. Now, he regretted his decision. He was sure Chief Uken was behind this manoeuvre, especially of the mill worker's memory loss.

The king looked into the panicked gaze of his queen. They hadn't expected this turn of events, but they'd not been unprepared either. They knew what each should do.

Boy, was I glad to know this. Because, it appeared I had no real power to affect anything that was happening. I was simply here to tell tales. How lame.

So, after a second of silent conversation between the royal couple, the type usual among long-time couples, Queen Jesam hurried off to one of the rooms in the palace, where the Atam priest had been ensconced since the throne room debacle. If anyone could locate the prince, the royal priest would.

"Everything will be fine," she muttered to herself, determined. Liman would call in the troops, and the priest would locate her son, she thought. Then she worried for her daughter-in-law. How would she take this crisis?

Well, the queen need not worry for Nkoyo since she was off on a mission of her own in the past. She should've been worried about the prince and the possible trap awaiting him.

***

When I zapped over to the prince's location, I came to find out the hunter had gotten confused several times to the annoyance of the mill workers with Onen. These men were revved to rescue one of their own and couldn't tolerate the obvious confusion of the hunter. Finally, the painfully skinny man had declared he would never know the way to that part of the forest from the backseat of a car.

Fleetingly, Onen wondered how his parents would react when they heard what he'd done. *They are not happy, Onen,* I thought in reply. Now, he knew Nkoyo would have his head for this recklessness, but to him, being a prince meant caring deeply and personally for his subjects. He mentally promised to explain to his wife that he'd done this because he believed if his child or children ever found themselves in a fix, the people of Atam would not hesitate to personally rescue them, too.

He was leading by example.

Urrg, I hated when he made sense despite this unreasonable situation.

This was the Atam he wanted, Onen thought as he noticed the fierce looks on his workers' face. An Atam where men took up arms and walked into certain danger for their fellow man. An Atam where love prevailed over petty squabbles—a tribe that strived on love would overcome all obstacles.

He drove into an unpaved path, searching for the perfect place to park his car, so they'd locate the right bush track into the forest on foot and rescue Eja.

It was an ambush.

I told you so, I sighed wearily.

Onen had barely turned off the ignition when a huge stone hurtled through his windscreen, causing him to duck almost under his steering wheel to avoid the brunt of the attack. The resulting shatter sprayed shards of glass on the occupants of the car.

"*ObaseWoden!*" God Almighty!

"*Oowoye!*" The general cry of pain in Atam, and other cries of pain, erupted in the car.

The foreman, God bless him, seemed entirely concerned for the safety of the prince. Though he saw the approaching mob of angry men when he raised his head from under the dashboard, he didn't run for his life. He prodded the dazed prince to get him out of the car and hoped he could escape.

However, the prince, even in his disbelieving state, was more concerned for the welfare of his men. God, could he be selfish for once, I wondered in frustration. Onen tried to reach out to one of his mill workers in the back who had a large gash on his forehead, apparently from a shard of his shattered windscreen, but was shocked to see the hunter raise his rifle.

Even in the mêlée that had erupted inside the car, with the occupants scrambling to get out, the hunter struggled with the length of his rifle. I wondered what he was going to do. When he righted it, he calmly blew a hole in the chest of the worker with the gash.

Oh my God! Even I wasn't expecting that cold-blooded action.

More screams of terror erupted, but Onen could only croak and stare at the bloodied, lifeless body of the mill worker. His eyes dazedly rose and met the sneer on the hunter's features.

The skinny man spat in Onen's face. "You are not my prince!" he declared with a vehemence that couldn't be misconstrued as anything but hate.

Onen wanted to ask the hunter why he was doing this. *Really, Onen*, I yearned to scream at him. Yet, his dazed mind wanted to know the reasoning behind taking another man's life. Thankfully, he was suddenly pushed down over the stick shift of his car when another mill worker tackled the hunter.

Grunts of effort and blows could be heard while the foreman put his mouth to Onen's ear.

"You need to run, my prince," he stated in a strained whisper, his hands shaking in fear as the rowdy crowd drew near.

Finally, someone was speaking some sense to this damn altruistic prince!

Another stone hurtled in from the windscreen at the back of the car. Ironically, the stone caught the hunter squarely on his temple. Good, the gods weren't asleep. As Onen scrambled down from the car, he saw the stone smash in the hunter's head, flinging his wiry body backwards and bent awkwardly over the driver's seat before going still.

He couldn't even celebrate the death of the hateful man, not when his men, the three remaining, pushed him towards the only available escape route, the forest, part of the land in dispute. With his heart hammering heavily against his chest, he stumbled into the forest and vaguely heard a shout behind him.

Apparently, they'd been sighted getting away, and an uproar of protest rose. Damn it, I was frustrated not having the power to fling that crowd away from the prince's tail.

"Faster, my prince," the foreman prodded while limping as quickly as he could beside him. Onen grunted, saw that he was injured, and put his muscular arm under his armpit, even though he could hear their attackers giving chase.

He almost vomited his heart when he heard clashes of machete on his right, not very far from where they were. He stumbled, especially as he carried most of the foreman's weight to enable them to run faster in the thick bush of the dense forest.

"Keep moving, Prince," one of the mill workers prodded urgently.

"Are they fighting among themselves?" Onen asked through a gasp as he kept moving, his voice shaking with uncertainty and fear.

"No, Prince," the other mill worker replied. He ran on the other side of the foreman, his face bleeding from tiny scratches.

Onen knew his own face would be the same—he could feel the sting as sweat dripped into the wounds.

"I think Yakpani has joined the fight," he concluded, and Onen nodded as he heard the distant clang of metal on metal, which sent a surge of terror hurtling into his throat.

He worried for Nkoyo and his baby. He worried for his parents. Had the crisis reached the residential areas? He really hoped not; he needed to find a way back to town. He had left his phone in his car.

"Does any of you have a phone?" he asked urgently and was disappointed when the men shook their heads with regretful looks.

"Do we know where we are going? We need to stop and get our bearings; we need to know which direction would take us to Yakpani. It is easy to get confused in a forest, and we don't want to end up in Umor at a time like this. We have no idea if the whole community is involved in this sabotage," he heaved, his anger at the stupidity of his people rising to the fore.

Running was a coward's way out. Thankfully, I felt him acknowledging there was nothing else he could've done with the angry mob approaching from both sides.

"Let's just keep moving," the foreman gasped, sounding tired, but Onen stubbornly stopped and carefully leaned the man on a sturdy-looking tree.

"If it isn't the crown prince of Atam kingdom. How nice of you to join us," Chief Uken declared, walking with confidence followed by some other chiefs and young men into the clearing, as though they'd been waiting.

Realisation finally settled on Onen that the attack had been staged to lead him here. They'd known the only escape for the prince would be delving into the forest, away from the angry mob. He could see the almost unrecognizable face of Eja as he sat propped against a tree, his neck bent awkwardly.

I couldn't believe that despite the danger to himself, the prince still wondered if the poor boy was still alive.

"Oh, he is," Uken replied his thoughts, and waved his hand dismissively at the unconscious boy.

Onen's heart stuttered and then started beating again so heavily and fast, he felt the terror might constrict his breathing. However, he managed to hide it. He wasn't from the royal family for nothing. He had been brought up with the fearlessness required of kings and the wisdom to serve his people right.

To my proud dismay, he smiled at Uken's words, underplaying the shock of the evil man's sudden appearance and his ability to read his thoughts.

"Is that so?" he managed to ask leisurely. "Why go through this elaborate hoax to get to me, Uken? Why take the coward's way?"

"You mean the coward's way of running from your car like a scared rabbit?" Uken laughed, his eyes darkening in a sinister way as he leaned heavily on his walking stick.

Onen swallowed hard and allowed his gaze take in his garb. The evil man had on only a wrapper around his waist, a multi-coloured towel on his shoulder, and *ekoo* painted on his biceps and limbs. It was the Atam celebratory style of dressing for chiefs during coronations or new yam festivals. The only thing missing was the feathery cap and the impossibly long chewing stick.

He allowed his gaze to drift to the chiefs clearly in support of Uken and his greedy acts. Also not surprising not just Umor chiefs were there.

"Why?" His gaze slowly stopped on each of the five chiefs involved. "What do you stand to gain in destroying your kingdom?" A couple of the chiefs fidgeted uncomfortably. "Why would you follow this man—"

"Enough with sentimental questions!" Uken commanded, raising his walking stick at Onen, not to smite him but charm him into submission.

"Your powers don't work on me, old man," Onen mocked when he stood his ground.

But, I swear, he felt a force rush past his ears when Uken pointed the walking stick at him. I was proud of Onen right now, but could he really stand the power of the ancient spirit at work here?

"I know this," Uken sneered. "The royal protection, but it didn't help you at the palace when we met last, did it?"

Onen swallowed his trepidation and tried to control his breathing.

"It wasn't for you, prince," Uken said, and raised the staff higher. His terrified mill workers started screaming with their hands covering their ears and grimacing in obvious pain. "You stupid fool! You feel since my powers don't work on you, I'll not have another way to snare you? You are just like your father in that regard, caring for the people." He sneered and cackled.

Once again, Onen was reminded of the evil priest of the past, but he had no idea how that knowledge would help him and his workers.

"The heroic prince to the rescue, eh?" Uken taunted while striding into the clearing fully, followed by his supporters. They were all dressed in the ceremonial Atam traditional garb of chiefs, too.

The screams from his mill workers had totally deflated his demeanour of courage. His foreman even went a step further to call out to him for help.

"Yes, Prince, help your people," Uken mocked while stepping closer to where Onen stood.

The prince noticed the chiefs hadn't said anything, yet they followed Uken like marionettes. They were probably hypnotized, yet that bit of information did him no good.

"What do you want?" he managed to croak through the terror constricting his throat while he prayed for a miracle deep in his heart.

"I want the Atam throne. I've always wanted the throne, and when my wishes aligned with that of these humans, I decided to take this body and take control," Uken said and laughed so hard, he bent his head and upper torso backwards.

Onen recalled a similar move had been made by the evil priest of the past, too, and he'd heard what he'd said about taking a body. He understood an ancient spirit determined to destroy Atam at all cost possessed Uken. On his own, Uken wouldn't have had the effrontery to take all the drastic decisions that had caused chaos in Atam, but being possessed and the chiefs with like minds being manipulated, the spirit was able to garner his minions.

The ancient spirit wouldn't have been able to control any of these people if they'd not always coveted the throne and had probably had clandestine meetings on how to go about taking it.

"You're right, of course." Uken's eyes shone dark with evil as he once again read his thoughts.

Onen knew what he had to do. It was what was expected of an honourable prince of Atam kingdom. "Let my men go, Eja included," he demanded, shouting above the painful screams of his mill workers.

Uken, or whatever possessed him, widened his eyes in mock shock.

"Are you sacrificing yourself, Prince?" he asked and then laughed because he couldn't hold onto the innocent look any longer. "Okoi's descendants are so predictable," he murmured, but Onen heard and swallowed hard in realization that he was a descendant of the man he'd seen in the past.

He believed, because he'd once compared himself and his wife to Okoi and Nnanke. At the thought of Nk, his heart bled, and he prayed harder for a miracle. His wife would never let him out of the house again when she heard of this situation. He would totally submit to whatever she demanded if only he'd be given an opportunity to return to her and carry his child in his arms.

"Okoi also sacrificed himself, but at least, it was for his woman. You are doing it for people who agree to take up arms and bring the royal family down." Uken sneered.

Onen's heart thumped hard against his chest. His white shirt had wilted with sweat, and his tanned trousers had dirty stains all over it. Fear inundated his entire body as he realized he might not survive this day. He wished he could be given a chance to speak to Nk and tell her how much he loved her and their baby and to ask her to be strong and bring up their child in the honourable way.

He refused to think about the fact that if he died, someone else would marry his wife because Nk was too beautiful a woman to remain a widow for long. He refused to think of the faceless man touching her intimately as he'd done—the thought brought a sob to his throat, but he held it back and looked up determinedly.

"*Waaaa,*" Uken mocked with the traditional exclamation of pity and a pout that made him uglier. "Don't worry, I'll take perfect care of your wife and your mother. You see, when you die here today—" Uken looked into his eyes. "—Oh, you will. The war will escalate. Your father's army will be useless against my powers, and guess who will be the new king? Me!" he exclaimed like an excited child, his eyes expressing his greed. "I'll have all the women to myself. The only problem will be deciding who would be my first wife, your mother or your wife."

"Don't you dare touch them!" Onen screamed, his tone higher and louder than that of his mill workers in desperation as he stepped threateningly towards Uken.

The possessed man stepped back and immediately raised the pain level of his mill workers by lifting his walking stick. Their screams increased. When Onen looked, his foreman, who was older than the other two men, bled profusely from his nose.

"Stop! Let them go…please," he begged. He'd rather die than allow innocent men to suffer unnecessarily. Even though the evil powers didn't work on him for whatever reason, well except when Uken physically touched him with his staff, he could feel the excruciating pain in the head and ears of his workers, and he wanted them released.

"I…" He had been about to willingly submit himself to Uken, but the possessed man moved with a burst of supernatural speed and touched the round, golden head of his staff on Onen's forehead, instantly weakening his knees. His legs folded beneath him, and he fell at the feet of Uken.

It was a heavy fall, as expected of a six-foot-plus man with bulging muscles. Yet, Onen struggled to get to his feet—his effort only got him to crawl. His head and body felt like it had been pumped with molten magma, which was systematically melting his bones and making him incapable of using his limbs.

"Let them go," he whispered continuously, his hand reaching out to touch Uken's ankle.

"He…he still cares for his people despite his own suffering," one of the chiefs finally spoke up in obvious awe of the Atam prince.

"As an intending king, you must honour your promise to release them," another chief declared, and they all stared at Uken expectantly.

I would laugh right now if Onen wasn't in so much pain. However, the ancient spirit found himself in a quagmire because of Onen's sacrifice. I heard him think: *thunder fire, the dratted honour of the typical Atam man!*

Greed reluctantly raised Uken's hand and ceased the pain of the prince's men. The hoarse screams subsided to moans as they lay listlessly on the forest ground, weak and drained from their excruciating experience.

"Now, tie the prince up," he muttered as though tired of the whole situation.

It was the plan for the youths, three young men who'd come with the chiefs, to tie up the prince after he'd been subdued. But at Uken's muttered command, two of them hesitated. They had seen the prince's act of sacrifice, and shame inundated their hearts. But Uken's driver broke out from their hurdle and heaved the prince from the ground. He could do this because he was tall and muscular, as well.

"You will do what you had agreed to do or regret it," Uken threatened and smiled when the young men jerked out of their sudden moral discovery and did as had been planned.

Prince Onen Liman Ikpi Egu was strung up like a common thief, all for greed in the hearts of men; all for the gem that was Atam kingdom.

***

"Where is she?! Where is she, you creature?!" Binah Yakpani screamed at the top of his voice.

If the whole village wasn't already aware of the sacrilege that had been committed by their priestess, Binah Yakpani's howl would've informed them of it.

The news spread like wild fire that a strange man had been caught in the forbidden forest and he had impregnated the priestess. Neighbours made sure to inform others on their way as they raced to the square where he was hung. Soon, the whole village gathered round the hardly breathing man.

"Maybe the strange man put a spell on her," Binah Ekori suggested quietly, trying to calm the situation fast becoming inhumane. He had noticed his friend, Binah Yakpani, had begun despising the very sight of Nnanke and had made several derogatory comments concerning her work for the spirits. It hadn't mattered that the village sang her praises as she always solved whatever problems cropped up. She was especially recognized for making Yakpani women fertile again.

He understood his friend became threatened over time when villagers directly requested for Nnanke when someone was ill instead of Binah Yakpani. As the binah, he was the leader, the highest authority — every decision, no matter how minute, passed by his consideration; the binah was king. But Nnanke and her powers threatened that position, causing his friend to react enviously.

Binah Yakpani pierced him with a withering look.

"How can this mere mortal charm our great priestess?" he sneered. His blazing eyes slowly met that of the villagers at the fore of the circle. "Your precious priestess, Nnanke, has broken the rule of the spirits, and the punishment is death," he declared with too much glee for such a sad situation.

"Uben is a true warrior and must be praised for his sacrifice. He risked a sojourn into the forbidden forest as the priestess has been slacking on her duties and discovered the abomination going on right under our noses," he announced and glowed in satisfaction when he saw the elders jerk their shoulders in shock and disgust of the monstruous sin.

"This has been going on for some time. Uben, tell them what you saw," Binah Yakpani encouraged.

Uben took uncanny relish in describing the completely carnal copulation he had witnessed in the forbidden forest and the largeness of Nnanke's belly that meant she was pregnant.

Uben's wife fidgeted uncomfortably in the crowd as her husband explained such intimate details about the priestess; she felt it was insulting to the woman who had helped them so much. Besides, she wasn't stupid, contrary to what her husband might think. She'd been aware he was about to marry Nnanke before she was chosen by the spirits, and since then, he'd always had tender emotions for her. She just wondered why men were so quick to forget Nnanke's works and unwilling to be lenient.

"Such sacrilege! And she knew what would happen to the village if she broke the rules of the spirits," Binah Yakpani insinuated, liking that the elders were becoming necessarily incensed.

"It was probably what caused a mysterious rat to bite a chunk off Uben's feet while he was on guard at the boundary."

"*Oh!*"

"*Oowoye!*"

"*Eya eh!*"

The crowd reacted to the scary development.

"*Eya eh!* It is true. When the spirits get angry, they start causing strange illnesses in the village. Haven't you people been experiencing unexplainable illnesses? So many boys have been hitting their big toes, even when they were not playing. Some of you men have complained pains inside your heads when you return from your farms." Men nodded to this, encouraging his tirade. "The other day, somebody was shaking with cold while his body was hot like fire; strange illnesses," he intoned, satisfied with the scary faces staring back at him.

"Why do you think she was the only one that knew how to cure these illnesses?" he insinuated, eagerly stoking their suspicion and distrust in Nnanke. "Hit him again and make him confess where the shameful priestess is hiding!" he commanded, and warriors, ready with huge sticks, began slamming Okoi one more.

It was an inhumane sight, and some women closed their eyes to shut off the violence. Okoi hung from his neck, his hands tied to his body with only his big toes on the ground. Even then, he had to stretch to touch those toes to the ground to create a balance and curb the tightening of the noose around his neck.

Nevertheless, when the warriors slammed those sticks on his back and belly, the control left his toes, and he swung from his neck, bearing the wounding pain and trying not to strangle. His legs scrambled in a wheeling motion trying to reach the ground and stop the swing of his body. He was completely battered, his eyes swollen shut from the beatings he'd received as they'd neared the village.

"Tell us where the priestess is, and we will make your death quick," Binah Yakpani declared magnanimously and poked Okoi's belly with his engraved staff.

The problem was, Okoi couldn't talk, not with the tight noose around his neck. If he could, he would've argued and made sure the villagers knew that their binah was lying. He didn't have to convince them—he just had to make them see a different perspective and be unsure of which to believe.

Okoi gagged and could do nothing when his wrapper fell from his waist, rendering him naked. He heard the crowd gasp, and some men covered their wives' eyes from his impressive manhood. Soon, the beating stopped, and he was able to press the top of his toes on the ground, relieving the tightening around his neck.

His swollen left eye, the only one he could see with, though in a blur, caught an even scarier sight. The cannibal priest that'd burned him—he moved among the crowd with an obvious smirk on his face.

Okoi's heart sank. Now he understood how this had happened. Nnanke had been right that he wouldn't give up so easily. Okoi could see why Binah Yakpani was behaving out of character as opposed to his friend, Binah Ekori. It only meant one thing—the cannibal priest was compelling them with his dark powers.

He worried for Nnanke, even more so than before. He couldn't help her or warn her about the danger. Binah Yakpani had no idea she was the last defence they had from the approaching war. Without her, the village would fall.

Tears dripped from his eyes at his helplessness. He might've been given a brief glance of paradise, but this was confirmation he was destined to die...violently. Okoi wished fervently Nnanke would hide when she returned and found him missing. He wished and prayed to the son of the white God that she would run away and not come in search of him.

He wished but knew it was useless, not when she'd ardently promised, "I would never let you die."

He sobbed with bitterness, the sound so distinct and heart-wrenching that a hush fell on the crowd. Tears could be seen in the eyes of women and some young men. The warriors stood back, fidgeting uncomfortably with no idea what they should do next.

"I'll die for you," he sobbed. "I'll die for you, Nnanke."

The hanging man repeated his solemn promise, and the villagers couldn't comprehend such a sacrifice. They stood in awe and discomfort, as they were unsure of the justification of his hanging.

Binah Umor saw the disintegration of his perfect manipulations as the villagers began to murmur among themselves. They were speaking of the dishonour of hanging a stranger without hearing him out. They muttered of the incredibility of a stranger liking their priestess to the point of sacrificing his life for her. The villagers were awed at the intensity of such emotion; they couldn't understand it.

While they tried to make sense of the powerful emotion expressed by the hanging man and before they could make a unanimous decision, Binah Umor spoke a spell directed at the heart of Binah Yakpani and Uben, increasing their envy.

Uben was envious of Okoi for having a more impressive manhood and having used it on the woman he'd coveted all his adult life. Binah Yakpani was envious of the power Nnanke possessed and her popularity among the villagers. Both men boiled with the intensity of their envy, becoming extremely furious as the villagers hesitated.

"String him higher! The traitor must die or else we, our children, and our land will be cursed!" Binah Yakpani declared, bent on righteousness.

The other warriors hesitated, but Uben rushed to the remaining length of the rope around Okoi's neck, tethered to a smaller tree. He cut it with the sharp edge of his spear, causing Okoi's legs to stand on the ground.

But then, he dropped his spear, held the rope with both hands, and dragged downwards. Okoi was lifted from the ground, dangling from his neck. His body jerked as he gagged, his swollen eyes gorging out in his last struggle for life.

The villagers moaned as one at the terrible sight. Some elders sided with Binah Yakpani and grinned with him at the justice the hanging represented. Binah Ekori shook his head sadly, and the unseen Binah Umor cackled in delight.

Even as the darkness of death engulfed Okoi's mind, his thoughts centred on his woman — his angel, his paradise.

In that moment, huts began emitting smoke, but the villagers were too captivated to notice that Umor warriors had arrived.

Chapter Twenty-Two

It was like a punch to her gut. The piercing pain made her double over, falling on her knees, her hand momentarily loosening its hold on the flap of her wrapper.

Nnanke knew instantly what had happened; she knew what had been done to her man. She knew she had failed in her promise never to let him die. Still, she screamed, "No!" her voice echoing eerily in the forest, causing a flock of birds to take sudden flight into the sky while animals in the trees fled in a scramble.

The villagers turned in one accord at the eerie sound from the forest. They saw the raucous flight of birds from the trees, and their hearts thumped with terror, for the sound was of intense hurt, pain, and anger. It was unmistakably the voice of the priestess.

***

The spirits had taken her through seven rigorous rituals she didn't understand. Nnanke had just been glad the overly bright beings didn't seem angry and had actually welcomed her. But she couldn't trust them until she'd left the depth of the river back to her forest, back to Okoi again.

Stranger things occurred under the river. She had seen a roaring fire in the water, and she'd had to walk through it seven times. Everything under the water had been performed seven times. By the time the goddess of fertility led her to the golden entrance and to the waiting spirit guides, Nnanke had been fagged out. The goddess, a glittering half fish woman with beautiful green shells covering her breasts, the green matching the hue of the lower fish side of her body, and long, dreadlocked hair draped alluringly over her pale skin, had reached out and touched her protruding stomach.

Nnanke had no idea what she had done, but she felt power flow through her veins, the surge so strong, she screamed and floated listlessly in the crystal water. Then, the beautiful goddess waved the spirit guides over, and the fish-like creatures took their places under Nnanke's armpits and began the upward swim back to real life.

When they arrived, the sun had just begun its return journey. They deposited her naked body on the river bank and swiftly plunged back into the river, swishing their blue tails in the air before they disappeared.

Nnanke had lain there for a while, wondering why Okoi hadn't seen her. He'd promised he would wait for her by the river even if it took her days to return. Groaning tiredly, for it felt like her pregnancy had doubled in weight, she twisted, turned, and placed her hand on the land, ready to lift herself to her feet. But the earth seemed to shift, covering her hands with soil, and then spoke to her.

She saw everything that had happened in the forest. Strange how the earth spoke to her as though they were old friends. She sank her hands into the muddy earth in appreciation even though her heart bled for what had been done to Okoi.

The earth hummed and vibrated around her, filling her with the strength she needed to get to her feet. As she made her way as fast as she could up the narrow path that led to the cave, she was shocked to find branches of plants leaning towards her as though welcoming her. Some with soft, curly branches wrapped around her wrist but loosened as she progressed up the path.

Her eyes widened at this wonder, but she had no time to think of it. She had to reach Okoi. She had to rescue him. She had to keep her promise of never letting him die.

Without waiting to properly tie her wrapper around her nakedness, she flung it over her shoulder, grabbed her staff, and raced into the forest. It took her a while to notice that brilliantly coloured butterflies, so many of them, followed her progress as she lumbered to the village.

But then, that piercing pain occurred, and she knew she'd lost her light.

Her scream scattered the butterflies in all directions but they fluttered back, surrounding her while she sobbed on the forest floor. Leaves grew where her tears dropped, plants reached out to her, flowers caressed her as though in commiseration.

Her hand touched the soil again, and she was shown his struggle behind the lids of her closed eyes. She could see the people, the ones who accused and the ones who didn't. She saw when Okoi noticed the evil binah, and she heard his thoughts of concern for her.

More tears flowed as she staggered to her feet and continued towards the village. Anger bubbled as she considered abandoning them to the brutalization Umor warriors would descend on them.

***

The villagers stood as though stunned in place when Nnanke stumbled from the dark thickness of the forest. If they hadn't just heard her scream or recognized the curly drape of her hair, they would've thought the hunched figure approaching them was an old woman.

Her white cotton wrapper draped from her shoulders over her body to her legs, the large flaps grasped together in one hand while the other stomped her staff on the ground as she staggered close.

Nnanke reached the square, a path magically opening in between the sea of gathered people, and finally, she looked up and beheld Okoi swaying from his neck.

Tears burned her eyes. Her face twisted. Her throat clogged. Fury built in her chest, and so did the wind. Dark clouds flew across the sky, and the villagers trembled in her presence but couldn't move a limb.

She sobbed as she walked towards the still figure dangling from a rope around his neck like a thief. This wasn't the man who had shown her life was more than what she'd known. This wasn't the man who'd held her with warmth. She lifted her eyes and beheld his nakedness, his shame.

They shamed him. The spirits accepted him, but man shamed him.

Her sobs increased into wracking cries. Still, the villagers stood quietly. Nnanke reached out her hand to Okoi's body, and a murmur broke out among the villagers, wondering what she was doing.

Before their eyes, the branch Okoi dangled from bent towards Nnanke, lowering his body. The ropes bounding him snapped, loosening his battered and broken body. The branch delivered him tenderly to the ground like a mother laying down her child.

Nnanke looked at Okoi's lifeless body at her feet. The earth bubbled around his length, creating a bed of soil for him to the astonishment of the crowd. Her legs wobbled beneath her, and she fell to her knees in grief, placing her head on Okoi's still chest.

"What did he do to deserve this?" she asked softly but was heard by all. "What did he do?" She sobbed. "My light," she murmured tenderly as though he were alive to hear her. She looked lovingly upon his face and touched his bearded chin with tenderness like she would do when she lay with him in their cave.

"I failed you. I let you die," she murmured, touching the wounds and bruises all over his body while tears flowed freely down her cheeks to soak into the soil bed he'd been laid.

Green sprouted like tiny shoots from the soil, all around Okoi. It grew rapidly into leafy vines that crawled all over his body, not just covering his nakedness but embalming his whole self. The leafy vines twisted like snakes, covering his face. Flowers sprouted on the vines, releasing sweet-smelling perfume into the air.

Nnanke struggled to her feet. Her heart broke in several irretrievable pieces as she watched the vine encompass Okoi's body until no piece of his skin showed. Then, the earth boiled, slowly swallowing the vine-covered body.

She watched him sink, and a ragged sob wrenched from her throat.

***

Nkoyo woke with a stifled cry, dragging me back to her side. The room hummed with power, and I suspected the ring had dragged her back home. I looked into her consciousness and was shocked to see what had occurred in the past.

Her face was entirely drenched with tears. Except, listening to her thoughts, I realised her tears were not for what had happened to Okoi but the replay of the past currently unfolding with her husband as the sacrificial lamb.

As the ring forcefully returned her to the present, the dark hole held snatches of pictures of the same betrayal through time; Greed was totally invested in destroying Atam kingdom. But they could defeat it by simply loving each other. They could defeat the influence of Greed by being satisfied with the abundant resources Atam is blessed with.

Without wasting time on what should be, Nkoyo hurried from the bed as fast as her large stomach would permit. Her white kaftan seemed rumpled, but she couldn't care less—she had to save her husband.

She shoved her swollen feet into flat, leather slip-ons, then grabbed her phone and car keys and hurried downstairs. Tears continued to stream down her face as she frantically called out for the gates to be opened.

Surprisingly, the security man, a jovial employee, didn't bother showing concern in the form of asking what the problem was. He instead jerked as though controlled and speedily opened the gate. Exactly what she needed.

Nkoyo dialled Queen Jesam's number, and the woman answered on the first ring.

"Darling!" she sobbed.

Nkoyo confirmed that what the ring had shown her was real. Onen was actually bound to a tree this moment.

She had to gasp several times to control her tears and fear. She had no idea what she would do, but she was sure of one thing, she was going to rescue her husband.

The queen rambled on about having called her several times but she hadn't answered her calls. Well, she couldn't have answered when she's been buried in the past, I thought. The comment made Nkoyo feel guilty that her husband had been in trouble while she'd been playing around with powers she'd been asked to avoid.

"Meet me instantly at the roundabout turn off… I know where Onen is being held," she announced and ended the call, unable to analyse why her voice didn't sound like hers.

Nkoyo wiped her eyes with her left hand while she sped down the road, pressing down her horn insistently to get people out of the way. As usual, her eyes drifted to her ring finger and found it empty. Realization struck her instantly—the ring was still stuck on her forehead. It must be how she knew the exact direction to where Onen was held.

Probably also why the roiling fury in the pit of her stomach felt like a volcano ready to erupt. Why she was confident that though she was a heavily pregnant woman, she would face down an unknown army to protect the love of her life. Love burned in her heart like a fiery furnace, filling her body with a buzzing energy, the kind that made it seem as though the air had just picked up.

Nkoyo glanced at the weather and wondered if it would rain. She shook her head at her mundane concern and sped down the untarred road she had just turned into. It took a few minutes for her eyes flick to the rear-view mirror — the king and queen and their army hurtled down the earthy road behind her, raising dust around their convoy.

She sighted Onen's destroyed Jeep first before taking notice of the pandemonium. Normally, the sight of dead bodies and burning houses should've terrified her, but Nkoyo was beyond angry; she was infuriated at the sight before her. She swore if anything happened to her husband, Atam would burn for his life.

Like a feature film in her mind's eye, she saw as Onen had stumbled out of his car, dazed, and wobbled into the forest with a handful of men around him. Nkoyo pressed down on the accelerator to hurry forward. Then, she was out of the car before the brakes had fully engaged.

She had no idea how the king and queen had gotten to her so quickly, but was shocked to be held back as she marched with the intention of plunging into the violent mêlée.

"No, Nkoyo," Queen Jesam shouted over the riotous screams, the army men quickly forming a protective arc around them, her hand tightly wrapped around Nkoyo's arm. "Allow the army to go in," she pleaded, her eyes showing how terrified she was.

"How did you know it was here?" King Liman asked, his hand flexing over the handgun in his grip. They had shed their royal garbs and dressed befittingly for war. A weird sight to see the monarchs so dressed. Nothing the army general said could make them stay home while their son was in danger.

Well, now we know where Onen got his stubborn determination.

When Nkoyo had called, after they'd been about to send some army men to Onen's house to make sure she was safe, they'd been shocked to hear she knew where he was being held. It made no sense, and they'd refused to suspect their son's wife, not when they knew she loved him with her life.

The king couldn't understand why his usually sweet daughter-in-law was refusing to look at them. He was grateful they stood quite far away from the riot, though they couldn't unsee the dead bodies and devastation caused by the clash. He sincerely hoped his son was okay, even though his car inspired terror and hopelessness. However, could someone tell the queen to unhand Nkoyo—she had a mission, for God's sake!

Thankfully, Binah Atam approached and touched the queen's arm. When she turned to him, he shook his head slowly and indicated she let go of Nkoyo's arm. Queen Jesam's brow furrowed in confusion as she didn't understand what the binah was silently saying.

The army men, complete with their camouflage fatigues and guns, passed the royal family and proceeded towards the pandemonium.

"Don't go any further," Nkoyo commanded, but her voice, though not shouted, was clearly heard. As though compelled, the army group of about twenty men, apart from the few protecting the royal family, stopped.

"Nkoyo—"

"I'll go first," she declared, interrupting the queen as though she hadn't spoken, then she turned to face her in-laws.

Queen Jesam immediately let go of her and stumbled back in terror. Her husband held her, and as a man, he curbed the need to show his own trepidation at the sight before them.

The wind wiped Nkoyo's white kaftan violently, plastering it on her body and emphasizing her protruding belly. She seemed fairer than usual; her recently loosened hair blew across her face and seemed longer. Yet, what inspired fear in the royal couple were Nkoyo's eyes.

It was as though she had three eyes. The ring stuck on her forehead glowed a fiery sapphire, the same colour that had taken over Nkoyo's naturally brown eyes.

"What is wrong with her?" Jesam asked the binah in blatant terror and concern.

Instead of answering, the binah prostrated before Nkoyo as the trees swayed violently in the strong wind.

"Nnanke! Yanen- woyee!"

"Nnanke! Yanen-wofai!"

"Nnanke! Yanen- woObasenfawa!"

"Kou annungwoyee! Kouannungwofai! KouannungnfawaObase!"

Go and do what is good! Go and do what is peaceful! Go and do the blessings of God!

Yes! Finally, a worthy confrontation to retell.

As though she had been waiting for the prod from the priest, Nkoyo—who was more Nnanke in that moment—rushed towards the riot. She passed her husband's car and marched furiously, the wind blowing after her like her personal bodyguard.

Nkoyo wasted no time. She pushed a couple of grappling men out of her way, and it looked like she'd shoved empty containers from her path as they fell heavily. She stood there and watched as the men of Atam destroyed their lives, their home, and essence in senseless war.

The fury hurtled from within the pit of her stomach and then burst out of her throat in one drawn out word, "*Komạạ!*"

A wave so powerful it shook the ground plied through the warring men, instantly setting them away from each other's throats. They turned in one accord to stare at the spectre Nkoyo made in her whipping white dress and hair and fiery blue eyes.

The men who moments ago were ferocious and willing to kill, even killed, cowered before Nkoyo. She spat on the sand in disgust, causing a whimper among them, before walking into the forest in the sudden silence that had ensued.

Darkness didn't deter her speed; her eyes glowed brighter, as did the ring on her forehead. I floated along, hearing snatches of thoughts from the army following behind. They wondered how she was seeing or how she could move so fast in the thick forest considering she was heavily pregnant. But after that strange show out there, they confidently followed the white-garbed figure. Their job was to rescue the Crown Prince.

When Nkoyo burst into the clearing, she did so with a gust of wind so strong, it flung the people gathered several feet backward on their arses.

Oh, what an entrance, I crowed, almost applauding. But, most importantly, that entrance paused Chief Uken from driving the dagger in his hand into Onen's heart.

Not pausing, Nkoyo continued with the momentum she'd used to enter the clearing and soon stood between Onen and Uken, her eyes flashing with challenge.

Uken — well, Greed — sensed the approaching army and immediately reached inside his wrapper and flung whatever it is he had grabbed from it towards the army without taking his eyes from those of Nkoyo.

The army men had just burst into the clearing, guns ready, when tiny black arrows hurtled in the air towards them. They had no time to dodge, their eyes widening in dismay. But then the knives suddenly stopped, only an inch from imbedding in the first soldier's eye. The man wheezed in relief and terror, his big gun shaking uselessly in his hands.

Binah Atam had the king and queen lying on the floor of the forest and had been in time to stop the diabolically created arrows. He twirled his engraved staff with both hands in front of him as he walked, muttering spells under his breath, and caused the arrows to fall harmlessly to the ground.

Uken growled angrily as his attack had been foiled. "You again!"

"Onen!" the queen screamed in dismay as she caught sight of her battered son slumped to the side on the tree he'd been tied to. She made to rush to him, but the king held her back.

Her cry of dismay distracted Nkoyo for a moment, and Uken seized that time to lunge over her shoulder, the specially designed dagger in his hand aimed for Onen's heart.

Nkoyo fell backwards, leaning her weight on her husband's slumped form to protect him. Her protruding stomach served as a barrier, stopping Uken from slanting closer. Her left hand rose to block his attacking right hand with the dagger, and she got nipped in the process but it didn't distract her.

"Yes! Me again," she finally replied his earlier sneer. With eyes flashing, her right hand blocked the attack from his left hand with a strength that made Uken's eyes widen in shock. Nkoyo immediately pressed her forehead bearing the brightly burning ring on Uken's chest.

She could see light from the ring piercing the darkness in Uken's body. He howled into the night, the sound a mixture of lost souls and nocturnal creatures. The evil fought the light and tried to expand its mass, which would mean killing its host, but the ring burned brighter, inundating the body with its brilliance.

The people watching in awe at a safe distance swore they saw a dark shadow flee from Uken's body when they retold their experience. Well, I cackled as Greed fled the fiery brilliance of light from the ring. Uken crumbled to the ground like an empty sack, and those that had been under his spell scrambled to their feet, looking around as though they had no idea how they'd gotten to that forest.

Nkoyo staggered, the colour of the ring and her eyes dimming considerably. The wiping wind calmed. Her arm cradled her baby bump protectively as she slumped to the ground.

The priest rushed forward, directing the army to arrest everyone, including the weak Uken, while he proceeded towards the prince and Nkoyo, the king and queen hot on his tail.

As Onen's foreman and workers were being helped to their feet, the priest wasted no time in grabbing Uken's dagger and slicing the rope binding Onen to the tree. The prince immediately slid to the ground and engulfed his weakened wife in a bear hug. The monarchs descended on them, engulfing both of them in a group hug.

Because Greed—that dirty, ancient spirit—had been vanquished, Onen felt released from the power that had held him bound in weakness. He didn't care for the bruises on his body but for his weakened wife. He disentangled himself from his parents' arms and tenderly grabbed her face in concern.

"I love you, Nk," he declared with ringing passion, the emotion surging so strongly in his heart that it choked him. "I love you, so much," he whispered fiercely, the relief of being alive causing tears to drip from his eyes onto her cheek, his hands roving her body in a bid to convince himself she was okay.

Nkoyo looked up at him with a smile. She was so tired and entirely drained, her limbs felt listless, and she knew she'd not be able to walk, at least, not soon. Her eyes drooped as she gazed at Onen lovingly. She caressed his chest, the only part of his body she could reach without raising her arm.

"I would never let you die," she murmured, smiled, and passed out.

Chapter Twenty-Three

Nnanke felt the devastation from the depth of her core. It twisted around her intestines and heart like the vine that had covered Okoi's dead body—only, these invisible vines twirling inside her had thorns that poked and wounded.

She was in excruciating pain.

A kind of pain that choked her breath and made her blood boil.

Wind wiped fiercely around her, flapping her wrapper and hair. Power sizzled in the air as total darkness engulfed the village. Lightning illuminated the sky, and the ominous flash matched the burning sapphire of her eyes and her glowing staff, contrasting sharply with the dull yellow glow of the markings on her skin.

Nnanke wheezed with the effort to control her fury. But she couldn't, not when she stood where Okoi had lain before the earth had taken him. She looked down, recalling how swollen and bruised he'd been. The memory weakened her fingers, and the flap of the wrapper slipped from them, blowing away in the wind.

Several gasps echoed among the crowd in the square.

As though her nakedness and obvious pregnancy had broken a stunned spell that had held the crowd in stupor, elders started muttering and spitting words of sacrilege and abomination and punishments. Simple villagers just wanted to return to their huts, but the wind blew them in, blowing up smoke of burning huts and sand from all directions. No one could leave the village square.

Binah Umor had been fast to recover after being shocked from the tree bowing to the priestess. Could the pregnancy have made her more powerful, instead of killing her as was expected? And what were those glowing markings on her body?

"You should be ashamed, Nnanke!" Binah Yakpani exploded. "You can no more be a priestess of Yakpani, not after you committed another abomination this day by allowing the elders to see your nakedness!" he shouted in an effort to be heard over the howl of the wind then spat on the ground in disgust.

Nobody seemed worried about the burning huts.

"You must face your punishment!" he declared with authority.

Nnanke shook her head, her hair flying in the wind as though they had a life of their own. Her hand tightened on her glowing staff as she tried…really, she wheezed louder in her effort to control the roiling fury in her belly while tears rolled down her cheeks as she mourned her loss.

Binah Ekori crept warily towards his friend, silently wondering if Binah Yakpani had gone mad. Anybody with a pinch of sense would know to keep quiet in the face of the priestess' fury. But the man had lost all sense of self-preservation and was stoking the woman's obvious pain.

He touched Binah Yakpani on the arm and shook his head at his friend when he turned to him. He couldn't shout over the howling wind, so that small gesture should've been enough warning. But his friend jerked away from him angrily and lifted his priestly staff in readiness to attack Nnanke, bent on administering justice.

Despite the violent wind, Binah Ekori fled from his friend's side as though he had a premonition of what would happen.

Nnanke turned her burning gaze on Binah Yakpani, sensed his intension, and finally let loose her fury.

It was the scream of a thousand souls—high-pitched, eerily melodious, and charged with numerous echoes. The strange, ear-splitting, and blood-curdling sound left her mouth with an explosive wave so powerful, it flung all gathered at the square backwards, except Binah Umor who stomped his staff on the ground and held on as the force blew against him, wiping his wrapper back, away from his thighs.

Binah Yakpani got the brunt of the scream's force. His staff disintegrated into dust, scattering in the wind while his ears, eyes, and nose bled. As he fell to his knees, blood dribbled profusely from his mouth, yet, Nnanke bent from the hip to focus the force of the scream on him.

The Yakpani priest died looking shriveled on the ground before Nnanke stopped screaming and stomped her staff, instantly stopping the violent elements.

Calm descended.

The waves of sand and wind quietened, no more lightning in the dark sky but stars, and the air smelled fresh and cool like it had rained.

In the sudden silence, the villagers dared not leave where the force of the scream had thrown them. They cowered where they lay, terrified for their lives. Especially as those courageous enough to raise their heads had found Uben stuck on the branch Okoi had been hung. The sharp edge of the branch had pierced his back and protruded through his belly, a copious amount of blood dripping to the ground. It was a gruesome sight.

Only Binah Umor stood in that square, brazenly staring at Nnanke's nakedness and grinning lasciviously.

"Little girl," he drawled and stomped his staff on the ground as he approached the priestess. "Your games do not impress me."

Nnanke said nothing. She calmly transferred her still-glowing staff from her left to her right hand, slowly stomped it seven times on the ground, and it transformed into a bright sapphire spear, glittering with diamond designs on it. With no prior indication of her next move, she lifted it and flung it directly into the centre of Binah Umor's chest.

The glittering spear struck, forcefully sending him backwards until he got stuck in a tree. Instantly, all the diabolic, manipulative tools in his wrapper fell to the ground in a clutter of woodcarvings, twisted palm fronts, and dead rats.

Yakpani people gasped and murmured questions of the strange man's identity.

Nnanke gazed at him blandly as he tried to pull himself from the spear. Then, she turned to the cowering villagers.

"Stand up, all of you." Her voice was barely above a whisper, but they heard her as though she had screamed it.

They hesitated and stared at her warily as though they expected her to fling thunder at them, for all those that had hurt Okoi had received retribution. Some of the villagers were worried for they had supported Binah Yakpani's decision to kill Okoi.

"Stand up and look at what greed looks like and what it can do to a people," she said, staring at Yakpani and the Umor warriors who had arrived just in time to see her spear pierce their binah.

The Umor men of valour had instantly dropped their weapons in surrender, for the sight of a naked, pregnant woman with glowing markings on her body, calmly subduing their powerful binah, proved terrifyingly awe-inspiring. Additionally, the spell holding them bound to the control of the evil priest had been broken when the spear of the gods pierced his chest.

Binah Umor struggled where he stood, blood dripping from his mouth and the wound on his chest, yet his expression remained an evil sneer.

Nnanke had no idea where the words were coming from, but they surged in her heart, and she knew she had to share it with the people...her people. She understood their actions stemmed from ignorance, but it didn't curb the burning pain of losing Okoi.

She faced them without shame that she stood naked in the centre of the square, seen by all. But then, a small woman broke from the crowd and approached her hesitantly with a wrapper in hand. Nnanke watched her, as did the whole village and visiting warriors, holding their collective breath in expectation of more violence.

Nnanke smiled at the woman through her pain. Women were more perceptive than men, and the knowledge she was about to impart would quickly be imbibed by women more than the men.

The small woman draped the wrapper on Nnanke's shoulders, covering her nakedness. In gratitude, Nnanke touched the woman's belly and immediately knew she was Uben's wife. But she was pure of heart, so she blessed her womb; she would be fruitful with her next husband.

"There will be more wars," she started, and the crowd gasped. "There will be more betrayals, more innocent people will die." She looked at them, her eyes glowing less brightly. "Unless we learn to desist from greed.

"Greed is strong—"

"Yes, tell them," Binah Umor, or the spirit in possession of his body, spat and sneered.

"—and it destroys kingdoms—"

"Kingdoms bigger than this!" he growled, coughing up blood in the process.

Nnanke ignored him and concluded, "—when you allow it into your heart."

She turned to where the Umor warriors gathered. "Greed didn't just decide to possess Umor. It was because you coveted power and wanted everything, so it settled and possessed your binah. It manipulated

Uben and Binah Yakpani," she said, turning to the Yakpani people and meeting their shocked and regretful eyes.

"…and caused the death of an innocent man. The warriors of Umor entered Yakpani to kill and enslave you!" she shouted angrily, her finger pointing at where the warriors huddled, looking guilty.

The villagers followed the direction of her finger and seemed to cower at the sight of the huge warriors, their bodies painted ominously with native chalk, looking ready for war.

Nnanke sighed wearily, her arm dropping. Anger was of no use—would it bring back Okoi? "The spirit of Greed will leave the children of Akpa today and will only return if you invite it."

She was reminding them that they all descended from the ancestral land—Lekanakpakpa, and were one and should remain one, instead of differently as they'd been.

Several shoulders shrugged in refusal, rejecting her statement, for they all thought after what they'd seen today, nobody would consciously invite Greed into their village.

But Nnanke knew better. Most of the time, the invitation wasn't conscious, and Greed was always fast to inundate the hearts of men where there is slight abundance.

And the children of Akpa, though living separately, had a lot of abundance. In the years to come, she was sure he would be given an opportunity to reign again, but today, she would vanquish him for a time.

"We are one. We are the children of Akpa. We all came down the hill together. Why then do we envy ourselves? Have you ever heard of the eyes envying the nose, or the mouth or the ears?" She shook her head wearily. "That cannot happen because they belong together and work together to make the face complete.

"If the eyes decided that it had the most important responsibility and set out to destroy the nose or the mouth, what do you think would happen to the face they all occupy?" She asked this fixing her glare on the Umor warriors, watching as they dropped their heads in shame.

"The face will become unequal," she replied in a sad tone. "The face will collapse, the face will be destroyed, and the eyes will be destroyed, too.

"We are one," she reiterated. "As such, the big settlements should be helping the smaller ones, not raiding them and leaving them desolate.

"Umor, Yakpani, Ekori, Agoyi, Agoi Ibami, Agoi Ekpo, Agoi Efreke, Idomi, Nigima, Assiga." As she called out the settlements, her voice echoed and sizzled with the power of cohesion.

"What are you doing?" Binah Umor grunted in alarm and struggled more to free himself, having been quiet for her speech the whole time. "You cannot mean to forcefully unite these tribes!"

Instead of answering him, Nnanke waved her hand, and the man struggled to speak but couldn't. She repeated the names of the tribes that had come down the hill from Lekanakpakpa, the motherland, seven times, and then she declared them a kingdom.

"Spread the word that Atam kingdom has been born this day and peace must reign in it. No matter how men decide to allow greed and hatred into their hearts, Atam must overcome evil with peace. Atam people must be willing to die for a fellow Atam person."

Nnanke pursed her mouth as though whistling and blew softly on the gathered people. They sighed in blatant relief as they felt the cool breeze against their skin and watched in awe as the air from her mouth swayed the leaves lazily.

"*Wofai.*" Peace, she declared softly and blew again. "Wofai."

She did this, repeating the process seven times. Then, she walked to Binah Ekori and grasped his hand, opened his palms, and blew on them, "Wofai," she blessed and touched his priestly staff, making it vibrate with power.

"You are the binah of Atam. Your heart is pure and peaceful. May greed never find you," she declared softly and placed her palm on his chest.

An excited murmur rose among the people at the declaration of a new binah.

"Where will you go?" Binah Ekori, now Binah Atam, asked with blatant concern and understanding, though he was silently stunned that a woman so wronged could do something good to a people who hadn't entirely accepted her.

"I cannot remain, my nakedness was seen," she replied and turned to face the evil priest finally.

Binah Atam followed her until they stood directly in front of Binah Umor who though couldn't speak, sneered his disgust at them.

Silently, Nnanke grabbed the hilt of the glittering spear and pushed the edge deeper into the evil man's chest. His screams and struggles were silent. She pushed, her hand shaking with the power she controlled as she rid the man of the evil spirit. Soon, unexpectedly, the spear exploded into tiny shards, and Binah Umor fell dead to the ground.

Nnanke could see Greed, skinny and ugly in his tattered robe, hurriedly flee the land. He couldn't stand being in Atam, currently saturated with light, unity, and peace.

The people jubilated, but Binah Atam bent and picked a sapphire piece of diamond, one of such that had decorated the shattered spear, the only one remaining, and handed it to a silent Nnanke. She took it, nodded her thanks, and walked slowly towards the forest.

"You could rule us," Binah Atam suggested, but got no reply as she reached the edge of the bush.

"Your child could rule us," he added desperately. Still no reply.

"What will you do?" he shouted at her retreating back from the edge of the forest, not daring to follow her.

What would she do? she silently wondered. This whole time, Okoi had become the centre of her life, but he was no more. What would she do?

The sadness she had been holding at bay suddenly engulfed her, and a keening cry erupted from her mouth. Tears blinded her eyes, yet she kept stumbling down the path to her cave while leaves and flowers reached out to caress her skin.

She entered her cave and stared. All she could see was the joyful times spent in there with Okoi. Nnanke rubbed her large stomach and wondered what good she was without him.

Flowers of different hues bloomed inside. She recalled how happy the colours had made Okoi, which always resulted in him holding her close and touching his mouth on hers.

Sadness clogged her throat, and she rushed out. Her life would be miserable. She would have no purpose. If the gods could choose her, then they could choose someone else now.

Nnanke tightened her hold on the remaining piece of sapphire, a gift for the spirits, as she dropped her wrapper from her shoulders and walked slowly towards the river.

Sobs wracked her body as she recalled more joyful moments with Okoi and how she'd promised she would never let him die. Nnanke believed she did not deserve to live.

She touched her protruding belly as though in farewell, turned her back on the river, and fell into it. She folded her hands over the piece of sapphire on the top of her belly as she allowed the river to slowly drown her.

***

Oh, no, it couldn't end this way. How sad for Nnanke that she lost the love of her life. Goodness, even though Nkoyo had fainted in the forest, the ring had dragged her back to the past.

Sighing wearily, I watched her wake slowly, but her eyes remained closed as she tried to curb her sadness for Nnanke. She couldn't imagine the pain in her heart if she'd lost Onen. Her sniffle caught Onen's attention, and he rapidly crawled into the massive bed and engulfed her in a hug.

"I'm fine, sweetheart. I'm good, the bruises were minor," he assured, even though his face had a collection of nicks and bruises that looked worse than they actually were.

Nkoyo sobbed harder, and Onen was at a loss as to what else to do. "I'm so sorry that I took a reckless decision, darling. I swear it won't happen again," he pleaded, his heart hurting from her obvious hurt.

"It's not that!" she exclaimed, bawling her eyes out and soaking his T-shirt with tears.

Okay, what is it then, Onen wondered. He pulled her from his chest and was pained to see how red her face was from her crying. "Sweetheart, talk to me," he murmured, smoothing tendrils of her hair from her temples.

"She killed herself," Nkoyo choked and stuttered through her tears. "She committed suicide because she couldn't bear the loss of Okoi. She killed herself with her baby in the womb. How could she do that?!" she raved while tears and mucus dripped down her adorable face.

"Shit," he swore — this wasn't good at all. He had experienced his wife go sad for days after watching a particularly emotional movie. This was no movie; this had been reality centuries ago, but it made no difference to Nkoyo.

"I'm sorry, baby. I don't know why she did that. But if I had…lost you out there today," he choked, realizing how lucky they'd all been. "I'd probably kill myself, too, as I'd be unable to live without you," he concluded in a sincere grunt, his eyes smarting with unshed tears.

His chest hammered as he recalled Nkoyo leaning over him to block the dagger in Uken's fist. It would take a long time to recover from how his heart had lurched frightfully in his chest.

"Oh, God, Onen, you say the sweetest things. I love you," she declared and hugged him close. Her tears subsided, and soon, her breathing evened, and she was asleep, tired from all the excitement of the day.

"I love you, too, so much," he whispered in her ear as she snored lightly.

Onen held his wife, thanking God for protecting and seeing everyone through the harrowing event. His hand reached out and caressed his wife's baby bump, and as expected, the baby swirled and bounced against the firm belly, announcing its presence.

"I love you, too, baby," he whispered, caressing his child's present home before joining his wife in sleep.

Epilogue

Hmm! What a tale!

I mean, it's spectacular!

I only wish the people of Atam would persist in recalling that the fabric of the kingdom was closely knit with peace and love at its creation.

Mankind needs to understand that greed is the root of all evil and not money as the cliché goes. Man's greed for power causes wars; greed for knowledge isn't necessarily a good thing. I mean, look at Hiroshima—that was a result of too much knowledge found. Coveting is a form of greed, too.

Speaking of the tattered ancient spirit, I always dodge whenever I sense his presence. I cannot forget how easily he'd flung me out of that car. Yet, my cheers are for Nnanke, the mother of Atam, who will forever watch out for the kingdom through the beautiful sapphire stone.

Having sounded relatively academic in my review, I, Gossip, will now move on to the juicy bits.

So, in commemoration of Nkoyo giving birth to the first twins of the Ikpi EguOkoi royal family, both females by the way, King Liman decided to create a new holiday for the kingdom, one he called Unity Day.

It wasn't so much a holiday as a constant, annual reminder for the people of Atam to remain in peace and love and unity. Of course, Nkoyo had regaled everyone about Nnanke and how she had dealt with the evil priest in the past, though she had only gotten to know that after she'd dealt with Uken in the present.

Prince Onen had held her close with a proud look on his face. Who wouldn't be proud of such a courageous wife, although the awe-inspiring acts were mostly Nnanke's spirit anyway. Still, it is necessary to praise Nkoyo for Mmatami had finally divulged the reason Nkoyo had been chosen to see the past and the origin of Atam kingdom. The old woman, who still didn't show signs of dying, had declared that Nkoyo was the only person with a strong enough essence to handle the powerful force which was Nnanke's spirit.

I'm beginning to think Nkoyo was blessed with twin females because of her strong essence. Mmatami had hinted she had to remain with the ring until her son arrived and until he turned twenty. Seems like quite a long time to me.

Nkoyo didn't seem bothered about the length of time she had to keep the ring, and neither did the prince, her husband. Not when they had two, beautiful daughters who had everyone cooing...even me.

I'm rolling my eyes right now, in case you're wondering.

***

After several *koke* of trying to drown herself in the river, Nnanke gave up. She was tired of being flung out of the water by spirit guides every time she tried.

Resolving to remain in the forest alone and not mix with the villagers, she regretted her decision when labour began. She wailed in her cave, thrashing about and pushing without prod.

The pain was excruciating, almost as much as when she'd seen Okoi hanging from that tree in the village square…almost, but not quite.

While she panted and breathed through her gritted teeth, she saw someone in a blur enter the cave.

"*Num mbuke eh!*" she exclaimed in pain, twisting and grunting and pushing.

"I would never let you die," the person replied.

Nnanke growled like an animal, angry that someone dared to speak her special words to Okoi. Who was this person? Was that a hand on her thigh? Why did it feel so comforting…like Okoi's touch?

Even with the bone-numbing ache of childbirth, she heaved herself up to a sitting position, and a scream curdled in her throat as she saw Okoi.

Was he a spirit? Had he come for her? Even though she had wanted to kill herself this past *koke*, actually seeing his ghost proved unsettling.

The scream in her throat finally burst out, and the pain of the child surging out from her secret place overwhelmed the terror of seeing a ghost. With her sight blurred with tears of pain, she watched as he confidently received the bloodied baby in his wrapper and proceeded to clean both mother and child.

Nnanke had no strength to remain in panic or entertain the dread lodged in her chest.

"Okoi," she whispered, hoping but not believing he was real. "Are you really here, or am I dead?"

Okoi, more handsome than ever and looking almost ethereal, lay beside her and touched his lips to hers, reminding her of the pleasures they'd shared.

Tears clogged her throat again.

"It is really you," she whispered in awe, her eyes glittering with tears and happiness.

"It is me. The goddess brought me back from the cocoon you wrapped me in. I saw every time she had to send you back, and I pleaded with her to return. I had to labour really hard in the never-ending garden of the spirits, and the goddess sent me out when your labour began, a reward for my hard work and sincere feelings for you."

Okoi couldn't keep his hands to himself. His eyes moved from his son to his angel and back. They were both beautiful, and he couldn't believe he'd been given another chance to live. He couldn't believe he was no more slaving in the never-ending garden. It was strange to be out in the real world; strange to feel the familiar softness of Nnanke's flesh. His manhood was already hard and painful between his legs, another familiar reaction when he was close to his angel.

Clearing his throat to curb his carnal desires and to remind himself he had forever with her, he spoke. "The goddess has asked that we rule Atam."

"The goddess has a lot of wisdom," she commented wearily, happiness making a mess of her heart. "I destroyed my staff so that I might never rule again," she spat, but with a helpless smile.

He returned her smile. "I saw. And when you dropped it the first time you drowned, the goddess picked it and made this." He presented an intricately woven golden ring with a diamond-shaped sapphire that winked in the sunlight flittering through the vines of flowers over the entrance of the cave. "She said it will bind us for eternity," he whispered, feeling the awe of the moment as he slid the ring onto her finger.

Nnanke shut her eyes as she felt invisible ties tightening her destiny with that of Okoi beyond time. When she opened it, Okoi gasped but then smiled because of another familiar thing he had missed — his angel's eyes glowed the same throbbing blue as the ring on her finger. He would definitely enjoy eternity with her.

With that thought, he leaned close and pressed his mouth on hers. She opened for him as he had taught her, and he groaned in pleasure, pressing his painfully hard manhood on her thigh.

Nnanke had just reached out and grabbed his hard shaft, moving from the hilt to the tip and smearing the wetness there around the smooth head of his shaft, when their baby coughed and suddenly started crying.

***

The cry of the baby brought her eyes open, and she surged off the bed only to see her huge, beautiful husband cuddling their one-week-old son. She stared at him lovingly, admiring how he patiently swayed the baby until the crying stopped.

"You're really good with that," she whispered as she left the bed and walked to him.

"I have practice." He grinned at her. "Besides, I didn't want him to disturb you. You need to rest more," Onen said with a tender smile for the love of his life.

He hadn't imagined this amount of happiness when he'd met her half-naked in his sister's room years ago.

Now he had four kids—a boy had finally arrived.

Nkoyo watched as he expertly placed his son in his baby bed, seeming reluctant to pull from the chubby guy. She waited until he sighed and straightened to his full height.

Slowly, she walked into his arms, her love for him increasing beyond bounds at the knowledge that he loved their baby so deeply, he found it difficult to be separated from him.

She stood on tiptoes and kissed him deeply. Onen groaned and took over the kiss, delving into the sweetness beyond her lips, and then he abruptly stopped and stepped away, holding her at arm's length.

"Stop, Nk, you know what happens when we kiss like that. I love my son to distraction, but he came a year too early. We don't want to make that mistake again. I don't want you going through those pangs again."

He looked so sincere and serious, it caused Nkoyo to melt into giggles. She had to smother the sound with her palm over her mouth.

Onen growled. "What's so funny? You know I can't control myself with you," he said sheepishly and grinned when she giggled more.

"And I love it. Oh, Onen, I'm so happy," she declared while dragging him to the bed.

The prince raised an inquisitive eyebrow.

"Do tell," he said and smirked, happy to see her happy.

"She didn't die!"

Onen had both brows raised now, as he had no idea what she was talking about.

"Nnanke! She didn't die, and neither did Okoi; their love survived," she whispered, and in that fierce tone, went ahead to tell her husband about her latest trip to the past.

By the time they settled down to sleep, they both agreed she'd seen that particular, unexpected vision because the crown prince had arrived.

Thank you for reading Pristine by Emem Bassey. If you enjoyed this story, support the author by leaving a review at the site of purchase.

A Ridiculous Royal Tale series:
Inside Out
Pristine

Age Is No Bother series:
Fine Wine
Fine Maple
Fine Scotch
Fine Ending

OTHER BOOKS BY LOVE AFRICA PRESS

Amber Fire by Aminat Sanni-Kamal
Tough Alliance by Kiru Taye
Locked In by Opemipo Omosa
Love and Handicrafts by Nana Prah

CONNECT WITH US

Facebook.com/LoveAfricaPress
Twitter.com/LoveAfricaPress
Instagram.com/LoveAfricaPress
www.loveafricapress.com